*For Grace*

# The Memory

## GERRARD COWAN

### The Machinery Trilogy

HARPER
Voyager

Harper*Voyager*
An imprint of HarperCollins*Publishers* Ltd
1 London Bridge Street
London SE1 9GF

www.harpercollins.co.uk

This paperback original 2019

First published in Great Britain in ebook format by
HarperCollins*Publishers* 2018

A catalogue record for this book
is available from the British Library

ISBN: 978-000-818152-9

This novel is entirely a work of fiction.
The names, characters and incidents portrayed in it are
the work of the author's imagination. Any resemblance to
actual persons, living or dead, events or localities is
entirely coincidental.

Typeset in Sabon by Palimpsest Book Production Limited,
Falkirk, Stirlingshire

Printed and bound in the UK by CPI Group (UK) Ltd, Croydon CR0 4YY

# Chapter One

**Turn back.**

That was all Ruin said to Brightling, as she walked down the stairs.

**Turn back.**

She was unsure how long she had been in this place. Her memories felt strange, at times: out of her reach. She forgot why she was here, in this darkness. She had to grasp for it, searching through the muddy waters of her mind. *The Machinery,* she told herself. *I am going to the Machinery.*

*Ruin is in the Machinery. Ruin will die.*

An image rose in her mind, and all her confusion disappeared. It was a picture of a young woman, pale-skinned and black-haired. *Katrina. I will destroy the thing inside her, and I will bring her home to me.* The mask burned against her skin, when these thoughts came. She had worn it since she had come here; it showed her the way through the darkness, down the never-ending stairs. It had such power, this thing. *I have power when I wear it. I will use it to destroy my enemies: the enemies of mankind.*

But she did not know how.

**Turn back.**

Ruin was afraid of her. This creature, feared by the world, Overland and Underland, was frightened. She could sense it, in his voice. She could always sense fear: even the fear of a god.

She caught herself. *A god? Is that what we call them now?*
**Turn back.**

*Yes. A god.* What else were they but gods, and what manner of mask was this, to strike fear into one of them? Jandell had fashioned it from a shard of a defeated enemy, in times long past, and he had given it to her. *The Absence.* A mask like no other: a mask that could carve someone's memories into little bits. The Absence was dead, now, but somehow, this little thing still thrummed with a dark power. It loved her. She could feel it. It did not wish to cause her pain. But it still hurt her. It licked its fiery tongue around her memories and longed to burn them away.

**Turn back.**

Each time Ruin said those words, she heard a noise behind, back from where she had come: a door creaking open. When she continued on her way, the door would close, only to reopen when Ruin spoke again.

Ruin did not speak for a long time. When he did, this time his words were different.
**You will not turn back, Brightling.**

She shook her head. 'No,' she said. Her voice sounded so small, here, and she despised herself for all her weaknesses.

There came a great sigh.
**You have always been special, Amyllia.**

The use of her first name made her stop.

**I know you very well. I have watched you for so many years.**

2

Brightling took another step. She knew what Ruin was doing. The doomed tried all sorts of tricks to stave off the inevitable. *Don't ever listen to the dead,* went an old Watcher saying. *The dead are full of lies.*

But she could not ignore Ruin. Not in this place.

**I see everything that has been and gone. I remember the first time you appeared as ... someone of** *promise*.

Brightling turned another corner of the twisting staircase. The steps were wider, here, the walls further apart. There was a door, to her left. It was slightly ajar, its edge glowing with a thin line of golden light. She reached out a hand, before quickly snapping it back.

'What is in there?'

**What else? A memory.**

Brightling heard a voice, muttering beyond the door. It was her voice; the voice she had as a girl. *Warmth. Contentment.*

**I have all your memories before me, Amyllia. Tell me where you would like to go, and what you would like to see again.**

Brightling turned away and looked once more down the dark staircase, through the eyes of her terrible mask.

'No,' she said.

The mask tightened on Brightling's face. *It wants to swallow me up.* She hesitated for a heartbeat, before removing it. She turned it over in her hands, running her fingers along its edges. Each mask was a wonderful thing, fitting its owner perfectly. *A second skin.* They were all different: some of them reached up over the head, some of them covered it entirely, others were just a thin piece of material. This one, though, was so very different to any other, flitting between man and woman, old and young, anger or happiness, all with that same sense of nothingness. She could not see its expression, now. She wondered what it looked like. She hoped it was wreathed with a terrible fury, and that Ruin saw it, and was afraid.

**You are a strange mixture.**

She put the mask on. The world around her was once again visible, glowing with a strange, green light.

'What do you mean?' Perhaps she could steer this thing, this Ruin, in a useful direction.

**You are cold. You are *focused*. You once thought of nothing but the Machinery. Now it is gone, and I have taken its place in your mind. You are devoted to my destruction.**

'I *will* destroy you.'

**There have been others, over the millennia, who were just as focused as you – many of them. No, it is not your focus that makes you curious. Nor is it your coldness.**

'Go on then. Let me have it.'

**You have another quality. It is unusual in one like you, so most people do not see it. You are *nurturing*. There have been people throughout your life who you turned into your children. Aran Fal was one.**

Brightling leaned against the wall, as the image of a blond-haired boy rose before her mind's eye.

**You changed him. I saw it happening. You took him, and when you were done, he was something else. Changed so subtly, yet with terrible finality. Aran Fal into Aranfal. A boy become a torturer. *The* torturer. A dark creature, yet he still has a little sparkle. I can see it in him.**

'So he is alive, then, wherever he is,' Brightling said.

**Perhaps, perhaps. Everyone is alive to me, Brightling, because all memories are here. All of them, from the beginning of everything. I have seen them *all*. I have *touched* them all.**

4

'You must have seen a lot, then.'

Ruin laughed.

**A nurturer to Aranfal, but also to others. To one above all. A girl, whose family was destroyed. I set that all in motion.**

Brightling winced.

**The Paprissis were destroyed. The girl was abandoned, and ended up where she belonged: with *you*, the cold nurturer.**

Brightling steeled herself. *It is testing me. It is only a voice: it has no power.* 'She was going to join you, no matter what happened,' she whispered. 'I feel no shame in that. That thing was always going to take her over.'

**Always? Always is a powerful word.**

A door opened to Brightling's right. There was no escaping it, this time, no walking away. Something in the room beyond called to her, pulled her towards it. She resisted, perhaps longer than Ruin expected; she thought she heard him muttering darkly. She was not one to give in to temptation. Not her.

But there was no refusing the draw of the room. It was the light that did it. As she stared at her feet, it gathered across the stones: the purple of the Strategists, spilling into the darkness, driving it away.

She began to tremble, and she cursed herself for it. She could resist no longer. She turned her head towards the light and saw *her*: the girl who changed everything. Her foster daughter. Mother. *The Strategist.*

Katrina stood alone in a small, confined space, more like a cell than a room. *No. This is not Katrina.* This was the creature, at its zenith: taller than the girl Brightling had known, stretched into unusual proportions. Her white rags had turned purple, as had her eyes. The same colour of light hung around her in a strange haze. She was standing completely still.

'It is not really her,' Brightling said. She felt a wave of relief. She did not want to face that thing, the parasite that had seized control of an abandoned, orphaned girl. But she perhaps feared meeting the real Katrina even more. She had failed that child. If she had been wiser, or more observant, she would have seen what was inside her. She could have gone to the Operator, and he would have done something. She was sure of it. But she had failed. *The greatest Watcher of them all, a Tactician of the Overland, and I let my girl be devoured from the inside out.*

**Isn't she wonderful?**

Brightling silently agreed. There was something incandescent about this girl. Something luminous.

**You did this, Brightling.**

Anger flared within the Watcher. 'I failed her,' she said. 'But your people put the demon inside her. Not me.'

**But what *are* we, Brightling? What are my people? We came from *you*. All of you. The memories of humanity. They gave birth to us. They feed us. We are *your* creations. You are the parents, and we are nothing but children.**

'Children don't live forever. They don't have powers that could break the world. They aren't called fucking Ruin, either.'

There was a laugh in the darkness. **I am a child, Brightling.**

There was a movement behind the image of Katrina. An old woman appeared, her face just visible under a dark hood. She threaded her arm through the Strategist's, and smiled at Brightling. Something crawled from her mouth, and flew away.

We are powerful beings, it is true. But all power has constraints. We are born of humanity; we cannot live to our true potential until we are at one with humanity. When we join a host, we become something more. An immortal, still, but one with greater *scope*. A *truer* being.

'And the mortal dies.'

The man that you see, when you look at Jandell – that is not Jandell. He is the host for Jandell. He was *meant* for Jandell.

The old woman turned and embraced the girl, before vanishing. Katrina breathed in deeply.

The host and the Operator must be *just right*, before the combination reaches its full potential. *You* made Katrina the perfect host for Mother. You gave her a certain strength: the mentality of a Watcher. Yet you weakened her as well. You filled her with self-doubt. Mother waited, and watched, and smiled, while you worked your dark influence.

Katrina disappeared, replaced with a flickering procession of images: Brightling and Katrina, Katrina and Brightling, over and over, as the girl grew up under the wing of the Watchers.

*I did this.*

The host was ready when the world changed. She was ready when the Machinery broke, and I sent such powers to her.

The mask throbbed against her. 'Say what you want: I am coming for you, with my mask.'

See what I have wrought, from my prison. See what I did to your world. See what powers I gave the One. You think I am weak?

'I think my mask is stronger.'

Ruin laughed, and the door to the cell slammed shut.

# Chapter Two

'The Machinery destroyed my family,' said Jaco Paprissi. 'The Machinery destroyed us all.'

The old man stared hard at Jandell. When he had first appeared before Drayn and the Operator, rising out of the grass like an animal, his features had been obscured by thick, green paint, the same colour as his robes. Now the paint was gone, but the wildness remained. His skin was raw, his grey hair matted with dirt. His face was deeply lined, but there was a certain spark in his dark eyes. *A drive.* It reminded Drayn of her mother.

He had taken them into this settlement, him and his men, through clusters of low, stone buildings, until they had come to this cold, dark hall, a damp space of wood and animals and smouldering flame. The other people had peeled off as they went, until they were alone, just Drayn and Jandell and this strange old man.

The wind howled outside the building. The wind always seemed to howl in this place.

*Jandell took his son away.* That's what he'd said, when they first met this man. Drayn had met a boy, deep in the Old Place, one who had stood at her side on her journey through her worst memories. *That was him.* Drayn knew it. She saw some of Alexander in Jaco. She wondered if she should tell him. *I met your boy, my lord. I met him in the land of memory.*

'No,' Jandell said.

Drayn was unsure, at first, if he was speaking to Jaco or to her. He was sitting to her side at the rough-edged table, hunched over, his strange cloak gathered around him, the faces staring wanly at the world outside their prison. 'I destroyed your family. I cannot hide from that.'

Jaco ran a hand through his nest of hair. 'Yes. But you're as much a victim as the rest of us. You may have built it and operated it, but the Machinery was its own thing. It spoke to Alexander. It told him such ... things. And it made you take him away.'

A new brightness seemed to enter Jaco's eyes. He was directly opposite Jandell, and he leaned in towards him. 'Is he alive down there?' But the light flickered out as quickly as it had come. 'No. He can't be. It's not a place for little boys.'

*A little boy. I met him. I knew him well ...*

Jandell shook his head. 'There is a boy in the Underland, but he is just a shadow. He is a dream. When I took him away ...' He bowed his head.

'He's just a memory, now,' Jaco whispered.

Jandell frowned. 'Just a memory? How do you know that?'

Jaco waved a hand. 'I've learned a lot, out here.' He took his gaze from Jandell, and looked again at the table. 'Did you hurt him, Operator?' he asked in a quiet voice.

An image came before Drayn: Alexander, chained to a chair, exhausted. Jandell was inches from his face, his mouth twisted into a sneer. He held something in his hand – a whip, perhaps.

'The boy was gone at the beginning. But the memories ...

I fought that creature of memory, for his knowledge,' Jandell whispered. 'Yet even when he told me the One had returned, I would not believe him.'

'But he didn't tell you everything, did he, Operator? He didn't tell you who the One *was*. He wouldn't have wanted you to hurt her. His *sister*.'

A new image appeared in Drayn's mind: a girl with black hair, a girl in white rags, slowly turning to purple …

Jandell rubbed his temples with thin fingers.

'Alexander did well to keep it from me,' he whispered.

'No,' Jaco said. 'Not Alexander. The thing that lives down there: a memory of a boy.'

'Perhaps that *is* Alexander. Why shouldn't memories be real?'

It was the first time Drayn had spoken. The others turned to her, and Jandell smiled.

'I was a dark thing, in recent years,' Jandell said. 'I was mad, and paranoid, and weak. Do you know what saved me, Paprissi?'

Jaco shook his head.

Jandell pointed at Drayn. 'This girl,' he whispered. 'This Fallen Girl, and her powerful memories. More than that, though: her memories are powerful indeed, but so is *she*.'

Drayn turned her head away. Part of her wondered if she should thank the Operator. *But why? How can I thank him for his praise, when I did nothing to earn it?*

'Operator,' Jaco said.

'My name is Jandell.' He sighed. 'A bleak name. The Bleak Jandell.'

Jaco nodded. 'Jandell. I want you to know …' He looked at the moss-covered ceiling, as if searching for answers. 'I do not forgive you, for what you did.'

Jandell bowed his head. 'You shouldn't.' He gestured at his cloak, at the faces inside. 'Someone made this garment for me to remind me of all the things I did, and all the people I hurt, when I was Jandell the Bleak.' He smiled. '*Was*. I am a fool; I will always be Jandell the Bleak.'

'I hadn't finished,' Jaco whispered. 'I do not forgive you for what you did. But I do not hate you, either. Because it was my fault.' He stroked his beard. 'I brought this upon my family. I could have stopped it.' His voice grew weary. 'Alexander told me about Katrina. He told me what she was. And I didn't believe him. I couldn't. I loved that girl as much as my son.' He placed his head in his hands and began to tremble. 'If I had told you the truth, you could have destroyed her, and Alexander would still be alive.'

Jandell shrugged his shoulders. 'Perhaps it is all fate,' he whispered.

There came a noise from outside: the whinnying of a horse. A man pushed open the door. He seemed to be middle-aged, though it was difficult to tell with any precision. His head was completely bald, without even eyebrows. He was tall, but strangely stooped. He had pale skin, but it was so weather-beaten as to almost be a shade of red, and he wore the same green robes as Jaco.

'Dark is coming from the beyond,' he said, pointing in the direction of the ocean. 'Not now, my leader, but soon, the dark will come.'

Jaco nodded, before turning to Jandell and Drayn. 'We have to go. This isn't a good place at night. There are raiders, further up the coast, and animals that come from the forests.'

They made their way on horseback from the small settlement, Drayn tucked in behind Jandell, with the faces of the cloak staring up at her. She felt something when she looked at them: things from the past, tugging at her.

She turned her head, back in the direction they had come from, squinting her eyes against the wind. The settlement was very small, only a handful of squat, broken dwellings. There were people, there, leaning against the walls or wandering around, armed with spears. But the only ones on the road were Jaco, Jandell, Drayn and the bald newcomer.

'Allos,' he said. He rode up next to Jandell and Drayn, and pointed to his face. 'Allos. Me.'

Drayn smiled at him and extended a hand. The man grasped it, perhaps a little too hard, and grinned back at her.

'I'm Drayn,' the girl said.

'Drayn,' said Allos. His voice was as rugged as the landscape, a thing of stone and hill. 'Drayn, from another place.'

Allos turned back to the road, and his expression fell serious once more.

'Where are we going?' Drayn called up ahead, where Jaco was leading the way. The old man came to a halt and turned to the girl.

'Up the road,' he said, jerking his head in the direction of travel. 'That place back there is just an outpost. We don't live there.'

'What's up the road?'

Jaco grinned at her. He was old, this man, but remained a powerful physical presence. She could feel the merest hint of his memories. They were full of wonderful things: things that no one else had ever seen. But they were tinged with sadness, too.

'Home is up the road,' he said in a cheery voice.

The road gave way to a dirt path. As the night came in, trees sprang up on either side, great sentinels that loomed over them, moaning and swaying in the air. The darkness beyond crackled with sound: the movements of animals among the branches and twigs of the forest floor.

Drayn did not know what she had expected when she first set sail with Jandell. In some ways, she was disappointed by what she had found: wind and rain and rocks and trees. But there were other things, here, that she had never experienced. The land was vast: she had seen that when they first landed. Even the smell here was different, coming at her in waves: the scent of a fire, fuelled by strange things.

'We are almost there,' Jaco said. It was growing difficult to see him, up ahead in the gloom. 'I hope you're not tired, Drayn.'

'No,' the girl said.

Allos spoke, then. She could not see him, but he was near her side.

'What powers? Why, when you will not turn to them?'

For a moment Drayn was confused. 'Powers? What powers do I have, is that what you mean?'

'He is talking to me,' Jandell whispered. 'He knows what I am. Perhaps he has seen my kind before.'

'Yes, before,' Allos said. 'For such a long time before, the powers were here.'

'He's wondering why I ride this horse,' Jandell said. 'He wonders why I don't lift us all up, with the click of a finger, and take us where we need to go.'

'They are things, indeed, that matter now,' Allos said.

Drayn searched for Allos, in the dark. He was nowhere to be seen. He was from this place, unlike Jaco Paprissi. The language he spoke was not his own. The land, though, was his, and he could disappear against it as he wished.

'I am a thing of memory,' Jandell said. 'But I am far from the only one. When I draw on the power, sometimes others can sense me: not all of them, and not always, but some of them.'

'And there are some you are hiding from, Operator,' said Jaco.

Jandell did not respond.

A light appeared before them. It was a torch, raised high in the centre of the path, far away from the trees. They took their horses around it, on either side.

'We are almost there,' Jaco said.

Drayn saw that the base of the torch had been shaped into a figure. No: it was many figures, stacked one on top of the other, naked human beings. At the top, one of them held the torch in his hand.

'Men and women,' Allos said. He emerged at her side. 'Together. That is the future: no powers but those of the world itself, and the people who live here.'

He nodded at the fire, before pushing on up the path.

They passed by more of the torches as they went deeper into the woods. After a while, the distances between the flames grew shorter, until they reached one every ten paces or so. The dirt path began to widen and became a road once more, paved with wide grey stones. Drayn felt something change in the world around her: more memories crowded in, cluttering her mind.

'Look ahead,' Jandell said.

She leaned around him. The road was coming to an end: before it was a high wall, formed of spiked wooden poles. There were figures walking along the edge, though she could not make them out clearly.

Jaco rode ahead of them, and the gate opened.

The road continued for another while. Signs of civilisation began to emerge: the smell of animals, the sounds of distant conversations. They passed through another gate, and then another, shell after shell of defences. The trees began to thin out, until they disappeared altogether.

Another gate came. This time, though, things were different. The roar of people could be heard all around them, even in the night, and the world was cast in a golden glare from a thousand torches.

Jaco turned to them, and grinned. 'Here we are, then. The heart of our little civilisation!'

The gate opened, the small party entered, and the world changed.

They had come to a town square, its surface a muddy mess, ramshackle dwellings of stone and wood leaning over its sides. The place was crowded with men and women, talking among themselves, drinking from wooden cups. Torches burned all around, though Drayn wondered if they were necessary: the moon above them seemed somehow larger than normal, a vast sphere of blue light, surrounded by infinite, sparkling stars.

No one seemed to notice the newcomers when they first passed through the gate. After a while, however, that began to change. Fingers pointed at them from small, whispering groups. Drayn glanced at some of the people and saw they were like Allos, pale skinned, but rough and raw.

Jaco led them away from the square. They passed through side streets and byways, all of them teeming with life. The buildings varied madly in their construction, from relatively stable stone structures to leaning piles of wood, though they were similar in one important way: none was taller than one or two storeys.

'We are here,' said Jaco.

In many ways, the building before them was much the same as the others they had passed: a stone structure, low and long. But there was something very different about it. Its lines were neater and sharper, the path before it swept clean. A man and a woman stood at either side, holding spears.

Jaco led them to the door, and nodded to the guards. He beckoned to the small group, who followed him inside. They were now in a large, well-kept room, its only furniture a great table surrounded by rough-hewn chairs. There were no paintings on the walls, no statues, no tapestries, only a handful of glowing candles. Still, there was an air of importance to the place: a sense of ordered authority.

Jaco whispered something to Allos, who nodded and vanished through a door on one side of the room. The old man took a seat at the table, and indicated to the others to join him. Drayn sat in a chair at Jaco's side, but Jandell remained on his feet, studying the hall.

'Do you like it, Operator?' Jaco asked, gesturing at the room. 'This is a minor version of Memory Hall, I suppose you could say. It's the centre of our world.'

'No,' Jandell said. 'I built Memory Hall. You made this yourselves, with your own hands.' There was admiration in his voice. Perhaps it was even pride.

'Indeed,' Jaco said. 'No fanciness here. No names, no titles. This is just the Hall.'

'And what are you?' Jandell asked.

Jaco shrugged. 'Just a Councillor. One of ten, elected by the people. Anyone can run for the job, as they like, no matter who they are. No children, though.' He grimaced. 'I think that was the Machinery's worst mistake. Was there ever a good child Strategist?'

Allos entered the room again, carrying a tray of food. It was simple stuff: white meats, wooden cups of water, bread. He placed it on the table, and disappeared once more.

'Allos there is a Councillor, too,' Jaco said. 'He won a seat in the last election.'

'Why's he serving you food, then?' Drayn asked.

Both faces turned to her.

'Because he likes to help.' Jaco frowned. 'You're not an Overlander. I can tell. Yet we speak the same language. Where are you from?'

Drayn was about to speak, but Jandell held up a hand to silence her. 'It doesn't matter. All that matters is where we're going.'

He took a seat opposite Jaco. 'But why are you hiding here, Paprissi?'

'Hiding?' Jaco laughed. 'Who's hiding? I came here for the same reasons as you, Jandell. To find answers.'

The two men – human and Operator – stared hard at one another.

'What is this place?' Drayn asked.

Jaco shrugged. 'We just call it the Newlands.'

'Is this the only city here?'

Jaco leaned back in his chair, and bit his lip. 'As far as I know, this is the only city in the Newlands. But we're not the only people here, not by a long way. There are communities all along the coast, and in the interior, far outside the forest's boundaries. We don't see them often. We try to avoid them, to be honest. It's a savage place.'

Allos returned and took a seat by Jandell's side. He held a strange object in his hands, a kind of spiked, purple fruit, which he began to methodically peel.

'Allos and his people lived in the forest, and along the

coast, when we came,' Jaco said, smiling at the bald man. 'They still do. But now they have a new life: a civilised life, speaking a civilised tongue. Here, in the city, they're still protected by the trees, still hidden from their enemies. But now they can enjoy ... stability.'

Allos fixed Drayn with a stare.

'Our language is foreign to you,' she said.

'Different, once, but not so different now,' Allos said.

The Operator stood. 'We have not come here to learn about language.' He seemed to grow taller; his shadow fell across the hall. 'I found this place in Squatstout's heart. *He* knew about it, though how much, I cannot tell. This place is so important ...'

Drayn found she could not turn away from Jaco, this proud, wounded, fascinating man. As she looked at him, the conversation of the others fell away, and the noise of the city outside began to disappear, replaced with an incessant drumming, thudding in her mind. She felt something, as she looked at him. She felt the corner of a memory, and she ran the fingers of her mind along its burning edge.

'There is an important memory here,' Drayn whispered. 'It's inside him. I can feel it.'

Jandell raised a hand. 'No,' he said. 'Jaco will tell us anything we need ...'

But it was too late. They had already gone inside.

# Chapter Three

'What is the Old Place? Is it a country, or is it a creature? Does it have thoughts? Does it know itself, any more? Did it ever? Once, when I ...'

Aranfal opened his eyes.

He was on his back, sunken into black sand. Above him was a dark sky, in which burned a red sun. *The Underland. I am searching for a memory.*

'... was very young, I played a game where I ran from one side of the Old Place to the other. Well, that's what I tried to do. But how can one travel through a god?'

There was a thin line of smoke in the sky: pale against the blackness. He had not noticed it before.

'And it did not like me there, oh no. It is capricious. It is harsh. Like its children. Like its *parents*.'

A face appeared above him, one that he knew well: the face of a young-looking man with long blond hair. He wore a green gown, covered with images of people and animals and shapes.

'Well, get up,' he said.

Aranfal climbed to his feet and cast a glance at the creature before him. There was something different about the Gamesman.

He seemed stronger, surer of himself. *Of course he is. He's the Gamesman, and this is a game: it's where he belongs.*

'Why were you lying in the sand?' the Gamesman asked. 'Was it comfortable?'

Aranfal glanced at the endless, black expanse. 'I don't know,' he said. 'I can't remember.'

The Gamesman laughed. 'Memories, eh?' He clapped his hands. 'What would we be without them?'

Aranfal looked into the distance. There seemed to be a structure of some kind far ahead, though he could not make out what it was.

'How is the game played?' he asked.

The Gamesman put an arm around him. There was a whisper in the desert.

'The Old Place guards the First Memory with the greatest care. It has never shown it to anyone, and it likely never will.' There was a sad look in his eyes, as if he was gazing at a condemned man. 'No one has ever found it. But it does love mortals, Aranfal. It does love you: its parents.'

'I'm here forever,' Aranfal said with certainty. 'I will never escape.'

'No one has,' the Gamesman said. 'Well, all except for Arandel. But he was so ... powerful.' He smiled at Aranfal. 'You have a similar name, but you do not have that power, Aranfal. You will be like the rest of them.'

'Where are they?'

'It doesn't matter.' The Gamesman shrugged. 'You can do nothing but follow the path ahead.'

With a bow, the Gamesman was gone, leaving Aranfal no more knowledgeable than if he had never appeared in the first place.

\*

The torturer walked and walked, across the black sand, towards whatever was before him, alone among the endless expanse. It took time for the image to crystallise. At first, he was merely aware of a change in the darkness. He could not tell what it was; he only knew it was there.

But as he went, its shape and outline grew clearer. *It is formed of stone and wood. There is something at the top. What is it? It is ...*

It was a well.

Aranfal approached it carefully. It seemed ordinary enough, the same as any other well he had seen before. A large bucket swayed above, though there was no wind in this place. The Watcher carefully leaned over the side and glanced below. *Anything could be hiding down there,* a cautious voice warned him. But he could only see the blackness.

'Hello?' he called into the dark, feeling strangely embarrassed.

His voice echoed in the deep, but no response came. He wasn't sure what he had expected.

A sound from behind seized his attention. A figure was approaching at great speed, a moving mass of hair and shawls, emitting exasperated shouts. Aranfal wondered at first if it was the Gamesman, but he soon realised this was something new. *And likely disastrous.*

'Five times we walked together, five times,' came a voice from the shawls. 'In all the trees in the orchard, no apples could we find. The dog sits alone in the courtyard: it is sick, and Father will kill it in the morning.'

The figure walked to the other side of the well, ignoring him completely. Aranfal darted around the structure, padding quietly across the black sand, trying to make out the features of this new arrival. But every time he came close, a thatch of wiry brown hair or a bunched-up mass of material would block his view. Even the creature's hands were hidden in a pair of dark gloves. The voice seemed female, though he could not even be sure of that.

'Are you an Operator?' he asked.

The newcomer did not acknowledge the question, but kept talking in her cascading spiel of nonsense.

'The candles are sparkling in the corridor, and there is a creak upon the floorboards. Nights are longer here, near the ice fields, where they never seem to end. When I walked into the street, there was a fire, such a fire, and none of my friends returned.'

The newcomer leaned over the side of the well, so that her words fell into the darkness and echoed within the pit below.

'I walked eleven miles to the next village, but my love had already passed. I kept a green bird in a silver cage. When I learned to write my name, I carved it upon my skin.'

The figure made a circle of the well.

'I found a straw man in the field. I kept a spider in a jar.'
*Is this a code?*

'I could not go that day, though I wish I had, for only I could have stopped him. My hounds are all three-legged. The clock in the spire is ticking, my love, the clock in the spire is ticking.'

Aranfal closed his eyes, and the words took on a different shape. They were building blocks, he realised; the speaker was constructing something. *But what is it? What is she making?*

'On the fourteenth night I wept for him. On the eighteenth night I laughed.'

22

*She speaks of memories.* He did not know if this was his own voice.

'In the stars I saw a name. It was ... *torturer.*'

Aranfal's eyes snapped open.

'What did you say?'

But the newcomer was not listening. She had climbed onto the side of the well, into which she poured her ceaseless words.

'Fire,' she said. 'I saw a fire, in the deep, ten thousand years ago. Such things were put there; such things.'

The figure leapt onto the rope, feet resting on the bucket, gazing into the pit.

'The cat is so unhappy!'

With that, she descended into the well.

Aranfal stood staring into the darkness for a moment, feeling utterly helpless in this desert. *Mother should have picked another.* He searched within for the Strategist's knowledge. *Mother, come to me. Tell me what to do.* But she did not speak to him.

He looked once more at the sand, at the blackness that rolled on and on. It seemed to shift as he stared. Was there a breeze here, now? The red sun flickered in the sky.

He turned back to the well, where the bucket was slowly creaking its way upwards. There was only one way to go.

'Where are we?' he asked in the darkness.

No answer came.

'Please,' he said. 'Let me see you.'

'I thought of something I wanted, once, and it came. That is the way to do it. There are five men and three women, standing at the doorway. The hat is on the stand ...'

*I thought of something I wanted, once, and it came.* Aranfal's mind turned irresistibly to home. He saw in his mind's eye the great fireplace, and imagined the light it cast, the scurrying shadows that played across his collection …

He opened his eyes.

'How?'

He had come to his quarters in the See House. Standing at the fireplace was the figure he had met in the desert, the person he had followed down the well. This time, however, she had revealed herself. She was a young woman, perhaps in her mid-twenties, though he was wise enough to know that appearances could be deceptive, especially in the Underland. She had a bedraggled, hunted look, as if startled from sleep. She was plump, and pale, with small brown eyes. Her thick hair stuck out from her head like a brush.

'How did we get here?' Aranfal asked.

The woman opened her mouth, and Aranfal steeled himself for another onslaught of nonsense. But this time was different. Even the way she spoke had changed; her voice was lighter and softer.

'Memories,' she said. 'All that matters in this world, or any other.' She seemed confused. 'Ah. We can think in straight lines, now. It isn't always easy for us.'

She looked at the fire. She flicked a glance at him, and it appeared as though she might say something else. But she seemed to think better of it and turned her gaze back onto the flames.

Aranfal took a step towards the woman. She glared at him, and he stopped walking.

'What were those things you were saying?' he asked her. 'Up above?'

She spun away from the fire and crossed the room, until she was an inch from his nose. She grasped him by the shoulders.

'Torturer! Is it you?'

Aranfal nodded, and the woman glanced at the ceiling with fear in her eyes.

'You are here for the game.' She turned her head and a hundred different faces flickered before him, men and women of many ages and complexions. 'There has not been a game since the last one. When was that? A moment ago, or a lifetime?'

'Ten thousand years,' said Aranfal.

'Ah – good, only a moment.' A look of confusion entered her eyes. 'The game has begun. Why are you here?'

'I do not know. I thought that perhaps you would show me the way.'

She looked over his shoulder. Aranfal turned and saw another room, far ahead, cast in a gloomy light.

'What is in there?' He turned back to her. 'Where are you sending me?'

The woman cocked her head to the side. 'Far from the road, it stood: the tree that never was.'

'What?'

'I saw a star, in the distance, though it did not see me.'

*Oh no.*

The woman smiled at him.

'There was a frog, and a pond, in the golden glade. But I could not go there.'

She turned away, and shadows surrounded her. Her voice grew softer as she faded away.

'I was with a child: my child. But it all soon came to an end.'

He was alone, then. He turned to face the new room, and went deeper into the Underland.

# Chapter Four

'Time is a funny thing,' said the King of the Remnants.

His prisoners did not reply.

'Not so long ago, I lived at the top of a pyramid,' he whispered. 'What was it called again?'

He gnawed at his lower lip. How could he forget the name of that place, the black monstrosity that had been his home? He toyed with it, plucking his way through possibilities, until it came to him, floating on the stew of his mind.

'The Fortress of Expansion,' he said at last, clapping his hands. 'Yes, that was it. I lived there, you know, for many years. I was pitiful, back then. I was like a little animal – do you understand? I feel so different, now. But it took a while to get me here, didn't it? I didn't just wake up one day, feeling better about things. It wasn't even my ... not even my powers, I would say. Not even the things I can do, and the titles I've got, down here. No – it was nothing but *time*.'

Far above, through a ceiling of thick glass, Canning could make out the sky outside. *Sky.* Could it even be called a sky, that tempest of storms? A swirling darkness hung above the Remnants; even in the daytime, the light of the sun peered

26

out only occasionally from behind the clouds, as if by accident. *What did that to the sky?*

'Was it you?' he asked, turning to his prisoners and pointing a finger at the great ceiling above. 'Did you do that?'

He smiled at the Duet. Once he had feared these creatures with such a burning intensity. He had feared their cruelty and their power, the sense that he was an insect, waiting to be crushed. *But I'm not an insect any more.*

They were lying on the ground, utterly still, curled together at the side of his throne. *My dogs.* He chuckled at the thought. They stared blankly ahead at the cavernous hall, this great space of steel and stone. They belonged to him now; they could do nothing unless he willed it. *How did this happen?* His recollection of those events was hazy. They had taken him to a memory, and he had trapped them inside it. *Him.* At first, they had been suspended in a kind of flickering light. Now, the light was gone, but they were still trapped; they were still in his power. *Perhaps the light was never there. Perhaps it was only in my mind.*

What had he done to them? They had gone to a great forest, high up in a tree. He had grown angry with them; he had felt himself capable of tugging at the memory, feeling his way through its power and using it for himself. And then he was back in the real world – if the Remnants could be called that – and they were his prisoners. When he looked at Boy and Girl, prostrated at his feet, utterly helpless, only one word came to mind. It was a word from the old books, a word from an age before science, before civilisation, before the Machinery.

*Magic.*

There was magic in memories, and he was very, very good

at using it. He was so good, in fact, that he had trapped two ancient powers and made them into his pets.

*I am a magician.*

'Your majesty.'

Canning snapped back to reality, to find Arch Manipulator Darrlan standing before him. The boy grinned, though it was uneasy. *He always seems so uneasy, these days.*

'How long have you been there?'

'Oh, five, six minutes, your majesty.'

'And I have been …?'

'In a reverie, my lord, positively in a reverie.' He giggled and cast a nervous glance at the Duet.

Canning nodded. He found that his own memories could take a strange hold of him, if he allowed them. *Getting drunk on the past.*

He glanced at his surroundings. *I am here. I know I am here. But somehow, it does not feel true. How could it be true?*

This was a throne room like no other he had seen or read about. It was a vast space, formed largely of metal, like so much of the Remnants: functional, durable, with no regard for beauty. The throne was a small, ugly affair, built into the wall itself and reached by a series of narrow steps. Canning was now sitting in this blackened metallic lump. There were no paintings on the walls, no tapestries, no artefacts to commemorate the history of this world. *Good. Why would we want to remember anything in a world like ours?*

The glass ceiling did nothing to relieve the gloom; on the contrary, it added to it, forcing the occupants to look at the world outside, that dark and bleak panorama of misery, torn and ruined by the wars of the Manipulators and Old Ones.

He looked down at himself, at the white robes he now wore: the uniform of a Manipulator. Pure, light, and free of blemish. Perhaps that was how the Manipulators saw themselves. *But none of us are spotless, are we? None of us can ever be truly clean. Not with our memories ...*

'Great Manipulator.'

Canning started again, flicking his attention back to Darrlan. It felt strange being called that. So many titles to remember: Darrlan was the Arch Manipulator, a grandiose mouthful for a child, and the head of the Remnants until Canning's arrival. But now he, Canning, the one-time Tactician of the Overland, was the Great Manipulator and the King of the Remnants, successor to Arandel, who led a war against the Old Ones ten thousand years before. *Titles, titles, titles, rolling through the endless years ...*

There came a sound from the far side of the room, in the corridor beyond.

'Ah!' Darrlan cried, clapping his hands. 'The Protector of the Secondmost City has arrived!'

The footsteps grew closer: great, thudding steps that echoed through the metal room.

'Who is this, Darrlan?' Canning asked. 'I didn't know there would be visitors.'

'Just one, my lord, just one!' Darrlan shot him a worried look. 'I am sorry to surprise you. But you must meet your people!'

The door to the throne room was a great gash, sliced into the side of the wall as if by some gigantic blade. Even it struggled to accommodate the figure that entered, a creature of greater proportions than anyone Canning had seen before.

'May I present to you, my lord,' Darrlan cried in the loudest voice the boy could muster, 'Arna, Protector of the

29

Secondmost City, Mistress of the Night Shore, Scourge of the Old Ones, Wielder—'

'Enough, enough,' the woman said. Her voice was surprisingly soft: not the great boom that Canning expected. 'Arna will suffice.'

The woman strode towards the throne, her dark eyes never leaving Canning. She was the tallest person the new king had ever seen. Her skin was a light brown, and her hair was entirely black, tied up into a functional bun. She wore a billowing cape that was as dark as her hair, folds of the material falling away from her powerful frame. She was not fat, though it was difficult to tell under her layers of clothing; rather, she had a solid look that made Canning think of the trunk of a tree. She held a walking stick, which she thumped rhythmically on the ground as she traversed the throne room. Canning very much doubted that she needed it for support. *Perhaps it is a weapon.*

He was briefly reminded of Tactician Brightling. *You are inferior. This is her world, her game, her rules. She will toy with you, and she will break you.* But he shook these thoughts away. This was not Amyllia Brightling, and he was not the same man that had cowered in the Fortress of Expansion. *You are the Great Manipulator. You are the—*

'King of the Remnants,' Arna said. She fell to her knees before the throne, and bowed her head, staring at the metal floor.

They remained like that for a while, Canning staring at the kneeling woman and wondering what he was supposed to do. He eventually glanced at Darrlan, who made a gesture with his head. Canning knew what it meant. At least, he thought he did.

'You may rise, my lady,' he said, in what he hoped was a suitably king-like tone of voice.

Arna remained where she was for a moment, before slowly unfolding herself into a standing position.

'It is a delight – a *delight* – to have the honour of meeting you, your majesty,' Arna said. 'Many of our people thought this day would never come. There were even times when I began to despair myself. But you are here, now – finally, we have a weapon that even the Old Ones fear!'

She glanced to Canning's side, her gaze falling on the Duet. Strange: this was the first time she had looked at them since entering the throne room. *Even now, she fears them. My little pets.*

'What have you done with them, your majesty?' she whispered. 'Your abilities are incredible. Once, you know, I held them for half a heartbeat – I was so proud of myself!' She laughed. 'I shudder with mortification, as I look upon what you have achieved. They are your prisoners completely.' Her eyes flickered towards Canning. 'What glories have you seen within their minds? They hold such memories, that pair: memories from long, long ago, from ages of savagery and glory. I saw such things in the moment I defeated them. What have you taken from them, my king?'

Canning glanced at the Duet. He had taken nothing. He had thought about trying, of course, but something held him back. He was unsure how to do it, in truth.

There was another reason too, though: something deeper. He was afraid of breaking the spell he had somehow cast, and which seemed now to operate entirely independently from any effort on his part. What if he tried something and accidentally freed the Duet? What would they do to him? Despite his newfound confidence, he knew the way of the world, and what would happen if he unleashed these beings. *If I freed these enraged gods …*

'I—' he stammered, before Darrlan interrupted.

'The king will discuss his activities when he sees fit,' the boy said. 'Until then, we should not ask.'

'No,' said Arna with a bow. 'Forgive me, your majesty.'

Canning studied the people before him, the wise little boy and the statuesque woman. His time in the Remnants played before his eyes, rolling forward in a river of memory: the weak man, proclaimed a king. *What is the point in your power? What have you done with it, except sit on a throne, gathering dust?*

Were these thoughts the workings of his mind, or was one of his guests doing this to him? He could not tell.

'Why have you come to me?' Canning asked. His voice was heavy, almost slurred. He felt out of balance. He turned his head sluggishly to the Duet, fearing for a moment that they would use his fragility to free themselves. But they remained just as they had before. He could still feel his hold over them, an invisible cord that ran from his mind to theirs, binding their vast and unknowable greatness.

Arna came closer to the throne. 'Your majesty – we need your help.'

It was the first time Canning had been outdoors since he had arrived in the Remnants. He had felt no desire for fresh air, no impulse to feel the wind on his face. Little wonder: there was no fresh air here, and the wind stank of death.

They were in a large courtyard, its surface paved with cracked and weed-infested stones. The main building loomed behind them, a great mongrel of a structure, stone and steel and wood. Scattered around was a mismatch of other structures, twisted and hulking shapes. Occasionally a pale sun would shine through the sky above, and the courtyard glowed with a dull light.

The space was filled with people, all wearing the white robes of Manipulators. Canning associated that uniform with power, with vitality, but there was none of that to be found here.

The Manipulators were lying on the ground, very still indeed. The Great Manipulator did a quick headcount of his prostrate subjects: eleven of them, crumpled up on the floor. He would have taken them for dead, though their eyes were open and burning white.

'They are Manipulating,' Canning said.

'Yes, sir. That's what caused the trouble,' came a voice from the edge of the courtyard.

A man appeared before them. Canning recognised him, he thought. *A face from another time: before I became a king.* The man seemed to be about as old as Canning, and just as bald, with dark skin and wide, lively eyes. He was no Manipulator, this man. He wore a brown cloak, and his gaze held no hint of the power of the Remnants.

'I know you,' Canning said, screwing his eyes up.

'Arlan,' the man said. 'I met you, your majesty, before you ... back before you came down here with us. When you were being held by the Duet – before you held them.'

Canning nodded.

'Controller,' he said. He placed a hand on the man's shoulder. 'I remember you, now.' He smiled. *Memories are such precious things.*

Arlan nodded. 'There's no time to reminisce, your majesty.' He seemed to catch himself. 'Apologies ... I did not mean ...'

Arna was at Canning's side, then. 'These are Manipulators from the Secondmost City, your majesty. Our part of the

Remnants has been under great … strain, in recent times. We've become the focus of a particularly nasty Autocrat, and it's almost broken us.' She gestured at the unconscious Manipulators. 'All of these warriors fought him at once – and all of them have been defeated. I took them here, to seek your assistance.'

'I've been keeping watch on them,' Arlan said. 'They've not moved a muscle. Sometimes you can see a Manipulator fighting back, even in this state, just by the flicker of a finger or the blinking of their eyes. But not with these ones. I think they might be gone for good.'

'Don't say that,' Arna snapped.

'Apologies, my lady.' Arlan bowed, before returning to the side of the courtyard.

Canning studied the Manipulators, glancing from one to the other. He felt something, as he gazed at them: a kind of presence, as of a great pressure bearing down on them all, or a fog blocking them from view.

'Where are they?' he asked.

'We don't know.' Darrlan was speaking, now. 'They've been taken somewhere, by this *thing*. We can't do anything for them. We've tried.'

'Perhaps you could help, Great Manipulator.' Arna's voice. 'This Autocrat would be no match for you. You could find them, and bring them back.'

There were more noises; more words being spoken. But Canning could no longer hear them.

'What did you say?' he asked.

He realised, too late, what had happened. He had gone to the other side of the fog.

# Chapter Five

'Who are you?'

The question seemed to come from far away, repeated in a pained voice. *Who are you? Who are you? Who are you?* Brandione paid it no mind. He focused on the sand, the black, black sand, as it fell away beneath his boots.

'Who are you?'

The desert was empty. The desert had always been empty.

'Who are you?'

There was no one there but him. The desert was empty.

'Who are you?'

He looked up from his feet. He looked away from the sand. And he saw that the desert was not empty at all.

There was a young man at his side: a man of many contradictions. He appeared youthful, at first, with unlined, pale skin and long blond hair. But there was an air of age about his watchful eyes, which could not be concealed. Stranger still was his gown, a green thing that writhed with symbols and shapes, numbers and figures and moons and stars.

How did this young man come to be here, in this desert of black sand, under a red sun in a dark sky? *Where* had he come from?

*This is the Underland, and things are not the same here.*

Brandione stopped walking, and the man came to a halt, too.

He grinned at the one-time General, and clapped his hands together. 'Who are you?' he asked.

'Charls Brandione. At least, that's who I was.'

'So you aren't him any more?'

'I used to be a soldier. Now I'm nothing.'

'Nothing? Hmm. You wouldn't be here if you were nothing.' He snapped his fingers together. 'I have it! The Queen. You are the Queen's pawn.'

Brandione nodded, and braced himself. He knew what was coming next.

'The Last Doubter,' the man whispered. 'I have heard your name. She has seen such things for her Last Doubter. Oh, I know what she thinks. I'm the Gamesman – I know what everyone thinks will happen, in all the games. She thinks you'll find the First Memory. Amazing!'

He laughed, and Brandione was struck with a sudden image of this man, long ago, standing before so many tables, a dominant figure, a power of the world.

The Gamesman, as he called himself, came up close to him. 'She is deluded. Do you know why, Last Doubter?'

Brandione shook his head.

'Because this is *the* game. The Old Place runs this game, Brandione. Hmm? We do not know what it is thinking. We do not know the rules. When it decides to ...' He snapped his fingers again. 'When it decides to end the pawns, or take them away, we do not know what forces its hand. All we can do is watch. Now tell me this, Last Doubter – why, exactly, would the Old Place want to show *you* the First Memory? Why would it reveal its most powerful secret, and risk losing it forever? It wouldn't, is the answer. It never has, and it never will.'

'Then how is it played?' *Always the same question, over and over again.* 'I think I should know, if I'm a player.'

The Gamesman shrugged. 'That's the delicious thing, Brandione. It changes all the time.' He looked up at the sun. 'It knows when we are coming to play. It knows what we want. And it does what it likes. The Operators watch you all, on my lovely table: helpless.'

'So I'm not playing a game at all. I'm only walking through a nightmare, until it decides it's had enough of me.' Brandione felt perversely piqued at the injustice of it all. 'There is no fairness, here. There is only death. It kills us in the order it wants, or throws us in some corner of this place, never to return.'

The Gamesman turned suddenly serious. 'Perhaps, perhaps. But to survive in the game, even for a while, is such an honour. The Old Place is everything, Brandione. I never question it, and neither should you. Its mind is unknowable, its highways endless, its thoughts too subtle to comprehend, even for the Queen herself – its first child!'

Brandione held up a hand. 'Enough. I can't listen to this nonsense any more.'

The Gamesman cocked his head to the side. 'Interesting. *Nonsense.*' He giggled. 'Well, here's something you'll understand. If one person lasts longer than the rest, it would be better to be that person, than any of the other pawns, wouldn't it? You would have time, then. Time to defeat the game.' He laughed derisively.

Brandione nodded, and looked out to the desert. 'That I can understand.' He thought for a moment. 'Where does it take them – the ones it doesn't kill?'

He turned back to the Gamesman, and found he was alone again.

Brandione walked on, through the black sands. At one point – he did not know when, or if 'when' even mattered here – he looked up and saw the outline of an object far ahead. He kept his eyes on it as he went. Once, he turned in another direction. But as he walked, the lines of the object reappeared. *It is meant for me.*

It became clearer over time. At first, he thought it was some kind of building: another tower, perhaps, like the one where he had met the Dust Queen. But soon he realised it was not a manmade structure at all: it was a mountain.

It was the smallest mountain the General had ever seen; so small, in fact, that it took him time to realise it even *was* a mountain. But soon it was clear. Rising from the desert before him was a sharp mound of rock, small but perfectly formed, its peak frosted with snow, its body wreathed in shadow.

Its size was deceptive. As he walked, the mountain seemed to leap towards him, growing with every jump. The experience was familiar; he had seen it many times before, in the Overland. In those days, he thought it was some trick of perspective or light. He wondered, now, if he had seen the Underland itself, back then, seeping into the real world. Perhaps there was no difference between them.

The sand at his feet began to slowly dissipate, giving way to rough, sparse grass. The mountain leapt forward again, until all the world before him was taken over by the rock.

Brandione began to climb.

A path had been laid out into the side of the mountain, cutting its way sharply upwards through jagged rocks. He was glad of his old boots, his military garb, as he made his way up the path, into the heights of the mountain. He stopped, once, and looked out at the world below. Blasted grasslands stretched away from the great rock, merging into the black sand somewhere far away. He thought he saw something else, out there: one of the great statues of the Strategist that now stood in the Circus. He thought she was raising her arms, but he could not be certain. There was a kind of fissure in the air behind her, like someone had torn out part of the black sky; a haze of blue light crackled in the beyond.

In the sky above, the red sun had gone. In its place was a moon, a vast, perfect sphere, casting a blue light down upon the desert.

Brandione turned back to the path and carried on up the mountain. The path began to twist and turn in tighter and tighter corners. Eventually he came to a wooden sign propped up on the rock before him, on which a question had been scrawled in black ink.

**Who are you?**

The one-time General stopped for a moment before the sign. Was he meant to answer this question? If so, how?

On he went, around another corner.

**Who are you?**

He stopped again. This appeared to be the same sign. He walked up to it, studied it, felt its edges; it was identical to the one before. He did not allow himself to feel any surprise. *This is the Underland.*

Brandione turned another corner, and there was the sign again, with those same three words leaping from its surface. Now, however, things had changed. He was no longer alone.

A young girl was sitting beside the sign, nestled among the boulders and smiling up at Brandione. Unlike the

Gamesman or the Dust Queen, this girl had no hint of humanity. She put Brandione in mind of a figure from a painting, sliced out of the canvas and brought to life: a beautiful drawing of a blonde-haired child in a white dress, but nothing more than that.

'Who are you?' she asked him. The voice did not belong to a girl of her age, or to any girl: it was more of a rasp than a voice, the pages of a book blowing open in the wind.

'Charls Brandione,' he said. 'I seem to always be introducing myself.'

The girl climbed to her feet. 'That is not you.' The voice rattled around his ears.

She reached out a finger and tapped Charls on the nose. 'Soldier, and scholar. Last Doubter.'

Brandione felt a sudden burst of anger. 'How do I play the game?'

The girl looked to the sky, whispering something incomprehensible, before she snapped her head back to Brandione. 'There will be no game,' she said. 'Not like the old ones. The game has changed.'

Anger burned in Brandione. The one-time General was a furious insect: a wasp, trapped in a jar.

'How?'

The girl became a man, then an older woman, then a thousand other people, changing madly in the course of a minute, before returning to the person he had first encountered.

She walked up to him and whispered in his ear.

'You are not here to have *fun*, this time. You are here to *help*.'

She nodded behind Brandione. He turned, to see a doorway in the mountainside.

# Chapter Six

'Death is coming.'

Drayn opened her eyes. Jandell and Jaco were at her side. She knew, somehow, in her bones, that these were the real Jandell and Jaco. There was something in the way they held themselves, something in the way she felt when she looked at them, that told her they were flesh and blood. But it was instantly clear that everything else in this place was a memory. *Does that make it any less real?*

A man sat at a desk before them. He was fairly young, perhaps in his late thirties, with neat black hair and smooth pale skin. He had an air of precision, of order. But there was something harried in his expression, something wan and fearful. The table was covered in papers, which the man sifted through with his fingers.

This was a younger version of Jaco. Drayn glanced from the old man at her side to his counterpart in the memory. There was a strange look in the old man's eye: a kind of affectionate disdain.

There came a great lurch, and Drayn almost tumbled to the floor. This was a ship like Jandell's, the one that had carried her into the East. But it was very different. On

41

Jandell's vessel she had sensed his power, carrying them across the waves. There was none of that here. There was only the peril of the *real*.

At the doorway stood another man, who must have been the speaker. He was a short, stocky type, who seemed to have sprung from the ship itself, a thing of seasalt and cold winds, his unblinking eyes making Drayn think of some animal of the depths. His head had been shaved with such severity that only the barest hint of stubble could be discerned on the gleaming pate.

'Who, Teel?' asked the memory Jaco.

The man called Teel entered the captain's cabin. He glanced at the floor and lifted a torn black cloak.

'Harra,' Teel said. He tossed the cloak to Jaco. 'She's above deck, my lord. It is cold.'

The younger Jaco stood and tossed the cloak aside. 'Let's go.'

They found themselves on the deck at night, staring at a dead woman.

Her corpse was positioned against a mast. A handful of other crewmembers were spread around the deck. Some watched Jaco, as he knelt down by the body of the woman called Harra. Others stared out to sea, to impenetrable blackness.

Drayn looked to the real Jaco. If he was surprised to find himself in a memory, he did not look it. Instead, he stared ahead with a dark gravity. Jandell seemed lost in thought as he watched the unfolding scene.

'How did you bring us here?' he asked Drayn, emerging from his reverie. 'Do you remember how you did it?'

'No.'

'And can you ... what do you feel?'

'Nothing,' Drayn said. But perhaps that was not true. Perhaps she was once more deploying her tricks, as if to ward off the Voice, that thing that had watched her in the Choosing. *It's gone, now. Isn't it?*

She *could* feel something: the edge of the memory. There was something there: a whisper of power ...

'What killed her?' asked the Jaco of the memory.

Teel crouched down beside the captain. 'It's the same thing that gets them all,' he said. 'Whatever *it* is. The Blight. She was fine this morning, or as fine as you can be, out here. And then ...' He shrugged.

The young Jaco nodded. 'The Blight,' he said. 'What is it?' He lifted Harra's arm, turning it over to study the underside. 'When I was a boy, I used to hear of terrible scourges. They came from the swamps in the South, folks used to say, from the festering waters. People would come out in blotches, and that would be the end of them. You never got rid of it, when it arrived in a town. You had to keep the people inside, until they were all ... gone.'

'Then perhaps you shouldn't be touching her, my lord.'

'That's just it, Teel – there are no marks on her.'

Jaco brushed a strand of thin black hair away from Harra's forehead.

'If it is the same thing, we're all dead already,' said Jaco. 'But I don't think so. I think it's something else. It's as if the spirit falls out of them, somehow.'

'It's a curse,' Teel spat. 'We are being punished.'

Jaco squinted. 'What do you mean?'

Teel clenched his fists together. 'We've gone too far from home, my lord, and we're being punished for it.'

Jaco smiled.

'The Machinery,' he said.

Teel nodded. 'Yes, my lord. We're from the Overland. We're a part of the Machinery. It felt us leave it behind, and it's punishing us. That's why we're lost, out here. We lost ourselves, when we left, and now we're lost at sea.'

There was a sound, in the dark – the screech of a bird. The crewmembers on the deck muttered to one another in hushed voices.

'Second,' Jaco said, 'the Operator has sanctioned our voyages. He would not have done so—'

'No, sir, no.'

Jaco's eyes widened. He seemed unaccustomed to being interrupted. He was so like Drayn's mother. *He's higher than the rest of these folk, and it's nothing to do with a title.*

'I'm sorry, my lord, truly.' Teel bowed his head. 'But the Operator is not the Machinery. They are not the same thing.'

Jaco looked back to Harra.

'Do you think it sees us here, Teel?'

Teel nodded. 'Yes, my lord. The Machinery knows all.'


They were back in the cabin.

'My lord.'

Jaco turned towards Teel, who stood at the door again. 'Death is coming,' said the captain. 'Who is it this time?'

But Teel shook his gleaming head. 'No. That's not it. Come.'

They all followed Teel through the memory ship, back up to the deck.

'It's land,' said Teel.

Jaco grunted, and stared out into the ocean, which glowed in the light of the dawn. Drayn saw it, then – a grey mass.

'Have we come home?' Jaco asked. 'Or back to the South?'

Teel silenced Jaco with a shake of his head.

'This is not the Overland, or the southern lands, my lord. We have not found our way by accident.' Teel squinted out into the greyness. 'I don't know where we are.'

Jaco nodded. 'Have we seen any other ships?'

'No. There's no sign of life here at all. But the coast … I cannot be certain, my lord, but to my eye, this is the edge of a wide land. It is no outcrop. If it's large, then it could be inhabited. And we don't know who they are, the people that live there.'

Jaco sighed. 'We have no choice. We must go there.'

The memory took them somewhere else: an expanse of pale-green grass and black, broken stone, at the side of a forest. The wind howled at them.

There were about a dozen crewmembers left untouched by the Blight. They had carved out a small camp at the side of the woods, in the shadow of three great boulders. They had food, and a supply of firewood: a hog was burning on a spit.

'Why's it stopped?' said a voice.

Drayn turned her head, and saw Teel and Jaco, sitting on one of the boulders. Teel seemed healthier than before: his skin was pinker, his flesh thicker, and there was even a thin layer of stubble on his scalp.

'The Blight?'

Teel nodded.

Jaco shrugged. 'I don't know. Perhaps it's the climate.'

Teel grunted. 'It's like we were being poisoned by someone, and now they've decided to … stop poisoning us.'

Jaco did not argue.

'If someone was doing that to us,' he said, 'I wonder why they've stopped?'

Teel glanced at the captain. 'Maybe they've got us where they want us.' He gestured to the other crewmembers, below the rocks. They were spread around in little groups, talking to one another and eating. 'Everyone's taken their mind off their work,' Teel said. 'Do you know what I mean, my lord?'

Jaco nodded. 'I do.'

'It's just that … I *feel* something here, my lord. That's all.'

Jaco stared at their surroundings.

'Then what should we do, Teel?'

Teel jammed a thumb over his shoulder. 'We should get back to the ship, my lord.'

Jaco glanced behind him, down to the shore beyond. Drayn could not see it, but she imagined the ship was there, tied to some rocks.

'We should get back to it, and take our chances on the waves,' Teel said. 'Death is coming here, as well. I can feel it.'

The memory shunted forward, into the night. The crew were asleep around their little camp, all except Jaco, who sat at the edge of a rock, staring out into the woods. Drayn glanced quickly around. She saw Jandell and the older Jaco, watching this memory with the same fascination as her.

A noise came from the woods, one that could not be ignored. It was the cry of a newborn baby.

Teel was awake and on his feet, staring out into the trees, tightly grasping a blade. Jaco scrambled down from the rock to Teel's side. The cry came again, closer than before. This time there were other sounds: the shifting of undergrowth, the crackle of sticks and twigs breaking underfoot.

'We should get away from here,' Teel said, in a quiet voice. 'Nothing good is coming from those woods.'

The memory Jaco shook his head. 'We don't have time. And we don't run away from crying babies.'

Teel grunted. 'It's not the baby I'm worried about. It's whoever's carrying it.'

The sounds came closer, almost as if the wanderers were at the very edge of the treeline, before they stopped altogether. Even the baby ceased crying. *Perhaps a hand has been placed across its mouth.*

'They've seen us,' Teel whispered. There was a tremor in his voice that was oddly unsettling. 'They're watching us.'

'Wouldn't you?' Jaco whispered back. 'If you were carrying a baby through the woods, and you stumbled across a group of strangers, would you run out into the middle of them?' He glanced at Teel's blade. 'When they're armed?'

The rest of the crew were awake now, too, on their feet and staring out into the woods. The only light came from the moon and the dying glow of the fire. 'Light a torch,' Jaco ordered a woman to his right.

He walked forward as the torchlight flickered around the camp. Teel grabbed him by the shoulder, but the captain shook him off. He approached the trees as quietly as he could, raising his hands in the air.

'I don't know if you understand me,' he said, in what Drayn took as an attempt at a friendly voice. 'We are from another land. We came here by accident, and we only wish to go home.'

There came a noise from the woods. It was not the cry of a baby, but a hushed whisper.

Another moment passed.

'Please, come out to us,' Jaco said.

There was silence. Nothing happened.

'Please,' Jaco said again. 'I swear, we mean you no harm.'

And then she came.

The woman was young to look at, somewhere in her twenties or early thirties. But there was an air of something old in the way she carried herself, and in the glances of her eyes. And what eyes they were: green as grass, green as emeralds, green as a snake. Almost as green as the dress she wore, a long gown that wrapped itself around her narrow frame, like it too was alive: a spirit of the forest. She wore her red hair long, the curls cascading past her shoulders, and her skin was a white so unblemished that it could almost have been porcelain.

Drayn heard a gasp: she turned and saw that Jandell had fallen to his knees, his head in his hands. The real Jaco simply watched, his face a slab of stone.

The baby was in the woman's arms, wrapped in grey rags.

'Can you understand me, my lady?' the memory Jaco asked.

The woman stopped walking. She was perhaps ten paces from their camp.

'Yes, oh yes,' she said, nodding vigorously. 'I am from your land, my lord, I know your words well, oh yes.'

The memory Jaco sucked in a breath.

'How did you get here?' he asked. 'We thought we were the first from the Plateau to come to this place – wherever we are.'

'Oh, it is a terrible place, a terrible place!' the woman cried. Her voice had a strange, sing-song quality. 'It is full of terrible people, my lord! They took me, you see, they sailed to our lands in their terrible ships, and they took me away!'

Jaco glanced at the trees.

'Is that your baby?'

'Yes, yes, my little girl!'

The woman began to move. The crewmembers tensed up, and Teel raised his blade, but Jaco quietened them with a flick of a finger.

The woman brought the baby to him, and Jaco looked down at the squalling child within the rags. Drayn hurried forward, to catch a glimpse of this infant. She had a thick thatch of black hair, and her wide eyes were the same colour. Strange, but she was not dissimilar to Jaco himself.

'They want to make her a slave too, my lord!' the woman cried. 'But I will not let them! I will throw her into the sea before I allow that!' She looked at the ground. 'They used me most cruelly, my lord,' she said in a quiet voice, gesturing at her child. 'But I am not sorry to have her, oh no. I will not allow them to take her!'

'Captain.'

Jaco turned to Teel, who was pointing into the forest.

'There are lights in the forest, captain.'

The captain squinted into the darkness. Drayn saw it too: a flickering line of torches, coming closer. Drayn could just about make out the sound of voices, shouting and calling, the words muffled by distance.

'It is them!' the woman cried. 'They are coming!' She grasped Jaco's arm. 'They will kill us all if you stay! Take my baby, and leave this place, oh yes, you must leave.'

Jaco seemed to thrum with a restless energy.

'Very well,' he said. He turned to Teel. 'We can launch the ship quickly.'

Teel nodded. 'Yes. But the instruments—'

'Oh your little tools and your maps, your little toys, they will work now!' the woman cried. 'This place sucks people in with its terrible tricks, but it cannot stop you leaving, oh no!'

Jaco nodded. He did not truly appear to understand, though he knew they had to leave: of that, Drayn was certain.

'Come with us,' he said to the woman.

'No, my lord, no. They will chase you if they see your ship. I will stay here, and I will distract them, oh yes, I am so good at distracting!' She thrust the child into Jaco's arms. 'Take her! Run!'

Jaco seemed to think this over for a moment. 'Very well,' he said.

The woman nodded, and turned towards the lights.

'What is your name?' Jaco asked.

The woman glanced back at him. 'I have many names, my lord, but none of them matter here.'

'What of the girl?'

The woman began to walk away. 'Call her what you will.'

They were back on board the ship, now, in Jaco's room. The captain sat at his desk with the child, wrapped in a woollen blanket. She was older than Drayn had first thought: perhaps seven or eight months old.

Teel came to the door.

'We will tell no one of this,' Jaco said, 'apart from my wife. I will keep the child in Paprissi House, until it is time to reveal her. My wife never leaves the house anyway. They will believe she is ours. As for our journey, we went to the South as usual.'

Teel shrugged. 'That is your concern, my lord.'

Jaco nodded. 'Yes. It is.'

'What will you call her?' Teel asked.

Jaco looked down at the baby.

'Strange,' he whispered. 'When I look at these eyes, sometimes I think I see the slightest hint of purple.'

Teel chuckled. 'That's love, playing tricks on you, sir. Makes you see funny things.'

Jaco's head snapped up. 'Love?' He looked down at the baby once more. 'She *looks* like one of us, doesn't she? A Paprissi.'

'Yes, sir. Pale skinned, my lord. A little Paprissi lady already, just by another name.'

Jaco smiled. 'She looks like my own grandmother. So there we are – that's what I'll name her.'

'Grandmother?'

Jaco laughed. 'No.' He touched the baby's nose. 'Katrina.'

# Chapter Seven

*Welcome.*

The word was scrawled into the wall in white chalk, high above Aranfal's head. He was alone. A narrow passageway stretched before him, formed of black stone and filled with a pale light.

He had been walking this same corridor now for hours, alone with his thoughts. He felt no tiredness, no hunger, no thirst. He was just a walking, thinking machine, mired in the past, and the present, and the game.

He began to walk again. But the wall was not finished with him, and another word waited up ahead.

*To.*

He studied it for a moment. *Welcome To. So I am collecting words.*

The next words came sooner than the others.

*The Hallway of Regret.*

He gave a sharp nod. *Welcome to the Hallway of Regret. I have a sentence now. That's progress, isn't it?*

There was a noise behind, a kind of creak. He turned, to find a door had opened in the wall. A golden light came from within, so bright it forced him to shield his eyes with an arm. He considered walking in another direction, back the way he had come or further down the corridor. But he knew there was only one way to go, now. The Underland would always take him there, whether he wanted to go or not.

The light was blinding, forcing his eyes closed. He had a curious sensation of floating. There was a sense of nothingness here, carrying him along with it. After a while the intensity of the light began to weaken, though he could still make out very little. He became gradually aware of a presence: he could feel it, rather than see it.

'I can't see anything.'

The light dimmed again, and the Watcher could finally fully open his eyes. He was in a vast hall, cut into the shape of a rough circle. All around were doors, carved into the walls in line after line, formed of all kinds of colours and materials. The room itself was empty, save for one, solitary figure.

The creature before him had the rough outline of a human, though human it was not. It was tall and thin, dressed in a blue gown that hung open to expose its birdlike chest. Thin fingers sprouted from webbed hands that sat at the end of elongated arms. Its red mouth was split open by a coruscating smile, sitting under a nose that was unusually *normal* on that strange face. It was completely bald, though this was not the baldness of a shaved head, or of one whose hair had fallen out: the skin had a strange quality, milk soft and satin supple, like that of a newborn baby. The creature had no eyes: just a smooth patch of skin where they should have been.

'Time drifts, and time is still,' it said. Its voice was familiar to Aranfal, yet he could not place it. It had a strange tone, as if it was not the voice of one being at all, but of many, somehow squeezed together into a single stream.

'Memory is strong, and memory is weak,' it said.

It did not appear to notice him, but to exist in a kind of suspended reality of its own.

'Who are you?' Aranfal asked.

'There was once a mother, who was herself a daughter, and a mother of mothers for evermore.'

'I don't understand.'

He walked around the creature, unsure of what to do. It remained perfectly still as he made a circuit of its ugly form.

'In the outside, there is a door. In the inside, there is a tree.'

His mind turned to the woman he had encountered when he first came to the Old Place. She talked in much the same way as this thing. He wondered if this was that same creature, or some twisted relation. She had spoken sense, in the end, pointing him on the path to take. But how could he draw some sense from the mouth of this monster, which seemed more distant than even the woman in the well?

'There is nothing but stars in the sea, there is nothing but droplets in the sky. The words of my fathers were unspoken, but my children sang in rhymes. When I found ...'

'Help me,' Aranfal said. 'Please.'

The creature ceased talking. It seemed to incline its head towards him, though he wondered if this was only a trick of his mind.

'The floor is on the ceiling. The roof is in the ground.'

He had seen people like this, in cells of the See House, men and women who drifted away on the contours of their own ravings. Perhaps they were trying to escape reality; he could not blame them. But floating minds were no use to a Watcher. A Watcher needed *answers*.

Aranfal had a lot of tricks, to bring someone back to reality. One always worked best though, a tried and trusted manoeuvre for which he had become famous: hurt someone they loved, or threaten to do so. Well, that was not going to work here. There was nothing here that the creature loved.

It occurred to him, then, that perhaps there *was* something here that the creature cared about. *He* was here: a human, one who had been permitted to play in the great game and not yet been killed or thrown into some nightmarish pit of memory. Perhaps he was his own bargaining chip.

'The night turns into more night, until day comes,' the creature said. 'But then, the night lasts longer than before.'

'Being of the Old Place,' Aranfal said. He did not know what else to call it, yet his words felt foolish. 'You are far away from me. Come closer, so that we may talk. I know you have summoned me here: allow me to understand you.'

'There is a world formed of green grass and blue ice. It is our own world, but it is upside down.'

'If you do not drag yourself away from madness,' Aranfal whispered, now standing directly before the beast, 'I will kill myself. I will pick my eyes out and bleed to death. I will make a noose of my cloak, and hang myself. I will die, creature, I will die, and I will not be able to help you.'

The creature was silent.

'I will die, and it will be your doing.'

And then all at once, the creature came to life: *real* life, engaged life.

'Torturer,' it whispered. A smile stretched across its unlined skin. 'We were gone, weren't we? We always go off on our journeys, floating away on the winds of memory. We cannot stop it.'

'I have met someone like you before.'

The creature only smiled.

'Who are you?'

'We are a face of the Old Place. We are the children of humanity, and the parents of Operators and all the other beasts that have spawned from this place.' It sighed. 'We are glad we can talk to you, now, as people. But it is hard for us. That is why we need our children: they are focused. They are more like you. We are … we cannot think straight. Sometimes it lasts for millennia.'

It cocked its head to the side, as if noticing Aranfal's expression for the first time: as if it could actually *see*.

'It's the eyes, isn't it?' The creature reached one of its spider hands up to its plum of a mouth and chuckled. 'It's always the eyes. We do not feel their absence. In fact, we pity those that have them.'

Aranfal glanced at his surroundings, to the doors that were all around. Some were slightly ajar, and light spilled out from the beyond.

'Where am I?'

The creature frowned. 'Didn't you see the signs? Did we *forget* the signs?' It seemed angry for a moment.

'I saw,' said Aranfal. 'The Hallway of Regret.'

The creature grinned, and clapped its strange hands. 'Indeed.'

'What do you want?'

It giggled. 'We will tell you about our eyes, torturer. We do not have eyes, because they are distracting. Do you understand? We do not want to *see* memories. Not ever. We simply want to *feel* them. The power in them is so much more than something one can see. And when we feel them – oh, well, we can see them all anyway.'

It reached its hands up and placed them on either side of the Watcher's head.

'It is so nice to have you here, in your true flesh and bone. It gives your memories more flavour. A great circle – we feel new memories being born within you, memories of memories, and on and on it goes ...'

The creature withdrew from Aranfal, and went suddenly still. 'We are many. We are eyeless. The Eyeless One, you can call us.'

Aranfal nodded. He felt as though the Old Place was beginning to show itself to him: starting to reveal its weaknesses. It was a god: he could feel that in his bones. But this god was born of mortals. This god lived for human memory. This god was a parasite. It *worshipped* him, and all the rest of humanity.

There came a great rumble, emanating from somewhere far beneath them. The room shook, and a piece of the ceiling fell, landing with a crack on the floor.

'Everything is changing,' the Eyeless One said. 'We all sit here, pretending to play a game, just like the others we have played for so many long years. But this one is *not* the same, Aranfal. How can it be, when we are subjected ... yes, subjected ... to that *thing*.'

Aranfal opened his mouth to speak again, but the creature held up one of its spider hands, palm facing forward. There was a new edge in its voice. 'The world is in motion, Aranfal. Can't you feel it?'

Aranfal nodded. 'I felt that, yes. What was it?'

The creature seemed suddenly fearful. 'Ruin is coming. We sit here, having a nice chat, and all the while, Ruin is coming. Ruin has grown so strong, now – stronger than us!'

'Us? You mean the Old Place?'

The creature made a flurry of tuts. 'Our children are such wonderful things.' It clicked two bony fingers, and suddenly they were joined by a group of spectral beings, hallucinations from a fevered dream: Shirkra, Jandell, the Strategist, the Dust Queen, Squatstout, a boy and girl Aranfal did not know, but who he knew in his bones were Operators like the others. 'We made them to help us, long ago, when we could not help ourselves. They are weapons: the power of memory, warped into creatures that can *use it* in such amazing ways.' The creature let out a long, rattling sigh. 'Among them all, one was the worst, and the best, all at the same time.' A gesture from a spindly hand, and a new figure appeared. This one, however, was no more than a shadow: a black silhouette, standing at the creature's side.

'Who is that?' Aranfal whispered. He looked around the room, and it seemed to him that the other Operators were cringing away from the shadow man.

'Ruin,' the Eyeless One said. 'He has no host, as yet, though he has been searching …'

'Ruin is an Operator,' Aranfal said. He felt himself backing away from the shadow man.

The creature nodded. 'Yes. And something has happened to him. Two of these children of ours – the lady of Dust and the Bleak Jandell – built something, in our heart, a little while ago. It is a terrible thing. They placed Ruin within, but they did not know what they were doing. They have made him stronger than he ever was before. He is now greater even than us: than the Old Place. *That*, torturer, is a power to be feared.'

The great rumble came again.

'What is Ruin doing to you? Are you dying?'

The creature shook its head. 'Not yet, not yet. But that child of ours knows so much about us, now: he has sat in our heart for so long that he knows all our weaknesses, all our soft spots. He knows how to use us as he wants. He is so very powerful! Soon he will take us over. Soon he will *become* the Old Place. Ruin, the god: within all memory, and all memory within him.'

The shadow man began to grow, darkening the room. As he did, the other Operators faded away, and the Eyeless One began to tremble.

'Only one thing can stop it. It is a memory, filled with such power that perhaps not even Ruin could stand against it. The object of the game, Aranfal: the First Memory of the Old Place.'

'Then give it to me! Or give it to one of the other players. Or use it yourself. Whatever it takes.' He looked at the shadow man, who was now as tall as two people, standing one on top of the other. 'Forget the game. That thing will destroy us all, if you let it. I can feel it.' He stepped forward towards the shadow, and some giddy part of him wanted to run inside it. He knew this was only a ghost, only a dream of the true creature known as Ruin, yet still he could sense its strength. 'It must be stopped.'

The Eyeless One gave a little giggle. 'Ah. There is the problem, our Aranfal. We have lost it. The First Memory. We have lost it.' The creature laughed louder. 'We lost it, just after the last game. We used to treasure it so carefully. But when the Machinery was made, during all that upheaval … we lost it.'

It clicked its fingers, and the images of Operators faded away, along with the ghost of Ruin.

'Then let me look for it,' Aranfal said. 'Point me to where you last saw it.'

'Point you? Hmm. We wouldn't know where to begin.' The creature seemed to think this over for a moment. 'There are so many places it could be. Here, in the Hallway of Regret – we are sure we had it here, once. Or perhaps in Chaos. Or was it in the Hopeful Chambers? Yes, we are *sure* it was in one of those places. We need mortal help, Aranfal. Your eyes see us in such a different way. Yet *you* cannot look through all of those places by yourself: not before Ruin comes.'

The creature grinned.

'It is lucky that there are two more mortals here, is it not?'

It reached up, gestured with one of those odd hands, and the floor opened up. Two people appeared from below, glancing around in fear and confusion.

It was Aleah and Brandione.

# Chapter Eight

The mountain was not what Brandione had expected.

'This is a surprise,' he said, as he found himself face to face with Aranfal, the pawn of the Strategist.

Aranfal nodded at Brandione, an uneasy smile on his lips. There was a change in the Watcher, and it wasn't just that his mask was missing. There was something new in his gaze, in the way he held himself. *Hesitation.* And something more: a lack of that hardness that had made him such a powerful force in the Overland. *Is this still the torturer from the Bowels of the See House? Or another man?* But Aranfal was not the only one who had changed. They all had. How could they not, when the world had fallen apart around them, and reality had collapsed into a dream?

There was a woman at the Watcher's side. *The Watcher Aleah, pawn of Shirkra.* She wore a faintly tattered black cloak, in stark contrast to Aranfal's brilliant aquamarine garment. She glanced around the room with a hungry gaze.

And then there was the other *thing*: a creature with over-sized hands, long limbs, and a vicious red smile. It had no eyes, but he knew it was watching him all the same.

61

'You,' said Aleah, pointing a finger at the creature. 'You took us here. What do you want?'

The creature giggled, covering its mouth with one of its odd hands. 'What do we want? We only want what all things want – we only want to live in peace!'

'Its name is the Eyeless One,' Aranfal said.

'A bit on the nose,' said Aleah. She sounded braver than she looked.

Brandione felt a well of deep power in this creature, greater by far than that of the Queen, but somewhat diffuse. He sensed that its powers were vast, but lacking in focus. It was an endless, placid ocean, while the Queen and the others were furious rivers.

'You are the Old Place,' he said.

The creature turned to him. 'We are many.' It grinned. 'You are the soldier and the scholar. The Last Doubter. Our first child sees great things for you. We hope you can achieve them. We hope that *one of you* can achieve them.'

'You *want* the First Memory to be found?'

'Of course! We need it, you see. You know why, Brandione.'

The General nodded. 'Ruin.'

The creature clicked its fingers, and a great shadow in the shape of a man appeared in Brandione's mind.

'Ruin is a creature,' he said with certainty. 'Ruin is an Operator.'

The Eyeless One gave a frantic nod. 'Yes! Of course! A demon child of ours, who will soon take us over, unless the First Memory is found.' The creature sighed.

'The game has changed,' the Eyeless One said. 'The old games were for our amusement. This one is for our survival. You must help us find the First Memory. You mortals can see things here that we cannot. Do you understand?'

'Where is it?' Aleah seemed disappointed. *She was enjoying the game, perhaps. I wonder where it took her?*

The Eyeless One raised its hands into the air, and wriggled its long fingers. 'We don't *know* where it is. We lost it, a while ago.'

'Ten thousand years ago,' said Aranfal.

The creature nodded. 'Yes. Not long. But now Ruin is coming!'

Aleah took a step towards the Eyeless One, who turned on her with a grinding smile. 'Ah yes, we know you. Ambitious, yet frightened. Very good!'

Aleah nodded. 'Perhaps.' She took another step forward. 'Let me get this straightened out, in my ambitious, frightened mind. You *want* to find the First Memory. And you want *us* to help you.'

The Eyeless One nodded.

'What do we get in return? I know what happened to the people who played the game in the past. What's to say you won't do the same to us, even though we're helping you?'

The creature shrugged.

Aleah's eyes widened, and she turned to Aranfal. 'We shouldn't help it. It'll kill us, or hold us here forever. Maybe they don't die, the ones it keeps.' She glanced around the room. 'I don't know which I'd prefer.'

The Eyeless One tutted. 'There are worse things than us in this world. Ruin has already gained so much power. Soon he will *become* us. Then you will have a very different god: a demon of memory, holding sway over the ever-growing past. He will seek out his favourite memories, and drown you in them: the nasty, horrible ones. The ones that you hide away. *Forever.*' The Eyeless One covered its face with its hands. 'Only the First Memory can hope to stop him. And we have *lost it*.'

'If we help you, you'll need to free us,' said Aranfal. He was unsure of himself, Brandione knew: making it up as he went along. 'We don't want to stay down here, and we don't want to die.'

The creature removed its hands from its face and scratched the underside of its chin with a yellowing fingernail.

'We promise to release you,' it said. 'And never play a game again.'

There was silence for a moment. The three mortals exchanged glances. Brandione could not say why, but he believed this creature.

Aleah, however, did not seem convinced. 'Why do *you* need *us*? What help could we give you?' She laughed. 'It's a trick, Aranfal. It's offering us hope, then it's going to snatch it away. It's the sort of thing you would have done, once.'

Aranfal winced.

The creature spread its arms wide. 'We are a child! When a child loses its favourite toy, what does it do?'

'Asks for help,' Aranfal said. 'From its parents.'

The creature nodded. 'Yes. That is all we are doing now. We are the God of Memory: but memories come from *you*, from all of you. You hold such powers, and only some of you have even begun to use them.' It waved its hands at them all. 'You can look at this place with different eyes. That is why you are such fun, in the game. We marvel at you. In the past, some of the players came so close. We need you to do that again. This time, though, we will not interfere. And when one of you finds the First Memory, we will marvel at your glory.'

Aleah's eyes were saucers. She was coming round to this

new proposition, Brandione realised. She liked the idea of finding this memory, and having the Old Place marvel at her glory.

He, however, was growing impatient.

'How is this going to work?' he asked. 'Where do we begin?'

The creature grinned. 'We think we remember seeing it in a few different places before we lost it. Three places, to be precise. Lucky there are three of you here!'

'Yes, very lucky,' said Brandione, who did not believe in luck.

'This is the Hallway of Regret,' the creature said. 'We think that ... *you* should look here.' It jabbed a finger at Brandione.

'As for you two – where to send each of you?' It jerked its head from Aranfal to Aleah, as if it was really looking at them. 'You,' it said, pointing at Aleah. 'You are the pawn of Shirkra – perhaps, then, you should go to Chaos.' It clicked its fingers, and the floor opened, swallowing up the female Watcher. 'And you – the Hopeful Chambers is the place for you.' It pointed at Aranfal. 'Be sure that you look very carefully, and mind your step.'

'Hopeful Chambers,' Aranfal whispered. 'Sounds like it could have been worse.'

The creature grinned. 'Don't read too much into the name.' It clicked its fingers again, and Aranfal disappeared.

The Eyeless One turned to Brandione. 'Last Doubter: welcome to the Hallway of Regret.'

Brandione glanced once more around the room. As he looked, he saw the hall change. The ceiling began to rise, gradually becoming more distant until it was no longer visible. The doors at the side of the hall were joined by thousands more, row after row, level after level, ever on and upwards, up into the darkness above. They were now no longer in a hall, but at the base of a vast, hollow tower. As he gazed at the ceiling, he thought he could just make out the faintest glimmer of light: lightning in a distant sky.

Brandione remembered, then, a place he had once visited with Wayward, back when the courtier was his guide through the madness of the Dust Queen's world.

'I've been here before,' he whispered. 'Wayward said it was a vision of the Old Place – *his* vision.'

'No,' said the Eyeless One. 'This is no vision. This is the Hallway of Regret.'

'Why would he lie?'

'Perhaps he sensed that you would come here, one day. Perhaps he wanted you to see it, but did not want to scare you, when there was no need.'

'I am not scared.' It was the truth. Brandione was not someone to hide away from fear. Fear was such a useful tool, if used to sharpen the senses. But he was not afraid, here, with this eyeless thing, among a hundred thousand doors. He was becoming more accustomed to the Underland. In a strange way, he felt it had grown used to him, as well.

'No,' said the Eyeless One. 'We sense that, in you.' It gestured to its right. 'We saw the First Memory here, in this place, we think – before the Machinery was made. We are sure of it. But then, we are sure we saw it in other places, too.'

'Where do I begin?'

The creature grinned. 'That is your path to walk, Last Doubter. I would not know.' The Eyeless One was now directly before Brandione; the former General felt the creature peering into him, if that were possible without eyes. It began to speak, but this voice was different than any the former General had heard before. It was not a voice at all, but a rabble of different voices, sometimes speaking together and sometimes individually, a young girl one moment and a group of men the next.

'You are the pawn of our first child: The Dust Queen. She was born in a dark time, born of desperation, a weapon pulled from the shadows. She is fire, and anger, and beauty. She sees great things in you; she believes you will wield the First Memory, and destroy Ruin.' The creature seemed to physically deflate, and it began to back away from Brandione, before speaking once again in its own voice. 'But we do not know. All of it remains to be seen. Nothing is preordained.' It shook its head. 'Prophecies – what are they, but lights in the fog? Who knows where the lights may lead? Often not the way they promise.'

'You are a god. You can stop Ruin alone.'

'No. Ruin is … too powerful. We tried to make him happy, long ago. We created a being for him to love – the One for him. But it was not enough.' The creature shook itself. 'What did we just say?'

Brandione screwed up his eyes. 'Do you not remem—?'

But the Eyeless One was not listening. 'Go, now. We are tired of you. Go, and find the memory of old, if you can. If you cannot, we will all suffer together.'

The creature gave a sharp nod, and Brandione was alone in an instant, without quite knowing how his companion had disappeared.

He gazed around the tower and considered the doors before him. *There are memories hidden within the maze,* Wayward had said. Did that mean every door held a memory, each of them tinged with regret? Was one of these the First

Memory of the Old Place? *Perhaps one memory can be hidden within another, over and over, until you're driven mad, peeling them all apart …*

He walked to the nearest section of the wall, feeling like a fool. Here he was, a soldier of an army that no longer existed, defender of a nation that had disappeared, and still he worried about what people would think of him if they could only see him now. *I am vain.* But he knew this was unfair. He had been trained, shaped, and moulded by the past, like everyone else in the world. He could not let that go, simply because the future was taking them all in a new direction.

*How can I tell which door to open first?* He closed his eyes and tried to sense his way around the room. But he felt nothing. He remembered, then, that Wayward had pointed to a door in this place. He glanced around, and sure enough, he saw it: light blue, with golden leaves painted into the frame. Wayward was always meant to be his guide. *Perhaps he was guiding me here, too.*

Brandione opened the door and walked inside.

# Chapter Nine

'What are *you* doing here?'

*The voice of a man? Not a man. Male, perhaps. But not a man.*

'I said – what are you doing here?'

Canning's eyes clicked open. A red void stretched away before him, as if he had been cast into an endless, sanguine lake.

'I've come to get my people,' he said, 'and take them back to the Remnants.'

There was silence for a moment. 'Take them *back*? That implies they *left*. What makes you so confident we are somewhere *else*?'

The stranger's voice was unremarkable, the sort one heard in a hundred places, on the street or in an alehouse or in the Cabinet of Tacticians. This red place would have been better suited to a voice like Shirkra's, that strange mix of girlish delight and guttural growl.

'You have trapped them,' Canning said. 'Let me take them, and I will not hurt you.'

Canning half-expected a peal of laughter to greet him, echoing out from the endless red. Instead there was a pregnant pause, before the voice spoke again.

'The walls are crashing down, my friend. You must feel it. The great divide is falling away. When Ruin comes, there will be no Old Place, and no mortal world, for he will swallow both. All will be memory: memory will be all. The memories you hide away, the ones you run from – he was born in that mess, and he will chase you through them forever.'

*He? Ruin is a creature?*

A black dot appeared in the redness.

'You don't sound happy about that,' he said. 'Not happy at all.'

'There's not much point in being happy, or sad, or anything else. It simply *is*. There's nothing anyone can do to stop it. Perhaps not even Ruin could stop it now. Perhaps it was always just meant to be.'

'You will die, won't you?'

'I will die, but I will live forever: within Ruin, the God of Memory. For mortals, it will be worse.'

Canning pointed a finger at the black spot. He could feel it, the contours and edges of it, its power, its weakness. It was a thing of memory, and all things of memory belonged to *him*.

'Reveal yourself.'

He gestured with a finger, and it grew before him: a patch of flowing blackness. *Black paint on a pool of blood.* The blackness surrounded him, until all the red was gone. It was alive. He heard a whisper in his ear, that same voice, hushed now and urgent all at once.

'You are strong in the power of memory. You feel it, don't you? Even when you don't want to, it's there.'

'Why have you taken this form?' Canning asked. Fear crept through him for the first time. He found his breathing was laboured. The creature was suffocating him.

A head appeared in the darkness: a woman. Canning recognised her as one of the Watchers in the courtyard, a victim of this Operator. Her face was perfectly still. Soon, her body emerged from the black, until she floated before him, a lifeless figure in a white gown.

'Do you know who I am?' the Operator asked.

'An Operator,' Canning said. 'A parasite of memory.'

'You do not *know* me. My name is the Outside. I was born just after the Absence fell, as the Old Place filled everything with its power alone. I am a power, Canning. And you *dare* to challenge me!'

The blackness burned white: it flowed over the woman, until she was consumed by it. There was a scream from far away.

'Do you know what that is, Canning? That is this woman, this *Manipulator*. She is suffering, Canning. Would you like to see her suffering?'

The whiteness fell away from the woman's face for a heartbeat, and Canning saw her. Her eyes and her mouth hung open, and she reeked of an animal terror.

'What are you doing to her?'

There was a laugh, and the woman was covered again.

'You mean, what have I *done* to her. I finished her, Canning, and I took her memories away. They will know she is dead, now, in the world above. They heard the screams as well.'

More faces appeared then: the other Manipulators. Men and women, like Canning himself. Voices reached him, panicking whispers. *They are still alive.*

'Can you hear them, Canning? They seek your aid. I would like to see that. Please, try to help them.'

The endless white turned back to black, then to red again, repeating over and over. Canning could no longer

71

tell which parts of this place were the Outside. *Is part of it the Old Place, or is it all the same creature, red and black and white ...?*

'This one is good,' the Outside said. The other faces disappeared, until only one remained: a very young man, perhaps in his late teens. 'New to the whole business, but good. A fine delicacy.'

Canning closed his eyes as the young man screamed. The other Manipulators had taught him nothing; they had left him to fend for himself. Perhaps his reputation was enough for them: *the Great Manipulator*. But they were wrong, and he had thought too highly of himself. Now he regretted his arrogance. He wished he had retained just a little of the old Canning's humility.

*I hope my instincts save me, because they're all that I have.*

He opened his eyes, to find that all was once more black. A new face had appeared in the darkness: a woman, perhaps in her sixties, her eyes framed by curls of brown hair.

'This one will be delicious,' said the Outside. 'She's all hard and brittle. She's probably quite a good one. When I break her, she'll be nice and crunchy, like a lovely nut.'

Canning felt a wave of panic. *You are just Timmon Canning. You are nothing but a fishmonger, and you weren't even good at that.*

But he knew this was not true, even now. He had grown into something greater. He would die here, if that was how his story was to end. But he would not die a coward. He would not die as the Tactician he had once been.

He closed his eyes again. He thought about where he was and what had taken him here. This was a construct of another being: a thing of memory, like Shirkra and all the others.

Perhaps the power of memory could break it. He knew, however, that he could not take it by surprise, trapping it as he had done the Duet. It was watching him far too carefully for that. He would have to fight this thing. *Somewhere, there must be a weapon I can use.*

'You are very impressive,' the Outside said. 'But the Old Place is memory; memory is the Old Place; and I am formed of memory. You cannot use the power of memory, as I can; you cannot use the Old Place, as its children use it. It is *not* your god.'

*You are wrong. All of you are nothing but children: the children of humanity. The children of our nightmares. Children must do as their parents wish.*

Canning felt a change. He touched a part of his mind and knew that he had created a barrier, beyond which the Outside could not pass. Suddenly there was silence, as his enemy's words disappeared.

He opened his eyes, to find he was still in the great womb of blackness. Now, however, all was calm. But he knew he was not safe. *Victory is more than defence.* He began to search within himself, casting his mind over the detritus of his past. He was hunting for a weapon, driven by an instinct that he could fashion something fierce and terrible. He would make one from the memories available to him, in this place: his own.

He thought of his years of hardship as a poor, thin, starving child, and his years of misery as a fat, cossetted Tactician. *There must be something in there. Where?*

'You are asking the wrong question.'

This was not the voice of the Outside. He knew this voice very well, and it sent a shiver through the core of him. Only two people in the world spoke with that voice.

The Duet, supposedly his prisoners, were standing before him.

'What are you doing here?' he asked. He glanced between them, at those two pairs of glacial eyes. 'How did you escape?'

Boy grinned at him. 'Escape? What makes you think we escaped?'

Girl moved forward. 'We're still in your prison, Canning. You called us here. Did you not realise?'

Canning shook his head. 'This is a trick. You are in league with the Outside.'

'The Outside!' Girl clapped her hands. 'The Outside is so *awful*. So *boring*, even when he's cruel.'

'Yes,' said Boy. 'So many of the young ones are just like that.'

'Be quiet,' Canning snapped. 'And don't move.'

He did not know what prompted his words: irritation, perhaps. But the result was remarkable: as soon as he had spoken, the Duet became utterly still and completely silent.

'You may speak again,' he said. On cue, Boy and Girl came to life once more, exhaling deeply.

'So it's true,' Canning said. 'I've called you here, somehow. You're still under my control.' He scrunched up his eyes. 'I'm not sure how I did that.'

'You were searching for ways to defeat the Outside and free your friends, or whoever those wretches are,' Boy said.

'A part of you realised you controlled a great weapon,' said Girl. 'Us.'

Boy snatched his hand up: he held a long shard of ice that had been carved into a blade. It had a slightly red tinge and dripped cold water. 'I will kill the Outside with *this*,' he said.

'No,' Canning said, shaking his head. 'I'll fight him on my own. I only need to know …' He nodded at the ice. 'That thing. How do you know it will hurt the Outside?'

Boy shrugged. 'I just do. It's born from bad memories. It's *horrible*.' He grinned, and his teeth seemed sharper than normal. 'I made it in a moment,' he said. 'I made it from things that the Outside won't like. Not. One. Bit.'

'You found it in a memory,' Canning said. 'Teach me how to do that, too.'

'You ask how?' said Girl. 'You really don't understand your powers. What natural talent you must have, Canning the Great Manipulator, to hold us as your prisoners, without even knowing how!'

He shook his head. 'I do not know. I do not know.' He nodded again at the weapon. 'Where do I find things like that? What memories must I look to?'

Boy laughed. 'You will find your way. You are the Great Manipulator!'

Canning shook his head. 'I don't understand.'

Girl opened her mouth, but Canning did not hear her words. His defences had vanished. The Duet were gone, and he was now once more in the presence of the Outside.

'You put up a wall against me, didn't you, Canning? You don't even know how you did it. I sense a certain power in you. But it has no direction. You do not …'

The words fell away, as Canning turned his mind to memories, searching for something powerful, something that *burned*. And soon enough, an image appeared. It was a woman with long white hair and a look of fire in her eyes. It was Brightling: the centre of so much of his suffering, threading the tapestry of her intricate webs.

For years, she had humiliated him. She had seen his weaknesses, and she had picked at them, tearing off the scabs and spreading the infection. She had turned him into a wretch. She had made him look a fool, in his own eyes, the people's eyes, and the eyes of the Machinery. And he had *allowed* her to do it. He had *agreed* with her. He knew he was worthless. She had made him realise what a truly miserable, scrabbling wretch he was, and he deserved it.

Now, though, he saw what she had done. He knew the truth of it. She did not humiliate him because he was weak. She did it because he was *strong*. She saw him as a threat, someone who could be Selected ahead of her as the Strategist, one day. She had turned him into the kind of man the Machinery would *never* Select.

A single memory came to him. He saw himself, sitting in the heights of the Circus, watching a play that Brightling had commissioned, a play in which all his failings were on display, a play designed to draw laughter, laughter aimed at him alone. It was so raw, so visceral: he could sense the very heart of it, the dark pulse of the pain within …

He looked down at his hands and saw that they held a long, dark sword. Red light played across the surface: the sparks of an inferno.

'You have formed this from the power of memory,' whispered Boy. Canning could not see him, but his words came from nearby. 'Use it against the Outside!'

Canning looked around him, at the great pool of blackness.

'Do not try to harm me,' said the Outside.

Canning grinned. He knew fear when he heard it.

He pulled back his arm and thrust the blade into the darkness.

'Is that all, Canning? Is that all you can conjure from the great pit of memory?'

The blackness fell away, and he was standing in a white space. A red circle floated before him and began to gently tremble.

'Do you know why I am called the Outside?'

Canning shook his head. He glanced at his hand: it was balled into a tight fist, as if that strange sword was still in his possession. But it was gone.

'It's strange, really,' the Outside said. His voice was hard, functional, devoid of feeling: the farmer, preparing to behead a chicken. 'I was always just a bit different to the others. I always liked the little memories, the ones the others would ignore: stubbing a toe, cutting yourself shaving. They all excluded me, after a while. I was on the outside.' He sighed. 'I've never had a host, Canning. Do you know what that means? I couldn't find anyone suitable, no matter how hard I tried. Too much of an *outsider*.'

There was a pause. 'Perhaps it could be you? You're quite impressive, in some ways. But no: I would've felt it by now.'

Canning's sword reappeared, hanging pathetically between him and the red circle.

'A nasty little weapon, this, formed from a horrible little memory, no doubt. Someone you don't like, I'd say. A lot of powers in those memories. But do you really think the power of one or two little memories means *anything* to something like *me*?'

A mouth appeared, then, in the red circle, displaying daggers for teeth. It grew wider as it moved towards Canning, swallowing his pathetic little sword along the way.

The mouth came to a halt before him, hanging open. Canning looked to the side and saw Boy and Girl, grinning at him voraciously.

'You made that weapon out of the power of memory,' Girl said. 'That's good. But it was a piddling thing, really.'

'Ask the Old Place for what you need,' Boy whispered. 'The power of memory will provide it, from all the memories that ever were. *Demand* it.'

Canning looked at the great, red mouth that hung before him. 'I can't do it,' he said. 'You should finish this thing. You should destroy the Outside.'

Girl giggled. 'You summoned us here, Canning. You control us. You did this through your hold over the Old Place, your mastery of the power of memory. And you say you cannot fight a little child like the Outside?'

'Besides,' said Boy, 'if you want us to truly help you, you would have to set us free. And I do not believe you want us to be free, Canning, as much as we would like it.'

Canning shook his head. 'No. I do not want you to be free.' He blinked, and the Duet were gone.

But the mouth was still there. And now it was moving again, floating towards him: the gaping maw of the Outside, coming to end him.

Strangely, he felt a new sense of calm. If he died here, in this terrible place, fighting to save a group of Manipulators, would that not be a good death? Would it not be honourable? If he had remained a Tactician he would likely have expired in the Fortress, slumped over a chair, a glass of Redbarrel falling from his outstretched hand. But that end would never come for him, now. He would never be a Tactician again.

*Old Place,* he said within his mind. The words felt alien to him. *Underland. Come to me.*

Nothing happened. The great mouth came closer.

A flicker of desperation sparked within the former

Tactician. How could he master the great secrets of memory in this moment, standing here, a weak, half-beaten creature? But the thought turned to a kind of resolution. *It has always been the same when you used this power. You have always felt desperate. You have always felt alone.*

He pictured the Underland as a great ball of twisting light. He plucked the light apart, formed it into shapes. He thought back to a moment from his past, when he was a child. He remembered seeing a man in a field, slicing crops with a murderous instrument.

The ball of light became a scythe, not formed of wood or metal, but *memories*. And not *one* memory, but a great host, all of them infusing the scythe with their power.

The mouth fell back.

'How did you fashion such a thing?' There was a note of panic in the Outside's voice.

Canning gritted his teeth, stepped forward, and swept the scythe in the air. It flashed as it went, cutting through the great mouth, splitting it in two. For a second both parts hung uselessly before him; the room flickered through different colours, the manic reflections of a crazed rainbow. The mouth vanished, and a great roar filled the air, a scream that crawled across Canning, into the corners of his mind ...

Images flooded him, the memories of a million souls: too many to remember and too many to forget. He turned them away, their anguish and their joy and their fear and their strength. He felt himself falling out of the Outside's world, back into reality, whatever that meant. But before the end, he saw them: his allies in this madness. Boy and Girl. Boy smiled at him and stuck a thumb in the air.

'What mastery of the Old Place,' whispered Girl.

*

He awoke amid a crowd of Manipulators.

They were gathered around him, staring down. There were Arna and Darrlan, the senior figures in this world, who had taken him to face the Outside. And there were the others, alive and well: the Manipulators whose minds and spirits had been taken by the Outside. *The ones who survived, at least.*

'Help him up,' said Darrlan. The others parted, allowing Controller Arlan to push through their circle and help Canning to his feet.

'What happened?' asked Arna.

Darrlan laughed in his boyish way. 'Don't you see? He's beaten back the Outside.'

'No,' Arna said, shaking her great head. 'There's more here than that.' She studied Canning intently, as if reading his soul. Her eyes widened. 'He has killed him.'

The other Manipulators emitted a collective gasp, and the smile fell from Darrlan's face.

'Killed?' he whispered, somewhere between horror and awe. '*Killed?*'

Canning nodded. He saw it again: that great scythe of shifting light. 'It can be done.'

He looked down, and the scythe had returned, held tightly between his hands. It was there for only a second, but the others saw it. They saw it, and they saw what their Great Manipulator could do.

They fell to their knees.

# Chapter Ten

**Turn back and live.**

Brightling had come too far to turn back. And there was nothing to live for back there.

'You know what's coming,' she said. There was a kind of whispering noise, close to her ear. The mask was urging her on.

*Destroy it.*

When Ruin spoke again, there was sorrow in his voice.

**Very well.**

For a time, she wondered if that was all. Perhaps the next time she heard him speak would be in person. *Within the Machinery.* She realised, then, that she had not considered this. The beating heart of the world was about to open for her. A childhood image bloomed in her brain, her infant imagining of what the Machinery actually looked like: a thing of iron, black and red, functional and beautiful all at once. She didn't know how she pictured it, now. *The pit of a monster.*

**I have been trapped here for so long. But I never saw another like you. Neither did Jandell. He loved you so much. He wanted to help you, in your ascent.**

There was a laugh in the darkness.

**All your efforts have turned to dust.**

A new room appeared to Brightling's left. She saw a younger version of herself: a girl, sitting in the library of the Watchers, alone.

The scene flickered and turned into something else. There she was again, a young woman amid a group of other Watchers, the only one without a mask. They were snaking out around the perimeter of an old house. Another change of scene: she was somewhat older, perhaps in her early thirties, and sitting at a great desk. Operator Jandell was behind her, his hand upon her shoulder.

The scene collapsed into a deluge of images, a crazed flow of visions of her past: a child, in the West, racing to the top of a hill; a young woman, playing with a blade; an older woman, interrogating a Doubter; and dozens more besides.

**You have a conflicted quality, which the Machinery has always admired. You are ambitious, but there is a moral quality to your ambition.**

The mask burned upon her.

**You did not seek power simply for itself, as so many have. You wanted it for a purpose. You wanted to be Selected because you *loved* the world you grew up in. You loved the Machinery.**

Ruin chuckled, and it echoed around the stairs.

**And now you are coming to tear out its heart.**

Brightling turned away from the room and once more faced the stairs. 'I am coming to destroy *you*. I don't care about the Machinery.' The words tasted bitter on her tongue, and she did not know if they were true.

**There is no difference. I *am* the Machinery!**

Brightling walked on, and Ruin fell silent for a long time.

Eventually, another doorway appeared, this time to her right. The image that appeared was unexpected. It was not an image from her past: not directly, anyway. It was someone she knew.

'Canning,' she said. 'Why is *he* there?'

The one-time Tactician for Expansion was sitting on a chair. No: a *throne*, formed of some kind of metal, and carved into a wall. This was not one of her memories. She had never seen that throne; it was not in Memory Hall, or the Fortress of Expansion, or anywhere else in the Overland. Canning himself seemed different. He was trimmer, harder-edged. There was a glimmer in his eye. *This is not the man I knew.*

'This is a creation of yours,' Brightling said. 'That throne isn't Canning's. And *that* isn't Canning.'

**It is real.**

She stepped towards the image. 'Where is he?'

**Far away from home, in a wrecked and dying land. But he is respected there. They call him *great*.** Ruin laughed. **He is powerful – *much* more powerful than you.**

Brightling shook her head. 'He was in the Circus, at the end – when Mother came. He should be dead, now, or rotting in the Bowels.'

**He used his powers to escape.**

'What powers?'

**This man is greater than you will ever be.**

Brightling nodded. 'I know that. I always saw it in him.'

**That is why you wanted to destroy him. I want you to know how much I admire you. Not because you are ruthless – because you are *perceptive*. You saw Canning's greatness, all along, even when no-one else did.**

Ruin sighed.

**Yet still you come to me. Still you want to face me with your little mask. Don't you see, with that great mind of yours, what is going to happen to you?**

The mask burned. It *hungered* to face Ruin.

'You are going to die,' she said. 'You will beg me, in the end, to release you.'

Ruin fell silent.

Down she went, further into darkness.

The doors opened regularly on either side, exposing her to rooms filled with memories. Some of these she recognised from her own past. Some were nothing more than the tiniest moments: a glass of water on a hot day, a cut finger, a coin on the ground. Others were more than one memory, a strange melange of moments. In one, she was a young girl, perhaps no older than seven or eight, yet she wore the half-moon crown of a Tactician, and sat in Cabinet with Canning and the rest of them. This was the stuff of dreams. *Perhaps not. Memories are funny things: we toy with them, we put them together, we mix up different ones like paints. What is the difference between dreams and memories? Perhaps there is none …*

Others, though, were truly alien to her. One showed a night-time scene: a dark pond, surrounded by black plants with glossy leaves and pink flowers. Beside the pond sat a man in a white cloak. His hair had been shaved to an outcrop of stubble, but he still seemed young. Despite his youth, a great sense of exhaustion arose from him; he held his head in his hands.

'It's you,' Brightling said. She did not know what made her so certain.

**Yes. Long ago.**

'You are ... sad.' *A small word, for such a creature. But the right one.*

This was in the early days. The Queen had been battling the Absence, alone, for a long time. The Old Place created me, to fight at her side. It called me Ruin. I was its most terrible creation. In the end, I fulfilled my purpose. I brought the ruin of the Great Absence.

The mask burned hot on Brightling's skin.

Here you see me, after a victory.

'You don't seem victorious.'

What kind of victory was it? There was only the Dust Queen and I. The mortals were just sparks of flame, dying in the storm. And the Queen ... she was the same as me, but so different, so very different. What kind of companion could she ever be? One cannot befriend the sun, or laugh with the moon.

Brightling realised, now, what this creature was describing: this ancient being, the child of a god, was talking about *loneliness*.

But the Old Place is wise. The Old Place saw the trouble in my heart. It would not allow its greatest weapon to drown in a pit of despair. So it created something else: something for me.

The water of the memory pond began to stir. A female figure rose from within, naked and glimmering, shining with such brightness that the Watcher had to turn away.

'Mother,' Brightling said.

When she was first born of the Old Place, I knew her as something else. She was the One. The One to break the darkness. The One to keep me company. The One to stand at my side.

'Ruin will come with the One.'

You all thought the One was a human, foreseen in prophecy. But the One is not a human. The One is the One. There is only her – she is the only One, and for ten millennia, she has been coming.

The scene changed, and Brightling was confronted with the chaos of battle. Before her was Jandell, bloodied and torn. He held a woman in the air, pushed up upon his hands, and his face was consumed with hatred.

**Jandell broke the One.**

The scene faded to blackness.

**He thought he had destroyed her, before he cast me into this prison. But she survived. She has returned in all her glory, and she will hold my hand in the end.**

There was a pause.

**It is too late for you now, Brightling. You have come too far.**

Brightling turned away from the room, and saw that the stairs had come to a sudden end. There was a doorway before her, lying slightly ajar.

**Welcome to the Machinery.**

# Chapter Eleven

'Did the Absence make the stars?'

Drayn smiled to herself. She had always asked questions like this. Cranwyl used to laugh at them.

The thought of Cranwyl made her wince.

Jandell did not laugh. He sat next to Drayn, in the garden of Jaco's home, at the side of a fire. He looked at the stars and whistled a low tune. He ignored her question.

'That place you took us was one of Jaco's memories,' he said. 'You know this already, of course.'

'Yes.'

Jandell nodded. 'That was when the One was brought to the Overland. She had found a host, in this baby.' He pointed to his chest. 'We need hosts, to bring us to our true strength. We must become one with a mortal: the right mortal. Sometimes we have to mould them and shape them. That's what the One was doing, all these years, inside Katrina Paprissi.'

'I gave her the opportunity,' said a man's voice.

Drayn and Jandell looked up to find Jaco and Allos walking towards them from the back door of the old man's house, a modest, clean, wooden building. The newcomers took a seat by the fire.

'Like a fool, I took her, and I allowed her to flourish,' Jaco said. 'I should have seen it.'

Jandell shook his head. He turned his focus to Drayn once more.

'You took us to that memory,' he said. 'Do you remember how you did it?'

Drayn shrugged. 'I think so. I just … *do it*.'

Jandell nodded. 'You are special. There have been other mortals like you, in the past.'

The fire seemed to flicker, and Drayn thought she glimpsed a man's face there. She did not know who he was.

'I would like to know more,' Drayn said. She pointed at Jaco. 'I would like to know what happened next.'

'I came back,' Jaco said.

'He saved us,' Allos said, gesturing at Jaco. 'After the lady went away, he helped us build new lives.'

'I don't understand,' Drayn said.

'We lived terrible lives,' Allos said. He began to tremble.

'It's all right,' Jaco whispered. He looked from Drayn to Jandell. 'The people here were slaves. For ten millennia, they were slaves. They scrabbled out lives in the forests and along the coast, while *she* used them as she wished.'

'Green Eyes,' said Allos.

'Shirkra,' Jandell whispered. He bowed his head.

'No one knows what this place was like before she came,' Jaco said, gesturing at the world around them. 'Perhaps it was advanced. Who knows? In the end, she made it into *her* land. She was looking for something, you see.'

'Host,' said Allos.

'A host for a spirit the people never saw,' Jaco said. 'A host for the one they call Mother. Green Eyes would come among them and take people away.'

'Other things as well,' Allos said. 'In the dark came other things. Torture. Torture of the past.'

They were silent for a moment.

'But she never found the right host,' Jaco said.

'Not until the end,' said Allos. 'The end of all that once was.'

'My daughter.' The words pained Jaco.

Allos looked to Drayn. 'Look in me, and you will see.'

Drayn nodded.

They were in a clearing in the forest, surrounded by skeletal wrecks of human beings, ragged and pale and dying. In the centre stood a red-haired woman in a white mask, a baby in her hands.

*Shirkra*, said a voice in Drayn's mind.

Purple smoke filled the sky above them. It spread quickly, covering the sun, until the daylight was gone and all of them cowered below in darkness. Drayn could not understand what the people were saying, but she could *feel* it.

*It is her. It is her. It is her!*

A voice came, then, a voice of many, as if all of the dead had spoken together. Drayn wondered if it was speaking within her mind: within all of their minds.

**Where did you find this child?**

'In the forest, Mother, in the forest!' Shirkra cried. 'She is wonderful! Her memories have a lovely little flicker ... they are so like you!'

The purple smoke roiled in the sky.

**I feel it. I feel her.**

There was a great crack, and a streak of purple lightning. Mother was a storm.

**She will be my host. You have done well, my daughter.**

The smoke began to contract, converging into a narrow patch of the sky, before floating down to them. It shrank as it came, from the size of a person's head to a fist to an eyeball, until eventually it floated just above the baby girl, no bigger than a fingernail. The girl's eyes burned purple for a moment, and the smoke was gone.

The people moaned.

'What now?' Shirkra asked. 'Where will I go?'

**We must return to the land we left behind. I will go alone, and you will follow.**

'How will you go? You are so weak …'

**Someone will come for me. I see it now. I will be safe with him. I *need* to go with him. It is the path for me.**

There was a bustle at the side of the clearing, and a man ran in among them, thinner even than the others. His eyes were wild, and he was pointing to some unseen danger. Drayn did not understand the language he spoke, but the meaning somehow reached her.

*Strangers have come.*

When the memory disappeared, the small group sat in silence for a while, staring at the flickering light from the torch.

'Were there any others here?' Jandell asked, glancing up at Allos.

'Others?' Allos frowned.

'Others like me,' Jandell replied, gesturing at his chest. 'Others like Mother and Shirkra – Green Eyes.'

Allos shook his head. 'No. Not till you. None before. None other than them.'

Jandell nodded.

'Why did you come back?'

The other three looked at Drayn. She had not meant to

speak – the words had come tumbling out. *Speaking without meaning to speak. Very, very, unlike a Thonn. But so very like me.*

She gestured at Jaco. 'Why did you come back here?'

'Good question.' Jaco nodded at Drayn. 'Why don't you take us there yourself?'

Drayn felt the edge of another memory, and gave it a little tug.

They were in a room in the tower of an old house. Jaco was there, decades younger. He was moving frantically around, searching behind chairs, looking under a desk, even sweeping down the contents of a shelf.

'He must be here somewhere,' said this memory Jaco. 'He must ... he can't have ...'

'What are you doing?'

A woman was at the door, a willowy presence, her face gaunt. 'What are you doing?' she asked again. There was a trill of panic in her voice.

'It's nothing. The boy is playing.'

The woman's eyes widened. 'Playing? Up here?' She cast a glance at the corners. 'Never. He never plays up here. You'd kill him.'

Jaco waved a hand dismissively. 'He's somewhere. I'll find him.'

He walked towards the door, trying to push past the woman. She grasped his arm.

'What do you mean, *find him*?' The note of panic had grown shriller. '*Find him* means he is *lost*. Where is he?'

'He was in the hall. He went down there ...'

'And now he's not there?'

'No.'

91

The woman let out a cry: a *yelp*. She opened her mouth to speak again, but this part of the memory faded away.

They were outside now, somewhere in the grounds of a great house. Jaco was with a woman: a white-haired lady, imperious, powerful.

'It was the Operator,' Jaco said. 'He took Alexander away. I know it.'

The woman gave the slightest of nods.

Jaco looked up at a window, high above. 'Amyllia – I have to leave. Will you look after Katrina?'

Amyllia's eyes widened. She looked at the window, too: there was a young girl there, with black hair and dark eyes, staring down at them. Drayn knew somehow that this was the baby Jaco had taken. She could sense *her* presence there. *Mother.*

'Yes,' said Amyllia. It seemed she was about to speak again, but the scene vanished.

They were at a dock, somewhere cold and wet. Men were hoisting equipment onto a ship, a sleek thing with billowing red sails. Jaco was standing by himself, watching them work, hands stuffed into the pockets of a pair of rough trousers.

A woman approached him, holding a child by the hand. It was the white-haired woman – Amyllia – and Katrina.

'Don't do this,' Amyllia said. She pointed at the ship. 'You have a daughter to think of. You're all she has left.'

Jaco raised a finger. 'No,' he said. He cast a strange glance at Katrina. 'She's yours to think of, now. She's a Brightling.'

Amyllia seemed taken aback by these words. 'Why are you abandoning her?'

But Jaco did not respond. He climbed aboard the ship,

without so much as kissing his daughter. He turned and glanced at her, though, before he disappeared: there was a strange mix of love and loathing in his gaze.

They were back by the fire.

'I came back to learn more,' Jaco said. 'This is where we found Katrina in the first place. I thought that perhaps there would be a way to free her from … whatever was inside her. And then I stayed. I am ashamed of it. I stayed because I did not know what else to do. My daughter was *gone*. I never had a daughter, in truth.' He glanced at the Operator. 'I should have gone back. I should have told you what I knew about Katrina. But I hoped … I don't know what I hoped. Perhaps that she would cast out that monster by herself, and become my daughter again.'

Jandell nodded.

'I was broken, shattered,' Jaco went on. 'Maybe if I'd listened to Alexander at the beginning …'

'Nothing would have changed,' Jandell said. 'We have all been manipulated by him. *Ruin*.'

'Ruin is an Operator,' Jaco said with certainty. 'He spoke to Alexander. It wasn't the Machinery.'

Jandell's words came in a quiet voice. 'Ruin wanted Katrina to be left with Brightling. He made that happen. Perhaps he thought she would make a better … mother. There she was, all that time, under my very nose. Alexander told me that the One lived, but he never told me where she *was*: inside his sister. He was protected. I am sure of it now. Ruin kept me away from those memories.' He whistled through his teeth. 'Ruin is growing strong indeed …'

Drayn turned away, and noticed something strange: the memory had not yet vanished completely. She could see it, in the corner of her eye: that dockside scene. Something there was calling to her.

She looked back at Jaco and Jandell. *Can they see it, too?*

She turned her gaze fully on the memory. It floated before her, superimposed on the real world, a kind of moving painting, torn from the fabric of the air. It was calling to her, dragging her towards it. A thrill coursed through her. *The power of memory. The power of memory is there.*

She glanced once more at Jandell and Jaco, who remained sunk in conversation about the vanished past. She stood, and returned to the memory.

But this was not the same memory.

The day had turned to night. Sheets of rain piled down upon them, and the sails of Jaco's ships billowed madly in a tearing, whipping gale.

It was as if the colours on a palette had been mixed, and one memory had bled into another. She could feel the mixture, in the air. There was something jarring about the scene. She looked up at the sky and saw lightning, burning in an unnatural, purple storm. She thought she could see something else there, too: a kind of line in the sky, like the seam of a piece of clothing, slightly torn ...

Something dragged her focus back to Amyllia. She looked at the girl by the woman's side: now her dress was purple. No: it was not a dress. It was a thing of rags. The girl turned to Drayn. She was wearing a mask. *A white rat.*

There was a flash of gold in the corner of her eye. Drayn spun around. She saw nothing but buildings and people in a darkening coastal town, an endless crowd, dozens deep, staring at her in silence. But who was that? Who was that face in the crowd? Who was it that wore a wide-brimmed hat and a dark cloak, who held a great stick in his hand, whose face was obscured by a golden mask with a long, sharp beak?

It was a figure from her past. It was a figure from the Habitation.

It was the ally of Squatstout. It was the Protector.

# Chapter Twelve

The Hopeful Chambers were not chambers, and held little hope.

Aranfal stood in an open courtyard, wide and dreary. The walls of a great, red-bricked house surrounded him on all sides, vast things that seemed to reach up into the sky. He knew, somehow, that this house was closed to him; perhaps it was closed to everyone.

A great, spherical pond dominated the centre of the courtyard. Aranfal carefully approached it and gazed into the waters. In the depths, he could see flashes of colour.

'Hope moves in strange ways.'

Aranfal turned his head sharply. There was a little boy at his side, a child with black, curly hair and large, inquisitive eyes.

'I thought I'd be alone,' Aranfal said. 'I'm not sure why. Maybe I'm just getting sick of you people.'

The child frowned. '"You people"? What do you mean?'

'You … things down here. You faces of the Old Place, like that thing with no eyes.'

The boy shook his head. 'The Old Place is a god of many parts.' The courtyard darkened for a moment, and a hard expression entered the boy's eyes.

Aranfal turned back to the pond, while the child continued to speak. 'Besides, you're wrong. I'm *not* a thing of the Old Place. I'm a mortal. Or once I was, anyway. I think I'm just a memory, now. Hmm – so maybe you're right.' He grinned and stuck out his hand. 'Alexander,' he said.

Aranfal took the boy's hand. *Is this Jaco's son, the one whose disappearance set this whole thing in motion?* He decided not to ask. *There are too many questions already.*

'I'm looking for something,' Aranfal said. 'The First Memory of the Old Place. I spoke with a ... well, a creature without eyes. It told me it might be here. It says the First Memory is the only thing that can stop Ruin from becoming a god, whatever that means.'

Alexander cringed at the word "Ruin". He looked up at the blue sky. 'He is almost upon us. I have felt him myself, though I am so weak compared with all the others.' He nodded. 'The First Memory might stop him. If it's here.' He smiled at Aranfal. 'What if Ruin already *has* the First Memory? Don't you think it would explain so much?' He laughed. 'Who knows, though? I suppose you must do what the Eyeless One asks.'

'It told me the First Memory could be here,' Aranfal said. 'It's my only way out. If I don't find it, I'm dead, or I'm here forever.'

Alexander burst into tinkling giggles. 'If you don't find it, we're all going to die or be here forever! Though we won't be dead. If Ruin takes over the Old Place ...' Alexander shuddered. 'If that creature takes over the Old Place – if he becomes the Old Place – then we will live in memory forever. And they will be the memories *he* likes. Memories we'd like to hide away.'

He frowned at Aranfal.

'On that cheery note,' said the Watcher, 'I'd better find

this memory as soon as I can.' He glanced at the pond. 'The Eyeless One said it might be in the Hopeful Chambers.'

'Hmm! It's possible!' The boy spread his arms out wide. 'Anything is possible, isn't it? Especially now!' He grinned. 'Did the Eyeless One say where exactly it might be?'

Aranfal shook his head. 'No. Only that I'm supposed to look in the Hopeful Chambers.'

'Ah!' Alexander clapped his hands. 'In that case, you should not be standing *here*!' He reached out and placed a hand on Aranfal's back. 'You need to *dive in*!'

He pushed, and the Watcher went under.

This was not water: this was something else entirely.

The colours moved across and through one another, knitting together and falling apart, blues and reds and greens and golds of every hue: a paint pot, turned into an ocean. He found he was suspended within it, watching the colours twist and turn.

He felt something at the top of his head. He reached up and found a kind of cord emerging from his skull. He wondered for a moment if he had suffered some kind of bizarre injury. *My brain is falling apart, or whatever's left of it.* But no: he felt no pain. He tugged at the cord, pulled it down before his eyes.

It was a wriggling string of black *something*, like the other colours that writhed before him. He felt a sense of familiarity. The more he looked, the stronger the sensation grew: this was something that *belonged* to him. It was something that mattered to him, something that mattered to his past. He saw a face there, in the blackness: *his* face. It grew, the colour snaking outwards, until it gathered around his head.

\*

He was in the See House.

It was one of the great halls. The people were sitting in groups on the ground, or standing in the corners, whispering to one another. All of them kept far away from the centre of the room, where a naked man was tied to a chair, his face caked in blood. He was unconscious.

Aranfal examined the room, until he found himself as a young man, trembling in the corner. He had no mask, then.

'What's this, then?'

He turned around. Alexander was there, grinning at him, totally out of place in this great, dark hall.

'An interrogation,' Aranfal replied. He looked back at himself, at that young man. Was this Aranfal, or Aran Fal, or something in between?

*You know what's about to happen, here.*

'I thought this was supposed to be the Hopeful Chambers,' he said to Alexander. 'There's nothing hopeful about this place.'

Alexander shrugged. 'Who knows?' He nodded at the younger Aranfal. 'Perhaps you don't remember how you felt back then. I can sense hope here.' He sniffed in a breath, as if tasting the memory, and for a heartbeat he seemed so much older than he appeared. He exhaled and grinned at the real Aranfal. 'There *is* hope, here, though one has to search for it.' He whistled through his teeth. 'Though – inter-rogation? Jandell used to interrogate me, on and on, over and over. Yes, interrogation was the word for it. But it was just the two of us. There are so *many* of you here. What kind of interrogation takes place in a crowd?'

'A lesson,' the Watcher replied.

'Ah!' Alexander cried. 'What an interesting school this must have been!'

A man walked to the centre of the room, near the unconscious wretch. Aranfal remembered him well: Derren Rever, a teacher of Watchers, though he was not much older than many of the Apprentices. He was a tall, nervous creature, forever tearing at his robes with fidgety fingers, his black beard quivering.

'He's almost dead!' Derren cried. The Apprentices in the hall glanced at one another. Some of them sniggered. They wouldn't snigger at the other teachers. *They wouldn't snigger at Brightling.* The teacher gestured at the man in the chair. 'Who did this?'

Two Apprentices were pushed forward by their loving classmates. Aranfal couldn't remember them, now. He had forgotten all their names when he stopped being Aran Fal.

'You two,' Derren said. 'You've made a nice mess of him, that's for sure. What did you learn?'

The two Apprentices – a man or a woman, or a boy and a girl, more accurately – stood with their hands behind their backs.

'We need to know so many things,' Derren said. 'We need to know ...'

Derren droned on, and the real Aranfal turned his attention elsewhere. He couldn't listen to that man back then, and he couldn't listen to him in a memory.

He looked to the side of the room. A wall was missing, and in its place was a low platform, lined with chairs. In each of these was a gigantic figure, human in shape but far greater in size. He could not make out their features: they were dark things, moving shadows, huddled beneath hoods. They held little balls of black material in their hands, which they pulled apart and knitted together, over and over. It was the same substance he had seen in that chaotic pond.

'Who are they?' he asked Alexander, gesturing to the figures beyond. 'What are they doing?'

Alexander snatched a quick glance at the shadowy creatures. For once there was no cheer in his voice. 'The Old
Place is full of many strange creatures,' he whispered. 'The
Operators are its children, but there are other beings here.
Shadowthings, I call them. I think it makes things less scary,
when you give them a name. No one knows what they are.
They're not like the others down here. They don't seem to
*love* memories. They drain away the power, until nothing's
left but a husk, and sometimes not even that. They don't
even seem to enjoy it.'

'Are they doing that now?' asked Aranfal, nodding at the
Shadowthings. 'Are they draining my memory?'

Alexander shrugged. 'Maybe so. How could I know? No
one understands the Shadowthings.'

'Where do they find this power?'

'It's everywhere, Aranfal. You just need to look with open
eyes.' The boy nodded back at Derren, back at this memory
from long ago. 'Memories have different kinds of powers.
There is hope, here.' He chuckled. 'Let's see what happened
with your hope.'

Derren was now frothing with rage.

'Is there *no one* here who can suggest what to do?' he
asked. 'Is there *none among you* who can think of a way of
getting more from this man?'

'Masks,' said someone in the crowd. 'Give us masks and
we'll look inside him.'

Derren snatched out his own mask from somewhere in
his gown: the face of a cricket. It seemed incongruous on
such a big man. He slotted it onto his face.

'Masks, masks, masks!' he cried. 'You always talk about
masks, don't you? You think the masks just let you open
someone up, hmm, like a key in a door, and show you

everything inside them? No. It's the *wearer* that matters. And if you're not a proper Watcher without your mask, you won't be a proper Watcher *with* your mask.' He turned his insect face onto the unfortunate in the chair. 'Besides – they are not all-powerful. You can get a feel for a person, depending on how good you are: the way they work, some of the things they have done. But it's not like reading a book, my children. It's not like you can flick through the pages and find what they had for breakfast! And sometimes ...' Here, he paused, and gave the man a hard look. 'Sometimes they don't work at all. Sometimes we come up against people who just block us out. The masks are wonderful things – but the mind is stronger.'

He shook his head sadly. 'Any other ideas?'

A silence hung over the room. No one knew how to respond. But then the prisoner began to stir; he pulled himself upright in his chair and blinked hazily at the Watchers. He broke into a grin.

'Where are the ones that were beating me?' He looked around the room through blood-caked eyes. 'I can't see them. They're probably hiding.' He gave a theatrical frown. 'Of course, there's a good reason they've got nothing out of me. I don't have any story to tell.'

Derren shook his head. 'You're one of the worst Doubters in the West, Yannus. We know about your groups. We know about your plays. You will tell us about your network. You will tell us about the others.'

Yannus shook his head, and laughed. At the side of the room, the real Aranfal closed his eyes. He knew what was coming. Aran Fal becoming Aranfal.

'His son is a Watcher,' said the young Aranfal, in a trembling voice.

'Who said that?' Derren cast his insect gaze across the room. 'Who just spoke?'

The memory Aranfal walked forward, emerging from the crowd of Watchers. 'His son. His son is a Watcher. He's in our cohort.'

The memory Aranfal pulled a knife out from his cloak. At the side, the real Watcher groaned. Alexander took him by the hand.

'What's the matter?' he asked. 'What did you do?'

The memory Aranfal seemed to steady himself. 'He's tough, isn't he?' he said. He pointed the knife at Yannus. 'I could cut out his eyeballs right now, and he wouldn't care. Would you?'

Said eyeballs did not move, but remained carefully focused on Aranfal.

'But his *son* – he loves his *son*. Everyone loves their children. It's the only thing that makes a difference, sometimes.'

He grinned, and it was a savage thing. The other Watchers had all gone very quiet, watching him carefully. *Aran Fal becoming Aranfal.*

'It wasn't anything new, what I did,' said the real Aranfal. 'Brightling taught me it all. She showed me the way, before … before this day.'

'What do you mean?' Alexander looked genuinely confused. 'What wasn't new?'

'What I did.' Aranfal nodded. 'It wasn't new. But I got a name for it. Maybe I was a bit more aggressive than Brightling and the rest of them.'

He believed he was changing, shifting from Aranfal back to Aran Fal. But he couldn't truly go back to that boy, could he? No one could ever go back. He would have to become someone else: a different kind of Aran Fal.

Back in the memory, the tide of his terrible history was surging ever forward.

'He has a son,' said the young Aranfal. 'Also called Yannus. And he's a *fucking Watcher*!' The last two words were uttered in a kind of hiss. He couldn't remember if it was real or forced. *Probably a bit of both.*

Yannus grinned. 'That's not true.' But he was lying. Every part of his face screamed his lies, and Aranfal needed no mask to see it. 'My son is in the West.'

'Your son is here. Yannus the younger, come on! Step forward!'

If anyone thought that Yannus the younger would remain hidden, they were sorely mistaken. A part of Aranfal wished, now, that he had.

A young Watcher shuffled forward from the others. He was a pathetic specimen, a short, pudgy boy, his face pock-marked with pimples and blemishes. His hair was dirty and unkempt, and he had a slowness to him that suggested a mental softness. No one seemed to know him, apart from the younger Aranfal. Yannus had helped him, once, in the library. That was where Yannus the younger spent most of his days. He had helped Aranfal find a book, and he had told him his name. His *real* name. He'd done well, keeping it hidden from the Watchers. But he told Aranfal the truth, and the Watcher never knew why. *He shouldn't have done that. His name was his weakness, in the end.*

But in this moment, the boy did not seem weak, and he did not seem afraid.

'Yes,' was all he said.

Aranfal pointed the knife at him. 'Your father is a Doubter.'

The boy glanced at the man in the chair and back at Aranfal. 'Yet I am a Watcher.' He shrugged. 'What a world we live in. But nothing will change either fact.'

104

Aranfal grimaced, turning back to the father. 'Tell us what you know, or I'll butcher him. I'll do it right now. We don't need the sons of Doubters running around the See House anyway.'

Yannus senior remained silent.

'Very well, then.' Aranfal looked at Yannus the younger and moved forward.

The memory froze. Aranfal was not sure why, but he was grateful.

'What happened?' Alexander asked. 'Did you kill him?'

Aranfal nodded. 'Eventually.'

'Hope,' Alexander said. 'There is hope here. *Your* hope. The hope of an ambitious man. Other hope, too. The hope of a teacher for his students. The hope of a son for his father, and the other way around. Hope! So widespread, so desperate, so powerful, so strange!'

'Why did we come here?' Aranfal asked. 'How will it help us find the First Memory?'

'There is no *help* here. You must help yourself. You must walk your own path, in the Old Place.'

Aranfal was distracted by the Shadowthings. They were slowly climbing to their feet, depositing the black magic of his memories onto the floor.

'Where are they going?'

'Another place,' said Alexander, with a shrug. 'Perhaps another memory.'

There came a scream. Aranfal saw that the dark beings were walking through a bright door. On the other side, for just a moment, he saw Aleah. She was in pain. She screamed again.

Not knowing what else to do, Aranfal ran to the door. Or perhaps it was Aran Fal who ran.

# Chapter Thirteen

Brandione had come to a village of the past.

The town was hardly deserving of the name: a rough, shit-strewn road, beaten into the ground between some hovels. Soldiers were milling around, dirty and tired, carrying their lives on their backs. Brandione knew where he was, all right. He had come to this place through the Hallway of Regret, and there was plenty of regret here.

It took him a while to find the younger version of himself. His hair was thicker, his skin unlined, his body thinner. He looked like the others, caked in mud, gripping his hand-cannon tightly. But he was the one in charge. The others fell quiet when he was near, keeping their jokes and curses to themselves.

The memory Brandione was studying a building at the end of the street, a hard look in his eye. Hard, and tired. As he looked at that structure, the older Brandione felt a hollowness in the pit of his stomach, a void that seemed to slowly expand.

'Leader Brandione.'

The younger Brandione turned his head slightly. Someone was beside him, an older man, his face a scrabble of beard and cuts, his small eyes casting shrewd glances at his surroundings. Nal, he was called, though they all knew him as Nail. Always respectful to Brandione, but not the sort of person the future General would ever have trusted. Clever, in his own way: the type who could always find his dinner. But not a man to trust.

The young Brandione nodded at Nal. 'Go on,' he said.

Nal shifted his gaze to the building at the far end of the road. 'Funny, to put a barn there, my lord.'

Brandione shrugged. 'Maybe the town was built around the barn.'

'Maybe,' Nal said, though he did not sound convinced. 'Or maybe it never was a barn. Maybe it is a … *depot*, of some kind. Hmm? Somewhere for these …' He was about to spit out a swear word, but held it in. They all tried not to swear before their Leader. It wasn't a rule, and it certainly wasn't something Brandione had demanded. Something just made them hold their tongues.

'Somewhere for these *traitors* to store things, my Leader,' Nal went on. 'Somewhere to keep their little weapons.'

Nal seemed to despise the westerners, but it was feigned. The soldiery of the Overland had learned to respect the rebels a great deal. None of them thought too much about the causes of the rebellion, not even Brandione. But they knew the consequences, all right. *The West*. It was half the Overland, and it was in flames. The war was fought in snowy mountains, in burning deserts, in soggy farmlands: the complexity was endless, and though the Centre won, in the end, it was a close-run thing. If the westerners had been victorious, the Overland would have lost its great bread-basket, its store of food and fuel and furs and fancies. *And a new rival would have been born.*

107

Such thoughts were very far from Brandione's mind on this wet day in the West. That man was up to his neck in war, and close to drowning.

'Leader, that's where they've gone now,' Nal told the younger Brandione. 'Those fuckers.' He blanched. 'I'm sorry, my lord. I didn't mean—'

The memory Brandione raised a finger. 'How long have they been there?'

They were on the hunt for a particularly troublesome group of rebels, who had harassed them all along the road between Erran Town and the Four Villages. Brandione could no longer remember the name of this group, or what they represented to the rebellion. Over time, they all seemed the same. *Enemies, enemies, everywhere.*

Nal shrugged. 'No way of telling, my lord. They last hit us three days back, on the Lower Southern Path. If they came straight here, they've probably been in there a full day.'

'And we know it's them?'

Nal nodded to the side of the road, where a pair of youngish women were standing, their arms crossed, bags of bones and stringy flesh. 'Aye. Those two know them well, my lord, and are a bit angry with them. I'd never ask why, though, as it wouldn't be gentlemanly.' He smirked. 'They saw one of them come out, an hour or so ago, to get something. Probably ammunition, knowing those ... fellows.'

'Then why haven't they fired at us?' Brandione pointed to a series of shuttered windows along the top of the building. 'They could have hit us long ago.'

Nal thought this over for a moment, gnawing at a red lip. 'They're afraid, my Leader. They hope we don't know they're there. Or maybe they don't want to anger us. Maybe they think we'll parley with them.'

'Or maybe there's no one in there.'

'Maybe, my Leader, maybe.' Nal's eyes narrowed. 'But I believe those girls.'

The real Brandione remembered this now, remembered the words Nal spoke. At least, he thought he did. *Don't they say that memories change over time? Don't they merge with other memories?* Yet this one rang true. If it was mistaken, then so was his recollection of everything that had happened here that day. This was the path to madness, where every doubt became a monster.

In the memory, his younger self was speaking.

'We should talk to them. See if they'll surrender.'

A ghost of a smile flickered across Nal's face, though he stopped himself from laughing. 'There's no way, my Leader. That sort are never very good. You saw what they did on the road.' He glanced up again at the shuttered windows, and a thought seemed to occur to him. 'Besides, they *have* fired at us. One of them took a shot at us earlier. Nearly hit Derrick.'

'Most of the country here is shooting at us. Doesn't mean it was one of them.'

'Well, begging your pardon, my Leader, but doesn't that make most of the country our *enemies*? It don't matter, does it, if it's *exactly* who we think it is or not.' Nal waved a hand at some of the other soldiers, wearily going about their business. 'Anyone'd think we were foreigners, down for the day from Northern Blown or one of those other shitty little fuckholes.' He cringed at Brandione, feigning embarrassment at his language. 'But we're all part of the same city, my lord, aren't we? Just 'cause we're in the country don't change that. They should behave according to their civic duty, my lord, and not try and fucking kill us all.' Another embarrassed hand gesture. 'Doesn't matter if they're the ones we're looking for or not, does it, if they're attacking us?'

Brandione nodded. 'Let's hope they see sense.'

He gathered himself together and began to walk up the road. He did not get far, though, before Nal grasped him by the arm.

'My Leader! Where are you going?'

Brandione nodded at the barn. 'To talk to them.'

'Don't be … don't be so *brave*, your eminence.' Nal gave a broad grin, exposing a fearsome set of broken yellow teeth. 'You don't want to hurt yourself, by being so brave. We'd be lost without you.'

He meant this last part, Brandione knew. They had all of them come to admire this graduate of the College, this soldier intellectual, who took risks that even these hardened men thought reckless. They admired him. He could see it in their eyes. They were grateful, too, perhaps.

*I could have had so much, if I'd just stayed in the College. I would probably be Provost now, lying on cushions and reading books. Or I could have been an Administrator. That would have been a good life, too. Rolling around the Overland, manipulating its direction from gilded towers … all glorious. But no. I wanted something else. I felt haunted by something: the fear of being a coward. And so I confronted it, and I ended up on this street, this street I will never forget.*

'What do you propose we do then, Nal?' asked the younger Brandione.

Nal whistled. 'Well, now, that's a good one. That is a good one. A good question, I mean.' He smacked his tongue against his teeth. 'We could just leave, sir.'

The younger Brandione shook his head, as Nal no doubt knew he would.

'No. If it's really them, they'll harass us all the way up the road. We can't have that, Nal.'

This was the moment that Brandione had turned over in his mind ever since.

Nal's eyes widened, and his mouth broke into a grin. 'Tell you what, sir – I've had an idea. I know just how to deal with them.'

Brandione nodded. He glanced back at the road they had come from. 'I've got to get back to the camp for a while,' he said. He looked at Nal. The older Brandione felt ashamed when he brought it to mind. He felt *regret*.

The truth was, an unspoken agreement had passed between Brandione and Nal, in this moment. *I know what you are going to do,* the future General had communicated to his man. *I know what you are going to do, because I know who you are. I need you to do it. But I also need you to do it on your own. I need to have no part in it.*

'I know what you need,' Nal said.

The memory was replaced with another. He had left the village, and gone back to the camp, perhaps three miles away. He was busying himself with mundane tasks. The older Brandione thought back on these moments, now, as he watched his younger self move energetically between the tents. He remembered the thoughts that ran through his mind. *Ruthlessness is needed in war. The rebels would do the same, if the shoe was on the other foot. You have no choice.*

That was the most common one. *You have no choice. No choice at all.* But there was always a choice.

Eventually, as dusk was drawing in, another soldier approached him. Brandione did not need the power of the Underland to remember this man. His face was etched onto the one-time General's mind. He was small, uncommonly so for a soldier, with a round, rodent-like face.

'Something's happened in the town, my lord,' the man said. Funny, Brandione could not remember his name, now. Everything else was clear and present, except the man's name.

'What?' Brandione screwed his eyes up, attempting to seem anxious, even surprised. He was never much of an actor.

'That barn,' the little man said. 'There's been a fire.'

Brandione stood very still for a moment, before slowly nodding. 'Thank you.'

'Do you want to know about the rebels, my Leader? Honestly, it was a stroke of luck for us. There were so many of them inside there. They must have locked themselves in, and then burned the place down, the fucking fools: probably some accident with their smokestuff. What a way to go, sir. Nail said you could hear them, scrabbling and—'

The memory Brandione raised a hand. 'That will be all.'

The little man nodded. 'It's a good thing, Leader, isn't it? Good they're gone? I would've liked to face them properly, of course. Still – nice that they're not around to bother us any more, isn't it?'

Brandione nodded. 'Of course.'

The young Brandione looked back in the direction of the town, and his older self remembered. *The smell.* Far ahead, he could just make out a tendril of smoke, rising in the air.

The older man closed his eyes, and the past washed over him. They had soon left the town and the camp behind, moving onto some other scene from the war, one battle folding into another amid endless nights in the cold rain. He was not naïve. He had no illusions about war, or the ways that people died. He would order soldiers to kill, and they would do it. He would do it himself. There was no getting away from it. He knew it would be this way, and so had the rebels when they took up arms against the Overland. But something about this episode, with the barn, always sat uneasily with him.

It was the *dishonesty* of it. He knew that now. It was the sly nods and winks that had led to those fiery deaths, lungs filled with smoke, flesh melted from bones. He had known what Nal would do. He should simply have ordered him to do it. *Or I should have done it myself.* A part of his self-mythology had crumbled that day. He was under no illusions about the people that had died: they had tormented the soldiers of the Overland for long enough, picking off wayfarers and torturing them to death. They deserved what came to them. It wasn't the *act* that dismayed the future General of the Overland: it was the shirking of responsibility, the game he had played with Nal.

When he handed responsibility for the rebels to Nal, he had given the man something else: a shard of his own power. He had asked him to carry a burden that was too heavy for him. That was weakness in its purest form. That was the old Brandione, the one he had run away from, the one who first went to the College. That was the action of a coward.

And he felt regret, all right. Regret for the man he once was, and never could be again.

He opened his eyes. The place was empty now; even the young Brandione was gone. *This cannot be my memory if I wasn't here.* He looked around, at the dying fires and the darkening camp, and was struck by a sense of immense loss, for all that he had once been, and all that the Overland had stood for. He thought of this thing that menaced them, this Ruin. *Wouldn't it be good, in a way, to let it sweep us all up in its arms? What is there for us, now that the Overland is gone?* But he knew this wasn't true. They had all been tools of these beings for too long. It was like Nal and the barn. They had given a nod and a wink, and allowed these gods, or whatever they were, to rule their lives.

That had to end. Ruin must be destroyed. Then – when it was over – they needed to free themselves from the other creatures, too, from all these parasites of memory, and from the power of memory itself. They could no longer live on the wheel of the past.

For any of this to happen, however, he needed to find it. *The First Memory.* He wondered if it might be here, hidden away somewhere. *No.* He did not know what he was looking for, but he would know it when he saw it. He was sure of that.

The memory began to fade. It started at the edges, in the corner of his eye: little flecks of colour and light began to peel away, disappearing into nothingness. There was a noise, like the movement of some machine, and he was back in the tower of endless doors. He was high up, now: the floor below was far, far away, vanishing into a circle of shadow.

He looked to all the other doors, and he felt a sense of despair. How could he hope to find the First Memory in this endless maze? Was he trapped here, wandering the chambers of his own regrets – or those of others – until he himself became nothing more than a figment of the past?

He turned to the nearest door – red, with a golden handle – and reached out to it. He hesitated. *Why open it? Why relive another moment like the barn?* As always in these times of helplessness, a swell of anger grew within him. *I won't do it. I won't be a pawn any more.*

He thought of what this place was – this Underland. This Old Place. A home to all the memories of mankind: a thing of many parts, manic and twisted and untrustworthy, like memories themselves. *We did not think about it, in the old days. We thought it was nothing more than the home of the Machinery, the domain of the Operator, and the place we threw our Strategists.*

The last thought struck him like a blow. *The place we threw our Strategists.* So many funerals, over so many millennia: venerated bodies, taken from the mortal realm and tossed into the Portal, to the Machinery knew where. He thought of Kane, his old master. *We threw his corpse in here.*

The one-time General of the Overland was seized by a sudden urge to see Kane once more. *He is in here. I can feel it.*

He looked up to the ceiling. He could see it now in detail for the first time, a swirling storm of light. *If this is a place of memory – and memories are human things – then the power lies with us.* He thought of what the Queen had told him, about Arandel and the things he had done in the game. *I will make the Underland bow before me.*

'Take me to Strategist Kane,' he said.

Somewhere, he heard a noise. It sounded like laughter, though perhaps his mind was playing tricks on him.

He pictured Kane. He brought memories before him of the times they had spent together, the old man's hacking and spluttering. He felt a sudden surge of power, which flitted away as quickly as it had appeared. He *demanded* it come back: he ordered it to return.

He grasped at the power of his memories.

He made them serve him.

And he came to a room full of corpses.

# Chapter Fourteen

Canning returned to his throne room after his battle with the Outside, and vowed to never leave it again.

The great torches had been extinguished, with a handful of candles struggling pathetically against the gloom. Canning was slouched in his strange throne, that thing of metal that had been hacked out of the wall. The Duet were not far from his side, sitting perfectly still, hand in hand, staring blankly forward. They remained his prisoners. His hold over them appeared to have strengthened since his battle with the Outside, though he could not say why. Before, he seemed to be connected to them by a kind of invisible string. Now it was as if they were held within the grip of a great fist: a fist that he controlled.

The paths of the Underland were opening before him. He had looked into the Old Place and seized a weapon to destroy the Outside. The memories of history lay at his feet, with all their secrets and power. Yet none of it mattered, because he did not know what he was supposed to do next.

He climbed down from his throne and began to pace. For a second it seemed that Girl's eyes were following him. He stared at her and saw that she remained as motionless as before. *You are a fool. She will be your prisoner, and so will her brother, for as long as you like.*

He walked to a wall of the throne room and ran his fingers along the metal. It was cold and dull, rough and worn over the years. As he touched it, old memories appeared before him, dancing through the room. *Ghosts from the past.*

He looked once more at the Duet. He was becoming frustrated. *I must move on. I must find the path forward.* But *where?* That was the great question.

*Ruin.*

The name exploded in his mind. It had been buried there all along, waiting for its moment. The Outside's words remained with him. *The memories you hide away, the ones you run from – he was born in that mess, and he will chase you through them forever.*

Ruin will come with the One. It had been more than a prophecy to the people of the Overland. In a perverse way, it was the foundation of their lives: the price they had to pay for the Machinery's greatness. *We worshipped it all the more, because we knew it would break. We were all of us Doubters, all along.*

The Outside had talked about Ruin as if it was a creature. Canning knew what that meant. *One of them. An Operator.* Even in their current state – even as his prisoners – he could feel the Duet's power, thrumming through them and thudding across the hall, an ancient, terrible drumbeat. *And these two are weaker than the others.* He thought of Shirkra, the vastness of her abilities. *The Duet are nothing to her. What power does Ruin hold?*

He needed to find out.

Canning walked to the centre of the great hall, across pools of wavering candlelight. He thought back to his duel with the Outside, and the scythe he had summoned from the depths of the Underland, imbued with the power of so many memories. He did not need a weapon, this time. *I need an answer.*

He pictured the Old Place in his mind. He saw it as a great ocean, an endless, grey expanse, strangely still and silent. In the depths of that water, he knew, was what he needed.

*Who is Ruin?*

The water did not stir. It remained as it had always been: an implacable, impenetrable sheet of liquid steel.

*Who is Ruin?*

There was the slightest movement across the surface of the ocean, as if a breeze had appeared.

*Who is Ruin?*

Over time, the wind gathered pace, and the waters began to swirl.

*Who is Ruin?*

The water was parting. Underneath, there was a kind of shadow. But it was more than a shadow; it was a thing of power, a thing of the endless ages ... a pair of red eyes appeared there, in the darkness ...

Fear took hold of him, and Canning tore himself away from the ocean. But the shadow did not leave. It was there, in his throne room, standing before him, shaped like a man but something else entirely. This was the only Operator that mattered, he now knew. All the others were pale, insipid, compared to this *thing*.

The shadow grew, losing the shape of a man, falling into smoke. The red eyes appeared once more, floating within the darkness, lowering themselves towards him, studying him with the patient hunger of a predator. He saw that they were not eyes at all, but flames, small sparks of a fire that would one day incinerate him: an inferno that would burn the world, and bring forth something new from the ashes ...

Canning fell backwards, towards his throne, pushing himself away from the shadow of Ruin.

'Leave this place,' he hissed. 'Leave me alone.'

He glanced at the Duet, hoping, perhaps, that they would help him, as they had in his battle with the Outside. But they remained as they were, staring impassively ahead.

'Leave me alone,' he said again, as the darkness filled the throne room, as it gathered itself around him, as the two flaming eyes came closer, burning against his skin. He glanced once more at the Duet.

'Help me,' he whispered. 'Help me!'

The shadow disappeared, and the Duet stood grinning in the centre of the hall. 'Truly, we see that you are Arandel's heir,' they said as one. 'We feel your power: the power to battle Ruin, in the end.'

Canning shook his head. 'I can't do it. I needed you to help me.'

Girl shook her head. 'No, your majesty. You cast the shadow away by yourself.'

'We remain your prisoners,' said Boy.

Canning hesitated. 'That was just a shadow.'

'Yes. When Ruin comes in all his glory, he will crush you like a bug.' Girl grinned at him.

Canning nodded. 'I know it,' he whispered. 'Where is Ruin now? When will he come?'

'Soon,' said Boy. 'He is in that thing you all love, Canning. He is trapped *inside* the Machinery, in the very heart of the Old Place. It is broken, but Ruin remains within its bounds.

It will not hold him for much longer. He is so powerful.'

He reached out a hand.

'The shadow of Ruin is growing, Canning. It is growing more powerful than the Old Place itself.'

Canning thought of the thing that had come to him. Perhaps it was nothing more than the memory of a memory. Or perhaps Ruin really had come here, to his throne room, to take the measure of him. Either way, he had felt the power of that thing, and he feared it.

'Only one thing can stop it,' said Girl.

'The First Memory of the Old Place,' whispered Boy. 'It is greater even than Ruin.'

Canning nodded. He felt the truth of this. *The First Memory.* The words seemed to burn and sparkle in a corner of his mind.

The Duet spun around, so that they stood directly beside Canning, and put an arm each around the King of the Remnants. With their other arms they gestured to the centre of the hall, where an image had appeared. The picture was entirely blue, cold and icy. It was not dissimilar to a statue, crafted by some artist of the Centre, though that was where the similarities ended. It was in fact a memory, depicting a table surrounded by chairs. In one of the chairs sat the Operator – Jandell. Three identical women occupied another three places. As soon as he had a clear image of them, they seemed to change, as if they were formed of some transient substance. They were so similar that he wondered if they truly *were* three women, or perhaps just three faces of the same entity.

Canning looked at the rest of the group. On one side sat the Strategist, the girl who had been Katrina Paprissi. She was leaning over the table, staring at it intently. To her side sat that figure from Canning's nightmares: Shirkra. She was not wearing her mask, and she leaned back in her chair, her hands folded behind her head.

And there, at Shirkra's side, were the two Operators he knew best of all: the Duet. They held in their hands a small figurine. Canning walked closer and saw that it was a tiny model of himself.

Canning thought back to a distant moment, when he had sat with the Duet in the branch of a tree in the middle of a great forest, before he overpowered them, before he became the King of the Remnants.

'You said you wanted me to play a game,' Canning said. 'To be a *pawn*.'

Boy nodded. 'You must do it. It is your only hope to find the First Memory. The only hope of the world.'

'But you will need to release us,' said Girl. She grasped Canning's arm. 'We can't take you to the game, unless we are free.'

Canning looked into Girl's vicious little blue eyes. 'How can I trust you?'

'You have no choice.'

'No. I don't believe you.' He shook his head. 'I will find a way into the Old Place by myself. I'll find the First Memory without playing any *games*.'

Boy smiled, and shook his head. 'Ruin's power is growing all the time. He will know if just *any* mortal enters the Old Place. But the game is beyond his control, as yet. He will not see you if you come as a player.'

'It is our only chance,' said Girl. She pointed a finger at the memory, at the little figurine of Canning. 'Besides,' she said, 'you are *meant* to be there!'

Boy opened his mouth, but Canning silenced him with a finger.

'I want to play the game,' he said. 'I want to find the First Memory. *Me*.'

The Duet exchanged glances. 'To do that, you will have to set us free,' said Boy.

'We would need to go to the table of our own will,' agreed Girl.

Canning held up a finger. 'Do not try to harm me.' He could feel the power of memory flow within him, now, stronger all the time. Without quite knowing what he was doing, he flicked a finger, and the Duet fell to their knees.

'We will not betray you, oh mighty Canning,' said Boy. His words were raspy.

'Good,' said the King of the Remnants. He made another gesture, and the Duet were free.

# Chapter Fifteen

The world fell into flames, but Brightling was not burning.

**Welcome to the heart of memory, Brightling: the fire of the Old Place.**

Ruin's words seemed to come from far away, but he was here. She could sense him. He was so close. She felt the anger of her mask ripple through her.

Brightling had been in a real fire, long ago, during the Rebellion in the West. She had pushed her way from a smoke-filled room and thrown herself into a river from the top of the building. *Anything to escape the flames.* But this was all wrong. She was consumed by the inferno, but she was not burning.

**It is not that kind of fire.**

What kind of fire was this, which burned with such ferocity, yet caused her no harm?

**It is the flame of memory.**

She looked behind, to find the door was gone. The world was fire: nothing more.

**You are here. It is too late for you.**

*He is right. There is no going back.*

She walked through the flame.

If only Jandell could see *this*. The two things he loved the most: the Machinery and Brightling, side by side.

Brightling walked on.

He lost you, on that island of Squatstout's. But perhaps you lost yourself. Perhaps you sought to escape him, before he broke you. He always breaks the things he makes, in the end.

Ahead, in the heart of the inferno, there was a moving patch of darkness: a shadow.

**You still think you can destroy me, Brightling. But how can you destroy me, if you cannot reach me?**

'I can see you.'

Ruin laughed.

*Destroy him.* The words thudded in her mind, a kind of mantra. *Destroy him.* The mask whispered to her, as she bore down on Ruin. The shadow seemed to grow.

She had faced Doubters with her mask: literally *faced* them, simply turned her gaze upon them. They had screamed for their minds, before the end. They had begged for their sanity. The mask had taken something away from them: stripped them of themselves. She had not used it more than a handful of times. She was not a cruel woman, no matter what the world thought of her. She always had her reasons.

**Everything you did was for the Machinery.**

She pushed Ruin away. She focused on the mask, allowing it to spread its power through her. She saw it as a web, woven within and beyond her. She could reach out with it. She could reach out to *him*. She could scrape out his soul, if he had one.

The fire diminished, until it burned ten paces away. Everything else was dark. She was reminded, absurdly, of her mother's cupboard, locking herself away when the thieves came, *yes, the thieves, I remember that now, they used to come in the dark* ...

She looked at the flame, and she saw memories there, playing across the inferno. In the centre was the shadow. *Ruin.* Panic jolted her. She reached to her face, but her mask was gone. It appeared in the flames, floating on the fire. It had formed itself into the face of a young woman, her features twisted into a scream ...

**Do you see how I am imprisoned, Brightling?**

The mask vanished, and something emerged in the middle of the flames. It put Brightling in mind of a grotesque bird-cage, its dark bars formed of some strange material, curling together to the curved summit of the weird prison. From this structure there stretched a bar of the same substance, which made its way to a great wheel, a twisted web of a thing. A pipe of the same blackness led away from the cage, disappearing somewhere far away, falling into a haze.

Within the flame, within the cage, was the shadow of Ruin.

'Where is my mask?'

Brightling moved slowly forward. She felt nothing beneath her feet.

'Where is my mask?'

The fury of the fire began to abate. The flames were disappearing, vanishing away into the pipe, until only a flicker was visible. The darkness in the cage had assumed a shape: the figure of a person, a moving silhouette. It walked to the edge of its prison and placed its hands upon the bars.

**Brightling,** said that voice that seemed to speak within her mind and all across the world.

'Ruin.'

The shadow man raised his hand, where he held her mask.

He turned it towards her; it was Brightling's own face that looked back, carved into that darkness, screaming in sound-less pain.

She walked to the bars.

'You are like the mask,' she said. 'You're a thing of night.'

**Night?** Ruin laughed, a hollow sound in his cage. **The night is filled with life. *This* is not night.** He held the mask up in the air. ***This* is not life. This is Absence.**

'All that remains of it.'

**The Great Absence: our creator, who realised too late that he wanted to be alone. Long gone, now, except for this rotten piece of *flesh*.**

Brightling's mask floated above the shadow man now, staring down at the Watcher. It shifted through different faces: from Brightling to Jandell to her father to Katrina to Aranfal, and a hundred more besides.

**Jandell and the Dust Queen betrayed me, ten thousand years ago. They tore me from my host, and imprisoned me in this cage.**

Brightling began to tremble. This, then, was the heart of the world. This cage and its wheel were the centre of her existence, the first thing she thought of when she woke in the morning and the last before she went to sleep, the glorious creation that had made the Overland an empire. This thing had Selected her, and Canning, and all the great figures of history, men and women, boys and girls, butchers and bakers.

'This is the Machinery.'

**This is my prison.** The dark hands pounded on the bars, though no noise came. **But *I* am the Machinery. Ruin, burning in the fire of memory: trapped within a cage.**

There came a great gust of fire from the pipe, and Ruin cried out.

'You fear the flames.'

**Fear the flames?** He gestured at the space behind him. **This is the heart of the Old Place. The power of all the memories that ever were burns in this place. I am a thing of memory. I love them more than anything else. But too much, Brightling ... too much *hurts*.**

Brightling nodded, suppressing a perverse sense of sympathy. *I need to get my mask.*

**The Dust Queen's treachery ... well, I should have expected that. She has always been capricious. But my son ... I am a father, and my first child betrayed me.**

Ruin made a hissing sound. His anger flooded Brightling; she almost toppled over, but steadied herself, reaching out to the bars. She thought she heard a whisper. *The mask. The mask. The mask!*

Brightling tapped the bars, which hummed back at her. She sucked in a breath, before she asked the question that had hung over the Overland for ten millennia.

'How does the Machinery work?'

**The Machinery is broken. But I will show you how it once was.**

The scene before Brightling did not appear to change in any significant way. The cage, the wheel, and the pipe to nowhere were there as before, and the shadow remained within the dark bars. Slowly, however, things began to alter. The space around the cage changed: black sand appeared at Brightling's feet, and a red sun burned in the sky above her.

Brightling turned, prompted by some sense that a familiar presence was near. She saw him, then, crossing the dark sands in his cloak of faces. *Jandell.* He seemed to leap towards them in fits and starts, until he stood at the cage, gazing in at Ruin. This was the Jandell that Brightling had known from her youth, the old man, his head bald, his skin pale and lined. The faces in the cloak glanced fearfully at Ruin, but Jandell's eyes were cold. His focus shifted from the shadow of Ruin to the great wheel, then onto the pipe, and finally to the cage itself, which he carefully prodded with his thin fingers. *A craftsman admiring his handiwork.*

Ruin began to speak. No, not Ruin: the *memory* of Ruin. **The great traitor.**

Jandell did not flinch.

'A Watching Tactician,' he said.

**Ah! Another one. You will need someone special. They are in a sorry state.** He laughed, and it echoed across the sands.

Jandell turned from the cage and walked to the great wheel. He continued staring at Ruin as he grasped the instrument.

'You know what I want now, Father,' Jandell said. 'You have seen my wishes. You know my vision for the Overland.'

**The Machinery is breaking, Jandell. Release me from this cage, and I will forgive you. We can stand together once more.**

Jandell smiled.

'The Machinery will never break.'

**I grow stronger than the flames. Soon, they will not harm me. You accepted the Queen's aid in building this *thing*, yet you do not believe her words. It is breaking, Jandell.**

'No,' said the Operator. 'The Machinery will never break.' He pointed at Ruin. 'A Watching Tactician!'

Jandell began to turn the wheel, and a screech filled the desert, as of metal dragged across metal.

'You know what happens when you defy me, Father,' Jandell said. There was a flicker of a smile on his lips. 'Remember I control the flames. I can burn you for as long as it takes, until I get my answer.'

The shadow stood very still. After a while, it seemed to nod.

There was a new sound: a distant rumble, the movements of some machine. And then the fire came.

It was different to what Brightling had seen before, somehow burning with a greater intensity, a special kind of fury. The cage vanished beneath the flames, obscured by tongues of red and gold and yellow. The Watcher staggered backwards. There was no heat from this flame, not in the sense of a normal fire. Yet all the power of the past was here, all the burning core of memory. She thought she saw things there, in the conflagration: images from older times, things she could never begin to understand, things that occurred in so many other lives.

There came a scream.

'What is this?' Brightling asked.

**My torture.**

While the real Ruin spoke to Brightling, the Ruin of the past writhed in the inferno.

**In the heart of the Old Place, I was cast into *all* of memory. All of the past burned into me, with its lessons for the future. With that knowledge, I saw the paths to Jandell's dreams. But I suffered, Brightling. I *suffered*.**

As Brightling gazed at the fire, new images appeared. These memories were familiar. They were *her* memories: a young girl in the West, a Watcher ascending the summit.

Jandell twisted the wheel, and the fire fell away, vanishing through the pipe. The shadow in the cage now seemed more like a living being than he had before, on his knees, panting, his fists on the ground.

**Amyllia Brightling.**

Jandell smiled. 'Good,' he whispered. 'Very, very good. I hoped it would be her.'

The voice spoke once more, in Brightling's mind.

**He always loved you. He loved you more, perhaps, than any other mortal, in the history of the Machinery. I sensed it within him.**

'So you Selected me. It was all down to you'

**No. I saw only what was in the flames.**

Something was happening in the cage. Ruin had climbed to his feet, and was whispering something. Brightling moved closer, but could hear nothing.

'What are you doing?' said the Operator.

Jandell had moved away from the wheel and was approaching the cage.

'Who are you talking to, Father? No one can hear you.'

Ruin spread his arms. When he spoke, it was not in that powerful voice that Brightling knew. This was the voice of a broken creature, the rasp of an old, broken man.

'The Machinery is breaking,' said the shadow. 'My powers grow with every Selection.' He tapped the bars. 'Already, my voice can travel beyond the cage.'

Jandell shook his head. 'You will not manipulate me. The flames will always control you. You will never be more powerful than the Old Place, Father. The Machinery will never break.' He nodded. 'Amyllia Brightling. Good. Good.'

He turned his back on Ruin and returned to the wheel. He twisted it, and the fire poured forth again, causing the memory Ruin to scream.

'Why is he doing that again?' Brightling asked.

Ruin laughed. **It was always the same. He liked to use the fire, for his little shows in the Overland.**

The flames swept upwards, disappearing into the sky, into some unseen space. Jandell leapt upon them and ascended. Brightling saw he had a piece of parchment in his hand.

'He is going to the Circus,' she said, remembering all those Selections she had seen, when fire had poured forth from the Portal.

**Yes. And he will let me burn until he returns. He always did the same thing. It does not matter. What matters is that Jandell was wrong. The Machinery *was* breaking.**

The scene changed. The cage remained in its position, beside the great wheel, with Ruin trapped inside. But they were now on a wintry mountaintop. The place was utterly unreal. All of it, from the form and colour of the rocks to the snow that lay on the ground, could have come straight from a painting or a tapestry. They were surrounded by the night sky, almost suffocated by stars.

In the cage, the memory of Ruin was standing very still before the pipe.

**Jandell's creation was built on two foolish mistakes, Brightling. He knew my powers would grow, every time I was burned. But I would never become more powerful than the fire, he thought. I would never be greater than the Old Place.**

In the cage, Ruin had raised two long, dark arms, great wings of shadow.

**Ten millennia were all it took to prove that idea a lie. Just ten millennia of burning in the flames, until *I* controlled the *fire*.**

The wheel began to turn, as if of its own accord. Flames emerged from the pipe: a purple fire, almost dragged from the depths by this shadow, who spun and moulded and twirled it before him like it was nothing more than string. He made a snapping gesture with his arm, and the flame flew from the cage, vanishing into the sky.

**I could do so much. I sent powers to the One. She took over your girl – your Katrina – and became the Strategist. All of you failed to protect that mortal.**

Brightling burned at Ruin's words, but only because they were true.

The scene changed again, and they returned to the cage in its hall of darkness.

**And now you come to hurt me – with this *thing*.**

The mask reappeared, still in the shape of Brightling's face. Ruin held it in his right hand, and toyed with a flame of memory in his left. He brought them close together, and Brightling's mask seemed to silently scream.

The Watcher took a step towards the cage. 'You told Jandell your voice could travel beyond the cage, as if you'd grown more powerful. But you have *always* spoken beyond its walls. You have spoken to Squatstout from the beginning.'

**Yes.**

A cold fear crept across Brightling. She had a growing feeling that she had been fooled. Not just her: *all of them*. All of the world, human and Operator alike, were somehow the subjects of a trick.

She walked forward and touched the bars. They felt like cold metal: nothing more.

'You said the Machinery was built on two mistakes,' she whispered. 'What was the second?'

And then he was there, so close to her, a shadow by her side. In the next moment, he was back in his cage.

Jandell thought the cage was perfect. It would always hold me in place, even if I mastered the flames.

Ruin laughed.

"Ruin will come with the One." That's what you all feared, for so long. Well, I will take the hand of the One, at the end. But I do not need her to escape this prison.

Brightling felt him, then, within her mind, pawing at her memories, pulling them apart and smashing them together, forcing her to see things she had tried to forget.

I have *never* been trapped, Brightling.

Suddenly he was by her side; in the next moment, he was back in the cage.

I *allowed* them to put me here.

I *wanted* to burn.

His words faded away for a moment, as he scrabbled through her mind.

Ten millennia. Ten millennia, to grow more powerful than a god. Soon I will *drink* the god. The Old Place will fall to Ruin. And oh, what memories we will wallow in!

He laughed. Ruin will come with the One! Ten thousand years of *nonsense*!

The world under Ruin opened itself before her, a world in which he ruled their minds. She saw memories from other lives, merged with her own: hard memories, the ones that people hide away. She saw things from her past, moments she had forgotten, moments she had *wanted* to forget. This would be the future; these memories were the heart of Ruin.

Ruin extinguished his flame, and raised the mask into the air.

I destroyed the Absence, Brightling. I am its *Ruin*. Why, then, would I fear its corpse, when I am stronger than I ever have been before?

He squeezed his fist together, and the mask shattered. Brightling thought she heard a scream.

I only need one thing. One thing that I have searched for, oh, for ten millennia. I never knew how to find it! But I see what I achieved, without even knowing it. I sent the One to you, so that you could mould her host.

Brightling felt icy fingers clawing at her soul.

And all the while, she was working on my behalf, forming you into the perfect host for *me*.

A sense of cold power came over Brightling, as Ruin took her over.

# Chapter Sixteen

Everything froze in the memory.

Drayn still stood at the side of the dock, with Amyllia and the little girl in the purple rags and the mask of a white rat. But there was no movement anywhere, now.

No movement, apart from the Protector in his wide-brimmed hat and golden mask, shuffling in her direction, slamming his stick into the ground. She had last seen him on the Habitation, just after Squatstout's death. He had leapt into the Endless Ocean and floated away, *above* the waters.

*He is one of them, and he will avenge his master.*

'You are a Thonn,' he said, as he thudded towards her. She had only occasionally heard the Protector speak, but she knew there was something wrong. This was not his voice.

Drayn nodded. 'Drayn,' she said. 'Though I'm not sure the name matters any more.'

The Protector held up a finger. 'The Thonns were the greatest House on the island.'

'Were? They still are. Or has someone taken their place?'

The Protector came to a halt before her. 'They've gone, haven't they? You are the heiress, fled from her shores.' He chuckled. 'It doesn't matter. It'll all be at an end, soon: Habitation, Overland, all of it. Ruin is coming.'

Drayn's eyes narrowed. 'Who are you?'

'You have such wonderful memories,' he whispered. 'I would love to play with them, you know. To see their contours and their colours … but I will not.' The golden beak nodded. 'I have a great deal to do.'

'Who are you?' Drayn asked again.

'I am old, so old … I was there from the beginning, almost.'

'The beginning of the island, when Squatstout first came.'

'No! The beginning of it all!'

He reached up and snapped open the helmet, throwing it to the side. He was a middle-aged man, rough and unremarkable. He had thinning black hair and thick stubble, and his eyes were wide and watchful. His red mouth sat sneering beneath a sharp little nose. She did not recognise this man by his appearance, but there was an aspect to him that was instantly familiar, the stench of something ancient and rotten.

This was not a man at all.

'Squatstout,' she whispered.

There was movement to the side. Drayn turned, and felt a rush of relief as she saw Jandell, striding towards them with Jaco at his side.

'Ah!' cried the new Squatstout. 'Jandell and the childless father!' He bowed to Jaco. 'What a man you must be, to have brought the One into the Overland, to nurture her, and then place her in that dark tower, where she became the perfect host! And you had another child, too … a boy …' Squatstout tapped his head mockingly. 'Let me see … let me see … what was his name …?'

'Squatstout,' said Jandell. 'Don't do—'

'By the Great Absence, brother – shut up!' Squatstout swiped a hand in the air, and a fountain of water rose up from the dockside, smashing into Jandell and knocking him to his feet.

'Alexander!' shouted Squatstout, turning his attention once more to Jaco. 'That was his name, wasn't it? You haven't seen him in such a long time, have you, Jaco? Not since my kind-hearted brother stole him away from you!' Squatstout laughed. He clapped his hands and a young boy appeared at his side, a child with pale skin and black curly hair.

Jaco staggered towards the boy.

'It is not real,' said Jandell, rising to his feet. 'It is a memory …'

'But memories *are* real, Jandell!' cried Squatstout. 'Soon the world will be nothing *but* memory – real and imagined! All the little loves of Ruin, all the memories mortals squirrel away, too frightened or ashamed to face them!' He laughed, and tapped Jaco on the shoulder, before pointing at Alexander. 'This *is* your son, *and* it is a memory.'

But Jaco was no longer listening. He was crouching down, his hands on his son's shoulders. His words came in a soft, pleading trickle.

'I'm sorry,' he said. 'I should have listened. I should have—'

Squatstout laughed. 'Should have, should have, should have! The great curse of humanity!'

He tossed his stick into the water, raised his arms in the air, and brought them down with a sharp motion. That was all it took. There was no cry, no blood. Jaco was dead on the dockside, and his son was fading away.

Jandell stood very still for a moment, before raising a hand to his mouth. He seemed suddenly shrunken, far older than before. A light within was flickering.

'I know what you are thinking, brother,' said Squatstout, nodding. 'You think I am so cruel, you think I am so wicked. But what did you do to stop me, hmm? What have you *ever* done? I will not stand here and listen to you accuse me of all the things you allowed to happen, and the things you have done yourself!'

Jandell began to tremble. 'I have tried to change,' he whispered. 'I have always tried to change. Not just for myself, but for you as well, and Shirkra, and the Duet. Even our parents. But I have always failed.'

'You are fighting your nature, Jandell. Though perhaps not. You were born from misery. Perhaps you are doing *just* what you were always supposed to. You make yourself miserable, because it is your destiny. But Ruin is coming, Jandell. Ruin has always been coming.'

The new Squatstout put an arm around Drayn, and they were gone.

'Do you know where I was born, Drayn?'

The girl could see nothing.

'Squalor,' she said. 'I sense it in you.'

A dull light grew around them. *Stones. Steps. An alleyway. It's night. It's raining.* The new Squatstout grinned at her, just visible in a pool of orange light that glowed from a lantern on the wall. He snorted the air. 'This is the kind of place you'd find a thing like me,' he said. 'A bit bad, but a coward too.'

Drayn heard a sound and turned to look the other way up the alley. She hadn't noticed the boy, at first, but there he was, sitting alone, his head in his hands. He was a thin child, all rags and bones; the mop of black hair on his head looked to weigh more than he did.

'Don't worry, boy. You'll get used to it.'

A door had opened behind the boy, and a man was standing there. Drayn knew this man very well, but at the same time, had no idea who he was. He was short, his bald head covered in a few strands of chestnut hair. He wore a hareskin shawl. But this was not Squatstout: this was only a man. She could *feel* his mortality; it hung over his every movement.

He took a seat by the boy's side, and touched the child's leg. 'Don't worry at all, not at all. There's all sorts of love in the world. You just need to get used to *my* love, that's all.'

The new Squatstout was at her side. 'I won't tell you how long ago this is,' he whispered. 'You wouldn't believe me.' He chuckled, then gestured at the man. 'Look at him!' he whispered. 'Such a horror he was. I can't remember when I found him – maybe a year after this. He'd spent all his life rummaging around in the dirt and the slime, the dirt and slime he made himself.' He grinned, and tapped his chest. 'That's me, Drayn, you see. I'm the king of dirt. I'm the lord of shuffles in the night.'

He giggled. 'I won't even tell you what this *new* host has in him.' He pointed to his head. 'I found him on the island, when I first came, and I just *knew* he'd be perfect for me, one day. But I didn't want to give up on my lovely old host, the one I'd had for such a long, long time. No, I couldn't do *that*, Drayn. So I held onto the other one as a spare. He'd die, though, like all mortals, if he didn't have one of us in him. So I made up a little thing of memory, and called it the Protector, and put him in this body, until I might need it for myself. When the time came, I just threw that Autocrat out. Ha! Oh, I would have died without it,

Drayn. I couldn't even have got by as a spirit in the air. I would've—'

'Get me out of here,' Drayn said.

They were in another memory. Drayn and Squatstout stood on a hill, staring down at a battlefield. There were no victors, here: just bodies and broken, blasted machines, strange things formed of metal that she did not recognise. It was early morning; the sun glared down upon them.

'You never had battles in the island, thanks to me,' Squatstout said, tapping his chest. 'I told you about them, didn't I?'

Drayn nodded. 'I'm glad I never saw one.'

Squatstout grunted. 'There he is,' he said.

Drayn followed his finger, until she saw a living figure, standing amid all that death.

'Come,' said Squatstout, 'let's go look.'

In a heartbeat they were down there. The young man was utterly alone; there was something strangely proud about him. This was Jandell. However, like the Squatstout she saw in the alley, it was not the Jandell she knew.

'Jandell has had this host for such a long time,' Squatstout whispered. 'His host was once such a wonderful man, you know, so regal and terrifying and angry, like my brother himself. Look around – do you know what you see?'

Drayn stared out at the carnage. 'Yes,' she said. 'The losing side of a battle.'

'Yes. But more than that – the end of an entire people. They picked the wrong enemy, long before this day, and were put to the sword. All of them, all ages, no respect for who they were, oh no.' He giggled. 'That man was the only survivor.' He nodded at Jandell, or the man who was to become Jandell. 'Do you know what he did, after this? He killed his own heart. He became pitiless. Somehow he raised an army of his own, and he went after those who destroyed his people, and he did the same to them. He fought with such fury. But it gave him no joy. It corrupted him, in the end. That is Jandell, you see: a man of terrible crimes, but no humour in them. *Bleak*.' Squatstout spat on the ground.

'He is a greater man than you.'

Squatstout threw his hands in the air. 'Did I ever claim otherwise? I know what I am. You never find my hosts out fighting battles, oh no.'

'I want to go home.'

'Home? The island?'

'No. To Jandell.'

'You think of Jandell as *home*? Hmm.' He clicked his tongue. 'I've seen people like you before. You just *know* your way around the Old Place. Amazing.' He leaned towards her. 'But you're not just a weaver of our magic, are you, Drayn? You're a mortal. And I can sense such lovely memories within your mind. They set Jandell free – what strength there is in them! I would like to play with them, before we all fall into Ruin. I'd like to finger them. I'd like to hide you away somewhere, far from Jandell, and prise your memories apart, to see what I can find.'

He moved towards her, smiling. His smile seemed to grow as she looked at it, expanding beyond his face, beyond his head, until the battlefield was gone, and all that was left was Drayn and Squatstout's smile.

'It is funny, Drayn,' said the great mouth. The voice was unmistakeably Squatstout's, but something about it had changed: there was a new weariness to it. 'We live for memories: we worship the past, the endless past. Is this a good way to live?'

The mouth receded, and Squatstout stood before her once more, on the battlefield again. An unfamiliar sense of melancholy had fallen upon him. He nodded to the bodies all around.

'All these people died this day, all of them but Jandell's host. They died, and yet they did not die: even now their memories live on in the Old Place. I can go to them, if I like: I can revel in their little stories. I can taste the power of them.' He sighed. 'But it is so much better to find a *living* mortal, truly alive, and walk through their memories hand in hand. Especially one like you.' He nodded at Drayn. 'We can do that, you and I. It would give me such pleasure.'

Once, when she was a younger girl, Drayn had seen a crow on a branch outside her bedroom window. She had gently opened the window, placed a stone in her slingshot, pulled it back, and killed the bird. She remembered standing in her room for a while and staring out at the empty branch, dumbly surprised at what she had done. Then she had gone downstairs, out to the tree, and found the bird. She took a little knife, and she began to cut it open …

She felt like that bird now.

The battlefield fell away and a burning power spun around her, growing and contracting, flashing between a thousand shades. When she focused on any point of the maelstrom, she could see strange little images, fleeting glimpses of *moments* of her past. All of them, though, were polluted; all of them were degraded; all of them stank of Squatstout. She could see him there, his face, his grubby presence.

**Such power is here, in these memories.**

The voice was Squatstout's, though it spoke within her.

I see, now, how you saved Jandell. Even *touching* these memories is enough to give one a kind of jolt! But I will drink them ... I will drink all of them, before Ruin comes.

She saw a cloud of grey smoke, floating through the storm of memory. It was *him*. He was within her: he had made himself a part of her essence.

**You should not think of your memories as individual chambers, Drayn Thonn. They are all a part of the Old Place. All of them can be brought together, things from the ancient past and things from yesterday ...**

For a moment the storm vanished, and they were at the Choosing. Drayn was standing very still, with one of the hands grasping her ankle. But this was all wrong. This was not the island. She was on top of a hill, and all around her were children, dressed in black, on their knees, weeping. The image vanished in a moment, and she was back in the storm.

I can feel such strength in your memories, Drayn. How did they become so powerful? She heard him laugh. We never know ... if we knew, we could do so much more ...

There was a brief silence, and even the memory storm stopped turning.

**What's this ...? What memory is this ...?**

The storm began to dissipate. An image emerged from far away, growing larger as it came. A young girl, standing over a man, a knife in her hand ...

**You have kept this one hidden. Come, we will go there together.**

Drayn heard a scream, and realised with a curious, numb sensation that it was coming from her own lips. *You cannot have this memory.* She focused on it, willing it to disappear. But it was useless. She could see Squatstout surrounding it with his strange smoke, tasting it ...

*This is delicious. Ruin will* love *this. This is what he lives for. This is where he was* born.

She was burning. *You cannot have it.* She moved forward and reached out her hand, as if the memory was something she could grasp. She stretched out her fingers to touch it, as thoughts gathered in her mind. *This belongs to me! You cannot have it!* She felt a kind of strength …

And they were back on the battlefield. Squatstout staggered backwards, his eyes wide.

'What have you *done?*'

Drayn looked down at her hand. There was an animal there, a snake, knotted around her arm. *No. It is not an animal.* It was a thing of pulsating power, a black rope that had tied itself to her. She thought she could see faces in the substance, people from the past: Dad, and Mother, and herself. *This is the memory, but it is changed. It is … it is magic.*

She looked up at Squatstout. His mouth hung open, and his eyes were creased with fury.

'Give it to me!' he spat.

He raised a hand; there was a spark there, a little flame, and Drayn thought she saw some unfamiliar moment, a dark scene, dancing at the tips of Squatstout's fingers. She felt herself being dragged forward, towards him, along with her memory.

'No,' she said.

She raised her memory into the air. She felt it form into something else: a spear, a dark weapon, a blade formed from the past, alive with power.

Squatstout's palms were spread open before her.

'No!' he cried. 'Come and join me … I can show you

things that Jandell never would. I can give you a castle, made of memory. A city ... a world ...'

Drayn lifted the spear and threw it at the Autocrat. He screamed, and the world filled with grey smoke.

She turned, and saw another being, far away, as if in another memory. It was a strange thing, a beast with long limbs, a bald head, and no eyes. It shook its head at her, willing her to turn away, to go to another place.

She did not listen.

# Chapter Seventeen

Every child in the Overland knew the Portal to the Machinery.

Brandione could not recall when he had first heard the name. Perhaps as a boy at his mother's knee. *That's the heart of the world, my child. That's where the fire comes from, the fire that brings us the names of our leaders. That's where we throw our Strategists when they die.*

*The Portal to the Machinery.* But that title could not be correct. Brandione had never laid eyes upon the Machinery, yet he knew it was not in this place. It was only bodies, here, lined up neatly in rows, eyes closed, hands folded on chests. Not just any bodies, but historical artefacts: the corpses of the greatest men and women in history, still wearing their purple robes. All of them were squashed together in a vast space, a hall without walls or a ceiling, a floating floor of white stone surrounded by flickering darkness. The stars in this nowhere land were not stars at all, but full-moon crowns like the Strategists once wore, gleaming down at him.

'Does the Old Place line the bodies up itself?' he whispered. 'Or is there an undertaker of the Underland?'

'Why not both?'

A familiar figure appeared at his side. He had seen this

146

woman in the Museum of Older Times, when he went on that strange journey with Aranfal and Squatstout so long ago, before everything fell apart. She wore the same dark veil, and her pale little hands still peeked out from her sleeves. The veil shifted as she spoke, so that her face and hooked nose were occasionally visible. He remembered that neck of hers, with its terrible web of scars.

The veiled woman pointed to the bodies on the floor. 'I place them where they belong. But I am a thing of memory, and a creature of the Old Place.'

Brandione nodded at the corpses. 'Do they rot?'

The woman shrugged. 'These are memories of the dead, of men and women and boys and girls that once were. A mixture of memories; the memories they brought to the world themselves, and the memories others had of them. Such famous men and women ... such wonderful memories. I try to keep them as they once were. I always thought someone might come to see them one day.'

'Has anyone come before me?'

She shook her veiled head. 'No.' She gestured at a nearby corpse. 'This is where the most recent arrivals are placed. Don't you *know* this one?'

Brandione studied the man at his feet. He was younger than the one-time General, with greying brown hair and a peppering of stubble. It took Brandione some time to recognise him as Strategist Kane, the man he had once served. *The man they thought I killed, all that time ago.*

'He's younger than I remember,' Brandione said.

The veiled woman nodded.

Brandione lowered himself onto his haunches and examined the face of his old master. He was not a good man, but he was Selected, and he ruled for more than half a century.

He oversaw Expansion to the ends of the continent. *But I would never have put you in your role. The Machinery was wise, and now it is gone, and the world is falling apart.*

Brandione glanced up at the veiled woman. 'I need something,' he said. 'We all need it. The First Memory of the Old Place.'

The veiled woman shook her head. 'I do not know where it is,' she whispered. 'You can ask the dead, if you wish.' She swept a hand across the corpses.

'Ask the dead?' Brandione glanced around. 'How?'

'Touch them.'

Brandione reached out to Kane's face. He felt a vague sense of danger; he turned his head sharply, half-expecting the woman to be moving towards him with some ill intent. But she was in the same position as before.

'Touch him,' she hissed. She twisted her head, and the veil fell away from her neck. Her skin was ruined: red and raw. '*Do it.* It will help you.'

Brandione reached out to the old man's face once more, before deciding that he could not hear that voice again.

'All the Strategists are here?'

The veiled woman nodded.

A thought crystallised. *Arandel was in a game, once. He fought the Operators. He learned how to beat them.*

'Kane is the most recent Strategist to die,' Brandione said. He pointed up the path. 'The first is down there, then?'

The woman nodded.

Brandione gazed at the hundreds of bodies that lined the sides, a highway of the glorious dead. He began to walk, half-expecting the veiled woman to stop him. After a while he turned back, but she was not there. She had gone back to wherever she had come from: the Museum of Older Times, perhaps.

And so on he went, past the corpses of the Strategists: people of all descriptions, closed books that he could open whenever he wanted, with just a touch of his hand. But he did not want to hear what they had to say. He only cared about one: a Strategist who had done it all before. The *first* Strategist.

He began to run, and the past seemed to run alongside him, to run behind him, propelling him forward. *His* past. A young man appeared at his side, driven by ambition, fighting against his own fears, falling into madness. For a moment he felt that *she* was there, watching him, urging him forward: a woman of three bodies, a woman of one mind, older than anything that lived.

His limbs grew weary, his body sore. He felt that he was running against some force. Perhaps it was only himself.

The pathway came to an end, at last, and Brandione turned his head, to gaze upon history itself.

Arandel was the most famous man in the history of the world. Children knew his name before they could walk. He was the greatest figure in the Book of the Machinery: the first person the Operator told of the glory of the Machinery, and the first to be Selected as Strategist, back when the city was not much more than the Circus, Memory Hall, and the See House. And here he was, lying on the ground before Brandione. The one-time General had expected something different. It was not that the face was unfamiliar, or that the works of art had been wrong. On the contrary, this was *exactly* the face that stared down from the apartments of the Strategist and the walls of the People's Level. Perhaps this wasn't the way the man looked in life; perhaps the Underland had altered his appearance to match Brandione's expectations. It did not matter. *I am here, and so is he.*

Arandel was young, no older than his early thirties. His corpse, like that of Kane, must have shown him from another point in life, long before his death. He had light-brown skin and delicate features: a sharp little nose, thin lips, long eyelashes. His hair was a tight mass of thick curls, and the number *1* had been written over and over upon his purple gown, interlocking in a graceful, looping style.

Brandione crouched down and touched the First Strategist on the forehead. After a while, the smooth little hands began to twitch, and the eyes clicked open.

Arandel pushed himself up into a sitting position and stared glassily ahead.

'Hello,' Brandione said.

Arandel did not respond. Brandione raised a hand and waved it in front of the First Strategist's eyes. There was no sign that the man had noticed Brandione's presence.

'Strategist,' Brandione said. 'Arandel. Prophet of the Machinery.'

Arandel remained silent.

'I need your help, my lord. I have been sent to this place … I have been sent to play a game.' He thought he could hear the old Brandione, commander of the armies of the Overland, laughing somewhere far away.

Brandione moved closer to Arandel. *One can speak to the dead, but no one can make the dead reply.* 'My lord, help me. Please. Tell me where to find it … I need the First Memory. It is the only way to stop Ruin.'

That did it: the word *Ruin.* Arandel grinned at Brandione, and there was a fire in his eyes.

'What do you know of *Ruin?*' The light voice was strangely familiar, as if it belonged to a man of today's Overland.

'Ruin is coming,' Brandione said.

Arandel snatched out a hand and grasped Brandione's wrist. He was surprisingly strong, and had a savage glint in his eye.

'Ruin?' he spat, before laughing. 'Ruin!'

'Is the First Memory here? The Old Place has lost it …'

'Why do you want *that*?'

'To fight Ruin.'

Arandel laughed; he pointed at his face. 'I tricked Ruin, long ago. I surprised them all. But there is no tricking any of them now. It is all at an end, and the First Memory will not avail you.'

He lay back down in his position and fell silent once more.

As Brandione stared at the corpse, he felt that old swell of anger. *He is right*. There was no point in any of this. *The game is a joke*.

An iron certainty took hold of him. He would leave this place. All he wanted was to stand at the side of the Dust Queen and face whatever was coming. He would go to her. If the First Memory was real – and he had his doubts – then one of the others could find it. It was beyond him.

He wondered if she would be disappointed in him. He hoped not. But regardless, he was leaving. There would be no more games for him.

He looked out into the darkness, to all the full-moon crowns.

'Take me to the Queen!' he shouted. 'Take me to the board!'

There was a whisper in the dark.

Brandione leapt upwards and *pushed* himself into the night sky, up among the crowns. He knew where he wanted to go. He knew the Underland would take him there, though he did not know why.

# Chapter Eighteen

'This is a bad place, Aranfal.'

The Watcher nodded. 'You didn't have to come with me.'

Alexander barked a laugh. 'No. But I couldn't let you go here alone.' The boy was trembling. 'Not to this place.'

The Shadowthings were directly in front of Aranfal and Alexander, moving slowly forward. He could hear Aleah's screams, somewhere up ahead, but he could not see past the creatures. *They're nothing but darkness. Oil on water. Smoke from the fire.*

'Where are we?' he asked Alexander. 'What is she doing here?'

The creature directly ahead of the Watcher stopped walking. It turned around, and it gazed down at him. There were no features in the depths of that black hood, but for two blotches of orange light.

The creature seemed to shake its head. It turned again and began to walk.

'I *hate* this place,' Alexander said, following the creature. 'I hate Chaos. But it's so hard to avoid, sometimes.' He tapped his head. 'Even within ourselves. You know?'

Aranfal nodded.

'Come on,' said Alexander. He grasped Aranfal by the wrist. 'Follow me.'

The boy led the Watcher up to the line of dark figures and squeezed himself between two of them. 'They won't hurt you,' he said. 'They don't care about you.'

They forced their way through.

Aranfal had seen many parts of the Underland by now, and had often wondered how he would describe his experiences to someone in the real world. But what he saw here, in this place, was something else entirely. This was something he could not explain to *himself*, and he was looking at it.

*Chaos*. Images paraded before his eyes, floating in the air around him, on and on into an endless space. A book danced past his head, followed by a row of coins. Far away, three men sat huddled over a dead horse, its stomach sliced open. A parade of dogs marched on a hill, and a man and woman fought for a golden spoon. A line of soldiers stood perfectly still, as black birds pecked at their eyes. A boy played a drum, while another cut his hair. On and on they went, a million scenes, glowing with an inner light, bursts of red and purple, on and on forever ...

'Memories are a great flow, Aranfal,' Alexander whispered. 'But there is so much to them, things that no one understands. There are memories that are not true. There are memories of other memories, and memories of imaginings. There are the memories of the mad. All of them are here, in Chaos. They say this is the largest part of the Underland.' He glanced at Aranfal. 'We must be careful, or we'll be lost. Lost like Aleah.'

Aranfal frowned. 'What do you mean?'

But Alexander ignored him. 'Can you feel *her* here, Aranfal? Can you feel Shirkra?'

'I can feel her,' he whispered.

'They call her the Mother of Chaos,' Alexander said. 'But even her name is the wrong way round. How can she be the *mother*, when this place has been here forever – as long as the First Memory itself?'

'She was born of this madness.' Aranfal gestured at the great expanse.

'Yes.'

Somewhere in the maelstrom, Aleah screamed.

'She is lost now,' Alexander said. 'This happens to many who come here.'

The Watcher looked out at the world around him. He listened to the howls and shrieks, and felt them tearing at him.

'This is a nightmare,' he said. Something flashed before him: a parade of tortured souls, driven mad at his hand. *You are Chaos, too, Aranfal and Aran Fal.* 'This is the true face of this god,' he whispered. 'Madness and cruelty. *Shirkra* is the face of the god.'

Alexander hummed. 'Ah! There she is.'

Aleah was sitting on the edge of a stone, floating in the air, her eyes locked open. Aranfal knew terror when he saw it: *true* terror, the type that no one understood until they felt it, the type that grabbed hold of you and couldn't be pushed away, not even by the so-called brave.

'She has been cast into the Chaos of her own mind,' Alexander said. 'All the little nightmares she dreamed up as a child, all the idle thoughts of terrible deaths – all of them are memories, and all of them are tormenting her.'

'Why? How has she become so lost?'

Alexander shrugged. 'She came to search inside Chaos. Perhaps Chaos didn't like it. Perhaps Chaos is searching inside *her*.'

Aranfal felt a weight at his back, and a Shadowthing pushed past him. It began to float upwards through Chaos, its hands woven across its chest.

'The Shadowthing is going to get her,' said the boy. 'She'll be taken from Chaos to ... somewhere else.'

Aranfal turned away from the nightmare. 'We need to go.' He felt a tremor in his voice. 'I'm afraid, Alexander.' The words felt pathetic, coming from the tongue of a grown man: a Watcher of the Overland, no less. But Aranfal knew better: all the Watchers did. Theirs was an order built on fear. They knew all its peaks and valleys, and none more than him. In an order of torturers, only he had been *the* torturer. He knew how to use fear as a weapon, because like all creatures, he was himself afraid. And this madness was too much for him, this Chaos and these Shadowthings. There was no reasoning with it; there was no escape. Not even the Strategist could help him here, amid this Chaos.

He cast a glance backwards, as the creature closed in on Aleah.

'She's brought this on herself. We need to go.'

When Alexander spoke, it was not in his own voice.

'Is there no loyalty, now, among the Watchers of the Overland?'

This was not Alexander. This was Aranfal's mistress. This was Brightling.

'There are two worlds,' said Alexander, or Brightling, or whoever was speaking to him. 'There is the See House, and there is the *outside*. We who dwell on the inside ...'

The words kept coming, but Aranfal could not hear them. 'Is that you, Alexander? Are you doing this?'

But the boy merely looked confused.

\*

Aranfal was in the See House. No: he was *on* the See House. It was night, and a rain was whipping in from the Peripheral Sea, washing over the Apprentices who sat shivering on the stone roof of that narrow tower.

In many of the memories that appeared to him in the Old Place, Aranfal had been a spectator, staring down at a younger version of himself. Not here. In this memory, he was inside the body of this earlier man: Aranfal within Aran Fal.

There was a group of them, up here, maybe fifteen strong, all of them folded up against the night, wrapped in their cloaks, their maskless faces open and fearful.

Brightling stood before them, and she was enraged. It was rare to see her angry. Her reaction to most events was cool, poised, even in the most extreme of situations. Not now. Now she trembled with emotion.

She paced before them, a knife in her hand.

'I tolerate a good deal, in this tower,' she whispered. 'More than my predecessors. Oh, you wouldn't have liked them, children. Not at all.' She nodded fiercely. She stood still, and gazed at the dark sky above. 'I tolerate a lot. But there is one thing I will *not* tolerate.'

She gazed at them all, flicking her head back and forth, as if daring someone to challenge her. No one did.

'We are a tower.' She said the words in a quiet voice, barely above a whisper, but the Apprentices remained in such dumbstruck silence that they had no trouble hearing their leader.

Brightling stamped her foot on the ground. 'I am not talking about this building. I am talking about *us*. The Watchers of the Overland. We are a tower, standing tall in society, casting our shadow across the Plateau. All look to us in wonder, and in fear.' She nodded, lifted the knife, and very gently tapped it against her skull. 'A tower stands on all its stones. And if one stone breaks ...'

She did not need to say more. Aranfal knew they were all picturing the same thing: the See House, falling to dust.

'There are two sides to our tower,' Brightling said. 'There is the inside, and the outside. We who are on the inside must place each other above all things. We are no longer members of any family, except the family of our tower. And one of you betrayed that trust.'

There was a whimpering sound as a tall, skinny girl rose to her feet. Aranfal couldn't recall her name, now, but he remembered the look on her face. *Torn*. She did not make eye contact with Brightling, but she somehow managed to speak.

'Madam, you are talking about me.' She sounded braver than she looked.

Brightling nodded. 'What did you do?'

The girl sniffed. 'I knew my sister was being investigated, and I sent word to her.'

'What happened then?'

'She escaped, ma'am.'

'Not for long.'

'No. The soldiers got her.'

At those words, Brightling stamped her foot on the ground again. 'The *soldiers* got that traitor! The *soldiers*!' She threw the blade on the ground, and the clanking of the steel echoed across the rooftop.

'Come here,' she said to the girl, who shuffled towards her with great, heaving sobs. Brightling grasped her by her cloak and dragged her to the edge of the rooftop. She put her hand around the girl's neck and lifted her, dangling her over the side. She had such strength. Few ever saw it, until it was too late.

Brightling gave a sharp nod. 'We are a family,' she said to the girl, though she was speaking to them all. 'We may hate one another – but we *never* betray one another to *anyone* outside the family. The day you do that is the day you are no longer a Watcher. And you have come too far. If you stop being a Watcher, you are *nothing*.'

All of them murmured the word back to her. *Nothing. Nothing. Nothing.*

Brightling placed the girl back on the rooftop.

'Sit down,' she said.

The girl looked up at her, eyes wide. 'Are you sure, madam?' *Stupid.*

Brightling nodded. 'That is your first crime against our family, and as your family, we forgive you.' She jabbed a thumb at the abyss. 'But this family forgives only once.'

In the land of Chaos, Aranfal halted. He cast a glance at Alexander, and wondered if the boy had brought that memory before him. He thought not. This was a creation of his own mind, brought to vivid life in this place: in this Old Place.

'You can't leave her here, Aranfal,' the boy said, speaking with his own voice once more. 'You can't leave her to Chaos and shadows.'

Aranfal shook his head, and turned back into Chaos, where the Shadowthing had now encircled Aleah. They both hung in the air for a moment, before vanishing.

'Where have they gone, Alexander?'

The boy's eyes bulged.

'Away. A bad place: worse than Chaos.' He spoke in a quiet voice.

'How do I follow?'

Alexander nodded at the other Shadowthings. 'You'd have to go with one of them. But I won't go with you, Aranfal. I won't go there.'

He looked to the line of dark figures. They did not appear to notice or care about him.

*Shadowthings, come for me. Take me away from here.*

But the Shadowthings were leaving; their backs were turned, and they were shuffling away to some other part of the Underland.

*Come for me! I am here!*

They kept on walking away from him, away forever, leaving him behind, leaving him in Chaos.

*Please!*

One of them stopped. It turned so slowly, and it gazed upon him with its orange eyes. It stood perfectly still for a moment. Perhaps it was considering him, assessing his memories, wondering if he was worthwhile. There was no way to see inside that mind, if it had one at all.

And then the Shadowthing lifted its arm. It raised it slowly, dragging it upward, until a finger of darkness pointed directly at the Watcher.

It felt Aranfal. It nodded. And it began to float towards him.

He was in a candlelit cell. The shadow creature sat in the corner, watching him.

There was a circular doorway leading out to a dark corridor. Aranfal backed towards it, watching the creature as he went. It made no effort to stop him. *It doesn't care where I go. It will find me, wherever I run.*

He walked out into the corridor, a place of cold stone

and damp walls, like the Bowels of the See House. A line of cells stretched away before him. He glanced at the one opposite and saw a young man lying on the ground, his arm across his head. One of the Shadowthings sat in a nook in the wall, playing with something in its hands. At first glance it seemed to be a sparkling ball of red light, but as he looked upon it, he could see things there: flickering images of the past. *A child playing in a garden. A man drinking wine. A woman crying.*

Aranfal turned away and began to walk up the corridor, past the other cells. All were the same: a man or woman on the ground, a shadow creature toying with their memories. *Draining them.*

His mind turned to strange things. He thought of other worlds: worlds without the Machinery, worlds without the Overland and the Underland, worlds without Operators. Could they live without the power of memories? Or would they all end up in cells forever, corpses without a spark?

And then, without expecting it, and without knowing how, he found her.

Aleah was sitting on a wooden stool in the centre of her cell, a prisoner. She wore her dark cloak, and her hands hung by her side, one of them holding her cat mask. Her head leaned backwards, exposing her neck. Her eyes were closed, and her blonde hair was slicked back with sweat.

She was not alone. A Shadowthing stood at her side, holding her in its hands. Yes, holding *her*: the essence of her, all that she had ever seen or heard or done, the memories of thoughts and mistakes, of unrealised dreams and petty ambitions. They were manifested here, in the hands of this beast, as a patch of blue material, which it stretched in its hands repeatedly, pulling tightly and retracting, over and over. Aranfal saw snippets of Aleah, there, and images of himself.

He stepped forward into the cell and bowed his head before her.

'She is dead already,' the creature whispered, in a shuffling voice, a voice of mud being scattered on coffins. 'All of you who live are dead, whether you know it or not. Your true self is here, in our hands. How can you claim to live when in a moment it is gone, and all that you once were is the property of another?'

Aranfal sensed a presence behind him and turned around. His own Shadowthing was there, glaring down upon him with those fiery eyes. Its patience was wearing thin.

He seized Aleah by the hand. It was cold. Anger burned within him. He had come here to save her and only succeeded in handing himself to these beasts. His noble act was in vain. He had not saved Aleah, and he sensed he was no longer able to help the Eyeless One. He had gone too far in the wrong direction.

As the Shadowthing surrounded him and began to claw at his memories, his own name echoed in his mind. *Aran Fal. Aranfal. Aran Fal. Aranfal.*

*Aran Fal.*

*Aranfal* ...

But the voice was not his own.

He was in a room, high in a tower, filled with sunlight. This was not the See House. This was another place, from long ago. He *knew* this, somehow, in the core of his being.

The room was a rough square, its walls and floors formed of smooth stone that gleamed in the sunlight. There was no furniture here, no clutter of any kind: only the Eyeless One, standing alone in the centre.

'Aleah's dead,' Aranfal said. 'I tried to save her, but I couldn't.'

The Eyeless One did not respond.

'We have called an end to the game,' it whispered. 'It is done. Everything is at an end. We have watched you all, and we see no hope. We sense, now, that the First Memory will never be found.'

Aranfal shook his head.

'Let me carry on,' he said. 'We can still find it. Nothing's changed!'

But the Eyeless One shook its head. 'It is too late. Perhaps it always was. The First Memory is lost forever, and we will not find it. Maybe it already belongs to Ruin.'

Aranfal grasped the creature by the shoulder, grimacing at the coldness of its skin. He despised it, in this moment: he hated its weakness, its casual embrace of defeat.

'No. This hasn't all been in vain.' *Aleah dead, for nothing.* 'There must still be something—'

'There is nothing.' The creature bowed its head. When it next looked at Aranfal, two eyes stared out at him, black holes that burned with flame.

'Ruin has won,' it said. 'We sense his power grow. Ruin won at the beginning. Our child will become our master, as it was always meant to be. The game is over.'

The eyes disappeared, and a dumb smile spread across the creature's face.

'The clouds in the sky are ships on the sea. In the old keep there is a light that burns for one night in the summer. I found my way to a castle, but the wrong people awaited me there.'

'No – come back to me. Please.'

The Eyeless One raised a hand, and cast Aranfal from its domain.

# Chapter Nineteen

Canning felt his powers grow, and it was a glorious thing.

He floated between Overland and Underland, travelling with the Duet on some strange current. They were going to the others. They were going to a great table, to play a wonderful game. He could *see* it.

Something sparkled and grew within him. Power? *Understanding* was a better word: his feel for the power of memories. Perhaps he had always had these abilities, even when he was a Tactician. But now it all seemed so much clearer; the paths were opening through this strange jungle. He could build a city from the fragments of memory, if he wished. He could turn the oceans dry.

He danced with the Duet. He felt himself flowing within them. He wondered why he had ever mistrusted them. *They are my friends. They are my allies.* A part of him warned him away from these feelings, but it was quickly smothered.

He saw things in their memories. He saw fleets of ships on red oceans. He saw machines beyond his comprehension. All the knowledge of the Remnants was taken from memories like these, snatched from tiny victories against the Duet and their kin. *I could do so much more. I could*

163

*seize all the wisdom of the world – all the knowledge of history!*

His mind thrummed with two words: *First Memory*. He could sense the awe in the Duet. *There is such a power in it*. He knew he could make it his own.

His mind occasionally turned to the game. *We should go to the table,* he thought. But the Duet smiled at him, and shook their heads. There was no rush, he realised. The game could wait, while he danced through power with his friends.

They spoke to him. They whispered of his greatness.

'There has never been a mortal like you, Canning,' Boy said.

'He is no mortal. He is something else – something glorious!'

He inwardly agreed. He was no longer Canning, the failed Tactician. He was the Great Manipulator. He was the King of the Remnants, ally of the Duet. He was their equal. No, he was their *master*, even if they were no longer tethered by his mind.

'We are almost there,' Boy said.

Nothing seemed to have changed. They flew through a sky that was filled with memory, flickering along the line between magic and reality. But up ahead, something was shifting. A building was stretching out before them, one that he knew, though now its stone was Strategist purple and its proportions were vast.

For the first time, a little breath of fear blew through him.

'This is the Circus,' he said. 'But it has changed … what is this place?'

'The game, Canning – this is where it will be played!' He was unsure which of them had spoken. It did not matter.

In a moment they were at the feet of a great statue of

Katrina Paprissi: the Strategist. Canning looked up and could see only rags. She was too gigantic, her face too far away.

A group of strangers were staring at him. Behind them was an enormous crowd, lined on stone seats, growling and cheering and spitting.

The smaller group came forward: a man and several women. *Operators*. He could feel it on them. But these were the weaker kind. He could break them in a moment, if he wished.

'Who's he then?' asked one of the women. She had the look of a drunk: thin and jaundiced, cocooned in the fur of some animal. She reminded him of the women of his childhood, the ones who had kissed and beaten him. She swivelled towards him and blinked her eyes. 'He's one of the powerful ones,' she said. 'Are they back, then?'

'They never went away,' said Canning. 'Not in the Remnants.'

The woman rasped a laugh. 'Dear me! Never went away, he says. Those down there are children. Not like you.' She reached out a hand. Her fingernails were painted: yellow and red. 'I can see you've done great things.'

The man spoke, then. He was a jittery type, in a dirty, thin, golden gown.

'You're too late. The game's over.'

Boy raised a hand, and the man fell silent. 'That's enough, now. I'm sure they'll make room for us.' An angry look crossed his face.

The man shrugged. He did not seem convinced.

'Come.' Girl was at Canning's side. 'Let's go up to the table.'

She took him by the hand and led him forward.

'What did that Operator mean?' Canning asked.

Girl laughed. 'He's just a young one, Canning! Created by one of us just a few thousand years ago. Maybe I made him! I can't remember.' She shook her head. 'Don't worry about what he says. Don't worry about him a bit. Why would you be here if there is no game?'

She pointed ahead. The table stretched away from him for as far as he could see, an endless ocean of dark stone.

Boy took him by his other hand. 'Come,' he said.

Walking hand in hand with the Duet, Canning made his way forward to the table's edge. Boy and Girl took him to a pair of chairs, which they clambered into.

'What do you think of it, Canning?' Girl cried. 'Isn't it beautiful!'

At first, Canning could not quite understand what exactly he was looking at. A manic dance of symbols and images played across the stone. He saw shapes, in the madness, living pictures of stars and moons, animals running across fields, stars sparkling in unreal skies.

'This is a map of the Old Place,' Boy whispered in his ear. 'We are not allowed to go into the game with you, so we come here to watch our pawns, as they run around that glorious realm, searching for the First Memory.'

'You have such powers, Canning,' Girl said. 'If you open your mind, you will be able to see the table as *we* see it. I am sure of it.'

Canning gnawed at his lip. Something here felt wrong. Somewhere, within his most pathetic recesses, he felt the old Canning begin to stir.

'But why am I here? Shouldn't I be *there*?' He pointed at the map. 'Shouldn't I be in the Underland, for the game?'

'Who says you are not already?' Boy glanced at the statues that loomed overhead. 'What is the difference any more?'

'No.' Canning shook his head. 'I shouldn't be here. I should be *below*.'

The board seized his attention. At first, he saw nothing but the haphazard procession of strange symbols and images. As he looked, however, he began to *feel* a kind of pattern on the stone. There was a burst of blue, which he somehow knew to represent Aranfal, the famous Watcher, the one who had treated him kindly when he languished in the Bowels of the See House. And there was a kind of haze of red ... *Brandione*. They were players, too.

But the board began to change. The colours faded, and the symbols disappeared. He was staring at nothing more than a stone table.

'What's happened?' He turned to the Duet. 'Where has everything gone?'

They grinned at him. He turned back to the table and, as he looked at that stone, cold realisation dawned.

'You never meant for me to go down there.'

'Of course not!' cried Girl. 'You betrayed us. You made us your *dogs*.'

Canning felt a void expand in the pit of his stomach.

'It was so delicious, Canning – your hopes!' said Boy. 'Your dreams! Your *delusions*!'

'Thank you for freeing us!' Girl was dancing at his side. 'Thank you so very much!'

In the background, the crowd began to laugh. They had all seen him. They had seen his foolishness, his belief that these gods were his *friends*. They were toying with him; he of all people should have seen that.

He did not turn to face them. He could not look at them, mocking him, as he had been mocked so many times before in his life. He cursed himself, and he tried to push their laughter away. But it would not be ignored. He closed his eyes; he bent forward, until he almost touched the stone of the table. Something within him began to shift; his walls were weakening, and his sense of himself was collapsing. He tried to reach out to the Old Place, to grasp its power and use it against the Duet. But he could not feel it anywhere. It was gone. It had left him, or he had left it.

The laughter crawled within him. He once more faced the Duet, willing it to stop. But it would never end. Boy and Girl had gone, now, and in their place were two curling bodies of pale light. Their eyes were now blue flames, and they burned at him.

**You hurt us, Canning.** They spoke as one, and their voice was everywhere, echoing within his skull. **You hurt us so badly.**

'I didn't mean to,' he whispered. 'Let me go. I will do what you want. We can do so many things together.'

**Together! Not any more. You took our love, and you threw it away.**

He fell to his knees. He could feel them picking at him. He was decomposing, under their glare: rotting from the inside out.

**We loved you. We wanted you to be our pawn, in the final game. Perhaps we would even have won. You did not want to help us, Canning, and now it is all over. You hurt us. You have wrecked it, Canning.**

'No … I would have helped you …'

The voice of the Duet spoke again, and this time it rang with the petulance of youth.

**You were meant to help us long ago! It would have been such *fun*: a little game before the coming of Ruin. But instead, you made us your prisoners! You tricked us!**

As Canning stared at the dirt, weighed down by the Duet and their fury, the memory of that moment came to him. He saw himself in that tree, tearing the surroundings apart with his mind, draining them of their power, and wrapping it around the Duet. He *was* a power, then, was he not?

'I was,' he hissed at the ground. 'I was better than you. I'll beat you again, one day.'

**That day will never come.**

He swore he would not fall easily. But it was no good. The pain became his world. *Pain is life, now. Pain is life.* When he was a boy he had worked in the kitchen of an inn, gutting fish. He got under everyone's feet, of course, as he always would, *forever and ever and ever*. One day he walked past the chef, and he dropped his little fish knife, and it stuck in the man's foot. There was such a roar, such a terrible scream, though it wasn't pain, it was *anger*. It was a *release*, almost of pleasure as much as pain: the pleasure of having a reason, any reason, to lash out at *fucking Canning*.

The man did something, then, to Canning's arms. The former Tactician would always remember how it felt, but he never knew what the bastard had done. He seemed to somehow grab them, and he twisted them, he *contorted* them, and it did something to that little boy that he still felt today. He could not remember screaming. He couldn't remember anything; he passed out, they said. But before he did, the screams filled the inn and bounced out onto the street; they turned the ale bad and scared the cats.

'Watch where you're going next time,' said the chef.

The Duet had grabbed his *essence* and twisted it, and they threw the King of the Remnants into the burning-white heat of pain, an agony that tore through his *mind*. But it was different. The Duet would not let go, and Canning did not pass out.

'Come with us,' said Boy. Through his twisted, hazy vision, he saw that they had resumed their old forms. 'Come and be our pet.'

Boy raised a hand and joined it with Girl's. Canning felt the pain ease. The world came into greater clarity once more, the sights of this giant, twisted version of the Circus. They were now some distance from the table, much closer to the spectators in their endless rows, an amorphous mass that flickered and burned with the power of memory. The crowd laughed at him.

The Duet had released him, but he still felt them within him. He was their prisoner now, for as long as they wished. He would be their prisoner beyond death; his memories would live forever, and they belonged to the Duet. There was no tricking them any more. They were a part of him. He would never surprise them again.

'Watch your thoughts, traitor,' said Girl. Her blue eyes flashed as she looked at him, and Canning saw for the first time that while she and her brother were two halves of the same whole, they were also *different*. There was a sense of anger in her, slow to burn but hard to extinguish, and he had ignited it when he defeated them. Boy was more the cruel schemer, the kind of child who lays traps for animals before plucking off their limbs. Girl was the fury of juvenile rage. *The memory of a little girl breaking a doll's head. The memory of a child stabbing her father in the leg.*

Girl snapped her hand into the air, and Canning was entangled in chains, metal loops that coiled around him tightly. These chains were formed of some dark place, some dread time from long ago. It was a time in his own life, but it had been taken apart and stitched together again, cut through with images and sensations from other existences. He looked at it and saw Annya. *Half-mad Annya, on the wall.*

These chains would hold him forever. He searched within, probing that strange land in his mind where his power lay, where he felt the connection with all memories and they revealed their powers to him. But the chains always held him back; the chains would always hold him back.

'We will pluck your memories from you, Canning.' Girl was at his ear, whispering in that fierce little voice of hers. 'We will hurt you for what you did to us. You will see things that never have been; things designed for *you.*'

'Ruin has made them, Canning,' said Boy. His voice was somehow sad. 'We will soon fall into him. All of us ... all the world ... immersed in his pain. All the memories you hide away, will be used to drown you.'

A thousand images flashed before him, glimpses of nightmares. *Half-mad Annya. Alone. Failing. Flailing. Dying, always dying, death without end ...*

Boy was grinning at him. He looked so cruel.

'Ruin is coming,' he said.

# Chapter Twenty

'You are the Old Place.'

The creature turned its head towards Drayn, as if it could actually see her. *Perhaps it can. Why should eyes matter in this place?*

'We are many,' the creature said. It pointed to itself. 'We are the Eyeless One.'

They were in a vast hall, its edges fading into nothing. A hundred thousand pillars curled upwards from the stone floor, reaching out to a ceiling that was nothing but mist, grey clouds tinged with gold.

'Are you like Jandell?'

'He is one of our children. Jandell, Shirkra, Dust Queen.' It sighed. 'Our beautiful children. We made them to save us, because we could not save ourselves.'

'You are more powerful than them. I can feel it.'

The creature shrugged. 'Power does not matter without *direction*. We cannot think like them. Sometimes, we can concentrate, if we need to. But then it fades away, and we forget what we were doing, and we fall into memories, into a million memories.' The Eyeless One stopped, as if grasping for the right words. 'Our mind is ... clouded. We may have a thought, but it takes us so long to understand. And so we made our children, to protect us. They are memory, as well. But they are memory as a weapon. They have been sharpened, and honed, and given focus.' It reached out a long finger and tapped Drayn on the nose. 'We modelled them after you: after our parents.'

Drayn nodded. 'I understand.'

There came a great rumble, from somewhere in the hall, and the ground beneath them trembled. The Eyeless One placed its hands upon its head.

'We saw great things for you,' it whispered. 'But it is too late. The game is over.'

'Not yet.'

Drayn turned, to see Jandell at her side. Relief coursed through her. Every time she lost him, he found her in the end.

There came another rumble, closer this time. The ground shook with a greater intensity.

'The First Memory was our last hope, Jandell,' said the Eyeless One. 'Now it is gone forever: the memory and the hope. We do not feel it anywhere ... the First Memory is gone.'

Jandell's eyes widened. 'I did not know ... There must still ...'

'It is too late, Jandell!' The Eyeless One sparked with fury, and for a moment it *did* have eyes, searing black things that smouldered in its strange skull. 'It is always too late with you. Ruin is coming.' A shadow grew in the hall, polluting every corner. 'You allowed him to gain such power, Jandell. You placed him in our heart. Now he is stronger than any of you. He is stronger even than *us*. Soon he will take us over, and you, the Queen, Shirkra, all of you. Ruin will *be* the God of Memory, Jandell, thanks to you and your mistakes. It will be a God of Pain; a God of the memories we want to hide.'

Jandell fell to his knees. 'Forgive me,' he said.

'Such arrogance,' the Eyeless One said, spreading its arms before Jandell. 'Only now, when your delusions have turned to ash before your eyes, do you see the truth.' The Eyeless One shook its head. 'There is nothing more to be done.'

Drayn watched the shadow. It was moving, crawling across the stone towards her. She looked at Jandell and the Eyeless One; they had not noticed. She could no longer hear them speak.

The shadow gathered into a pool before her and formed into the shape of a man. The man reached out a dark finger and touched her on the forehead. The room disappeared. She was standing on a dark beach, the sand as black as the shadow, the sun above her a burning red. The shadow was not visible, but he was everywhere.

**I know you.**

A patch of the sand began to move. It gathered into the figure of a person, and a single word echoed through her mind. *Ruin. Ruin. Ruin.*

The sand creature approached her.

**Your family are mine.**

She was plunged into a memory: her mother, in the dining room, picking at a fish, the shadow gathering behind her.

**Your friends are mine.**

Cranwyl – *Cranwyl* – on a path, somewhere on the island. The shadow danced around him.

***You*** **are mine. Your memories are mine. You hid this one away from me, in the Choosing. What talent! But you cannot hide now.**

The worst memory. Her father, on the ground, a bloodied wreck. She, standing over him, looking at the knife.

A new place. A dark room.

**I will explore your memories forever. I will show you *new* memories. Memories that are not of the past; memories that have not occurred.**

A candle bloomed to life. Cranwyl was here, tied to a chair, naked. Another Drayn was standing before him. She held the candle in her hand; she moved it to his chest, and back again, over and over, while Cranwyl screamed. She was smiling.

'No,' said the real Drayn. She turned away from the scene. But it was no good; everywhere she turned, it was there.

**I was born in the memories you hide away. Think of what I will create when I *am* the Old Place.**

'No.'

**Soon, Drayn Thonn …**

Drayn turned her mind to Jandell. *I want to leave this place.*

And she did.

She was back in the pillared room. Jandell was before her, with the Eyeless One.

'The shadow,' said the girl. A sudden coldness came upon her, and she began to tremble.

Jandell nodded. 'Ruin is cruel, because he was made that way.' He glanced at the Eyeless One; there was contempt, there, in his eyes. 'The Old Place made him that way.'

The Eyeless One shrugged. 'He was *such* a thing to see. Only he could destroy the Absence. Only he could fight for memory, against the great destroyer.'

'But what memories does he love?' Jandell asked. 'The

dark things that people keep locked away in their minds, the ones that shame them or terrify them. Ruin is *made* of them.'

'He wants to take you over,' said Drayn, nodding at the Eyeless One. 'He has so much power. If he does, he'll …' She thought back to the false memory. 'He has to die.'

The great rumble came again.

'I'll find this First Memory,' Drayn whispered. She saw a weapon in her mind, a thing without form or substance, and felt a new sense of certainty. 'I'll destroy Ruin.'

'Then we will go,' Jandell said. 'We will go to the table.'

The Eyeless One shook its head, but Jandell and Drayn were already gone.

They had come to a strange place, like a giant version of Squatstout's Courtyard, the part of the Habitation where the people gathered for the Choosing. This was a walled structure, though the walls were difficult to make out: they stretched far away from them, vanishing into shadows. Four great statues hung overhead, each depicting the same woman, displaying different expressions. At the sides were thousands of seats, thronged with shadowy groups of spectators. It was daytime, but the sky above rolled with grey cloud.

None of these things, however, were important. All that mattered was the table, an endless outcrop of dark stone, the board of some game she did not know. Shapes and figures moved across it in a kaleidoscopic dance. A sense of pain rose within her, and she longed to be back in the Habitation, seated at her mother's side, preparing for whatever the future held for her and the House of Thonn. As she watched this board twist and contort in all its strangeness, she saw only pain, unyielding and eternal. *Why didn't I stay on the island?*

*Why did I get on Jandell's ship?* Her mother's image grew in her mind, assessing her with harsh, uncaring eyes, warning her of her impetuousness, and where it would lead her. *She was right.*

She felt a hand on her shoulder. She looked up, away from the terrible board, and her eyes met Jandell's.

'You are a warrior,' Jandell said. 'You know that, don't you?'

Drayn nodded, though she was not sure.

'We need warriors now.'

His eyes moved away from her, to the side of the board. A great pit had been carved into the ground: a vast, black hole.

'That's the way in for players like you,' Jandell said. 'You'll have to leave, now. But I'll be watching you.' He nodded at the board, with its swirling, crazed surface.

'Come with me,' she said. 'Help me.'

She knew what his response would be, even before he shook his head and gave her a sad smile. But she had a strange faith in this creature. There was something in him that gave her hope. He came from darkness, she knew: a bleak pool of memory. But he wanted to change. He wanted to help humanity, not crush it. He had hurt many as he struggled to make the world a better place. But she had tasted the nightmare of Ruin, and she would always prefer the destructive dreams of Jandell the Bleak.

'I can't help you, down there,' Jandell said. 'The game is not for Operators. It is for mortals like you – and you will win. You will find the First Memory.'

Drayn smiled. 'And you will watch me.'

Jandell nodded. 'I will watch you, Drayn, until the end.'

The girl nodded. She turned to the pit, and her hands

curled into fists, the fingernails biting into her palms. She walked to the edge and gazed into the depths. There were faces there, in the dark: fleeting glimpses of creatures from the past.

A great cheer erupted, somewhere to her side. She looked towards the stands, that amorphous grey mass. She turned back to the pit, steadied herself, and jumped.

But Drayn did not fall. No: she was frozen in the air.

A woman stood at the side of the pit: the woman from the statues. She was grotesque, her limbs stretched out of all proportion, her skin so pale as to be translucent, her eyes as purple as the rags she wore. She held her right hand up, and in the other grasped a mask, an ugly, pale thing, carved into the shape of a rat.

*Strategist*. The word filled Drayn's mind, crawling through her. *Strategist. Strategist. Strategist*. She thought of a little girl she had seen in a memory, dressed in rags.

'No game for you,' the woman said. 'The game is over.'

The Strategist snatched her hand in the air, and Drayn was raised upwards, far above the great pit. That same great rumble came again, the sound Drayn had heard in the pillared room. Now, however, it came from the table. It was *growing*, expanding outwards until it covered the hole entirely. The Strategist nodded, and Drayn fell onto the rock. The surface no longer swirled with colour. It was nothing more than stone.

'What have you done?' Jandell was standing on the table, at the side of the Strategist.

The woman turned to him, and her smile was a terrible thing. 'Jandell! What a way to greet me. What have I done, indeed.' She laughed, before reaching out a hand and tickling her son under his chin. 'Such a rude thing to ask Mother.'

'This is a trick,' Jandell said, glancing at Drayn. 'The game is not over. Drayn needs to play.'

Mother shook her head. 'It *is* over, Jandell. Can't you feel it? Look at the board. It is dead.'

Jandell stared at the stone, and his eyes were filled with sorrow. In that moment he was truly a child, a boy who had tried to trick his mother, only to find that all his plans, all his little schemes, meant nothing to her.

'There is nothing you can do, now, Jandell. Ruin is coming.'

'He is still trapped,' Jandell said, backing away from the Strategist. He smiled, though there was no hope in his eyes.

The woman cocked her head to the side. 'Everything has happened as the Dust Queen foresaw.' There was a hint of genuine sympathy in her words, pity for her wayward son. 'This will be the same. She will take me to the Machinery, now that the game is at an end. I will open it, and Ruin will come.'

*Ruin.* Drayn still sensed the shadow man, crawling through her memories. The world that was to come stretched before her: endless journeys through the worst of all memories, to feed the desires of a god.

'The Old Place will be one of *us*, my son. It will live to aid us!' She gestured at Drayn. 'Not these bags of flesh and bone.'

Jandell raised a hand. 'I will stop you, Mother.'

The woman laughed.

'No,' she whispered.

The sky above fell dark, and great torches sparked to life far away, along the walls of this monstrous structure. Drayn became aware of movement all around, a great, shadowy shuffle. She turned to see the stands were emptying, and thousands of people had gathered at the table. *Not people.* These were things of memory, creatures like the Strategist and Jandell and Ruin. They piled up together, line after line, men and women and children, and other things besides, shadows of nightmares and flickering colours. All of them danced with memories; she saw the past in them, moments from long ago, and all the power of the Old Place. But these things were not the same as the others she had encountered. They were weaker by far: the eternal servants of their older brethren.

Jandell and the Strategist stood opposite one another, perhaps ten paces apart. Silence fell across the giant stadium.

'You killed me,' the Strategist said. 'You *thought* you killed me. Your own mother.' She flicked her hand, and a flower appeared in her fist, a dark, glossy thing with purple petals. It seemed to grow within Drayn's mind, until its thorns and its petals filled her up. But this was not a flower. This was a memory, born from poisoned soil. She saw a vision of Jandell, in his terrible cloak, holding a woman aloft. Drayn could not make out this woman's face, but she knew who it was. *Strategist.* There was a scream, and the vision fell into rotting petals.

'You tore me from my host,' the Strategist said, trembling upon the table. 'You made me into *nothing*. Only my daughter stayed by my side.'

Another woman appeared on the table, a red-haired creature in a green dress. She wore a white mask, through which a pair of eyes were visible, the same colour as her dress and burning with a *hunger*. All the while they focused on one person: Jandell.

'Now I am whole,' the Strategist said. 'I have become one with my host. She has given me strength, and Father has given me *power*. But it is only a taste, only the smallest taste, of what I will become.'

She raised a hand, and Jandell fell to his knees. His great cloak began to coil around his frame, the faces glaring out at the Strategist, enraged and terrified.

The Strategist paced forward, to stand directly before her trembling son.

'I love you,' she said. She reached out a hand and touched him on the top of his head. 'But I must destroy you.'

*Coldness.* It fell across them all, the ice of a deathstone, a frigid, grasping power. Snow fell from the dark sky, and each flake was a memory.

'No,' Jandell said. He stood, and the snow fell away from him. 'Ruin is not here yet.' He gave a sharp nod and his cloak curled forward, the faces snapping and growling, burning with a new ferocity. The dark material curled around the Strategist, and the faces began to leap from their prison.

The Strategist smiled. She reached out and plucked a face from the air, holding it between her thumb and forefinger: a piece of strange material, cut into the features of a wailing man.

'A terrible memory, that, terrible, terrible.'

Drayn turned, startled. A man was by her side, old and bearded in appearance, but a creature of the past like all the rest of them. The Strategist's snow was lying on his head.

'He doesn't like the things he's done,' the old man said, nodding at Jandell. 'He regrets so many things. The cloak means he can never forget the creature he once was.'

The old man smiled at her, before fading back into the crowd.

'I do not fear your cloak, Jandell, and I do not fear your little faces,' the Strategist said.

Mother was as tall now as five Jandells, as tall as Thonn House. She reached out a great finger and held it just above Jandell's head. She began to move it in tight little circles, and the cloak moved too, retreating from her and coiling itself around its owner. The faces were back in their prison, watching the Strategist with fearful gazes.

'No,' Jandell said. But that was all he could manage, as the dark material gathered around him, tighter and tighter, suffocating him. It shifted around his neck, and he closed his eyes. *Death is coming.*

The Strategist clapped her hands together and shrank before their eyes. Jandell tumbled forward, collapsing onto the table, utterly still. Drayn felt a shadow gathering within her, and all around the crowd. Strange, but she did not feel fearful. Instead, she was seized with a sense of dread inevitability. *It was always meant to be this way.*

But then something rose within her, pushing against this notion. *Always? Why always? Because these parasites tell us so?*

She stepped forward. 'Stop it,' she said to the Strategist.

'Ah. The Fallen Girl.' The Strategist grinned at her. 'The destroyer of Squatstout. A brave thing, like my own host in so many ways. Perhaps I will keep you, as a spare.'

Drayn raised a hand and sought that feeling of power she had used before, the weaponry she had deployed against Squatstout. But she had not even begun, when the Strategist struck her down.

# Chapter Twenty-One

'The game is over.'

Aranfal was in the Circus, the new version that had been built for the Strategist. The sky was dark, but light flickered from distant torches. Purple rags hung from the walls, and statues of Katrina Paprissi stared down at them. All was the same as before, but all was utterly changed. The Circus now was gigantic, the statues monstrous. The table he had seen before – the one the Operators used to play the game – was now a vast outcrop of stone. The symbols that had danced across its surface were gone, and it was nothing but cold rock.

He looked around for the Strategist. She was speaking to him, though he sensed she was far away.

'The game is over,' she said again. 'But it was not a game at all, was it, Aranfal? The Old Place *wanted* you to find the First Memory.' She laughed. 'The spectators are not pleased. They came to watch a game of old, not that … *nonsense.*'

Aranfal heard a great roar. He looked in the direction of the sound and could just make out movement, the shuffling of a great crowd. He remembered the creatures he had seen before, when he was in the Circus with Shirkra and the Gamesman: minor Operators, come to watch the game.

'Did I fail you?' he asked aloud.

The face of Katrina Paprissi appeared in his mind.

'Fail?' She said the word dreamily, as if she had never heard it before, as if it was some new language. 'No, Aranfal. There was no way to fail in that charade. Everything has always been going in one direction: to Ruin. You were wonderful.' She grinned. 'And now we are almost at the end. Come – watch me destroy my son, before the coming of Ruin.'

Aranfal looked again. He could just make out movement, far away on the table. There was a hint of purple. He climbed onto the board and began to walk across the stone.

'Strategist,' he whispered.

'Yes, my torturer?'

'Who won the game?'

The Strategist laughed.

'There is no winner but Ruin. And soon he will have his prize.'

The table seemed to grow before Aranfal as he walked. The stone was cold through his boots.

There was a roar of sound, a din of conversation at the side of the table. *The spectators.* He could not make out individuals; it was a great choir of noise. What did they want, these creatures? What entertainment did they seek? He concentrated and, for a moment, he thought he heard questions coming from their distant ranks. *Who are you, Aranfal and Aran Fal, you man of two parts? What memories do you hold?*

'I am a torturer,' he said. Shame tapped at his shoulder.

*I am a torturer.* Why was he ashamed now, in this place, after all his years in the Bowels of the See House, scraping answers from the agonised? *You have always been ashamed, you fool. You put it away for too long. But these things always come back.*

It was such a simple feeling, such an obvious little emotion. *I feel bad about the things I have done.* Even here, in this outrageous pastiche of the Circus, he could not escape it. A parade of victims danced before him. The ones he tortured were often guilty of nothing at all. That was the whole point. *The guilty wouldn't talk, many times, until their loved ones were with me. Then they talked, all right. Some of them took longer than others but, in the end, almost all of them talked.*

But not all. A man floated into his mind's eye, a man who did *not* talk. He was not the toughest-looking inmate Aranfal had dealt with in the Bowels. Not the toughest *looking*. But looks meant nothing. Aranfal had seen so many big men cry, men with muscles on their muscles, men with filed teeth. This one had none of that: he was a plump sort, innocent looking, with a mound of blond curls. But he hadn't talked. Not even when his children were brought before him. Not even when his children bled.

Aranfal squeezed his eyes closed.

'There is no escaping the past. In the new world, the past is all that will matter.'

Someone was at his side. It was someone the Watcher knew all too well: a younger version of himself, from another age. This boy wore a black gown over clothing of the same colour. His face was unlined, and even his blond hair seemed to hold a youthfulness that the man of today had long since lost. Yet the difference between them was something beyond the way they looked. It was something beyond the years themselves. It was the space between Aran Fal and Aranfal.

'Ruin is coming,' said Aran Fal the memory man.

Aranfal reached out to Aran Fal and stroked his cheek. It felt real, but so had all the memories he had encountered.

'Yes,' he said. 'And there's nothing to be done.'

Aran Fal cocked his head to the side. 'You cling to me: your former self.'

'I know you're gone, and never coming back.'

'No. You long for me. Aranfal wants to be Aran Fal again. Blaming others for your transformation. Blaming *her*.'

Brightling came to his mind's eye.

'I blame no one but myself. I turned myself into this. I cut you out.'

Aran Fal laughed. 'That's where you're wrong. I never existed. The boy who came down from the North was not as you remember. Nothing is ever as we remember. He was a complex thing. But he was always *Aranfal*. You didn't *change*. You were always the same man. It just took you a while to realise.'

Aranfal nodded. 'Perhaps you're right,' he said in a low voice. 'I've always been the same.' He turned from Aran Fal and looked along the table. Far away, he could just make out a small group of people. Among them was the Strategist, that twisted version of Katrina Paprissi. He could sense her from where he stood.

'Ruin is coming,' he said.

'Yes,' said Aran Fal. 'The spirit of our worst memories: the things we hate and the things we hide. He's like you, Aranfal.'

The Watcher twisted his head towards this memory of his younger self. 'What do you mean?'

Aran Fal laughed. 'He sees goodness in himself, despite everything he has done. He was born from anger, forged from pain. He was built as a weapon from the darkest impulses of humanity. He cannot be anything except what he *is*. Of course he sees goodness in himself. He is the weapon of the Old Place. When he takes it over—'

'The world will be a procession of our most hated memories – the things he loves,' Aranfal said. 'And he will not be satisfied with the past. He will hurt us, to make new memories. He will twist them into something new, something worse. It is what he is, and there is no way to change him.'

'He is what he is,' Aran Fal said, 'as are we. But perhaps we *are* different. Perhaps we can do something new.'

'Yes. Something good, before the end. Something to help ...'

'Yes ...'

'But how?'

It was too late, then, for any more questions. Aran Fal had gone.

On he went, across the stone expanse. The cheers and chants of the crowd came to him like a mantra, the songs that ancient savages sang in a strange land long ago. He smelled death on the wind.

'Your death.'

A being had appeared before him. He said *being*, though it looked like three people, three women formed of sand or dust, swirling before him, their feet vanishing in fogs of dark cloud, their features obscured under the mania of their beings. They wore crowns of glass.

'Dust Queen,' he whispered. He had seen this woman before, long ago, as an image in the Strategist's garden. Even there, her power had seared him.

The three heads nodded. 'You are going to your death, Aranfal.'

'Good. I deserve to die.'

The Dust Queen sighed. 'I have seen so many like you, over the long years. Cold, but conflicted. It always ends the same way.' She nodded. 'But you can write a different tale, Aranfal. You can *choose* your death. I see that before you.'

Aranfal knew, then, that he *wanted* to die. It was the only thing left that he could control. Even if his memories would live on forever, his flesh belonged to him alone.

'I would like it to mean something,' he said.

The Dust Queen smiled, and disappeared.

He met Aran Fal again, before he reached his destination.

'Where are you going?' the younger man asked.

Aranfal looked to the distance. He could see the Strategist clearly, now; her purple rags surrounded her, clawing at her frame.

'Her,' he said.

Aran Fal nodded. 'Mother. Born from memories of fierce nurture; the lioness with her cubs.' He chuckled. 'Death is coming.'

Aranfal sucked in a long breath; the air of this strange place filled his lungs with the sparkling core of memories. 'But we will choose our death, Aran Fal. It is the one thing we have left.'

'Yes. Let's make it a good one.'

'I will.' He nodded at the memory of himself, and set out on the final stage of his journey across the board.

'And now the torturer arrives, in all his twisted glory.'

Aranfal knew where he was. This was where the Portal

had once been, though now it was covered with the stone of the board. The crowd were closer, gathered at the side. Occasionally he could make out faces amid that grey gathering, leering at him.

The Strategist was standing near the edge of the table, her back to Aranfal. She turned to face him, and he staggered backwards. This was not the woman he had known. She was still that grotesque version of Katrina Paprissi, clothed in purple rags, her eyes sparkling with the same colour. She held her mask in her hand, that ugly face of a white rat, the same one she had worn since she completed her apprenticeship. But everything about her had changed. She burned with a new power; it was in her eyes, those purple things that saw everything at once. Her very frame *trembled* with possibility. He knew what she was thinking. *I have won. Ruin is coming.*

And Aranfal could see the source of her triumph. There, at her feet, entangled in his own cloak of a thousand faces, was Jandell: the Operator, the creature they had once treated as a god. He was perfectly still, and utterly defeated.

But he was not alone. To the other side of the Strategist was a young girl that Aranfal did not recognise, passed out on the table as well. She was a tough-looking creature, brown-haired and wiry, with a kind of regal air. He could always see things like that. He always knew where power lay, born or earned.

'Torturer,' said the Strategist. 'You were a good pawn. But the game is over. We have all felt it.' She gestured at Jandell, and then to the prostrate girl. 'You have done better than many of the other players. Jandell did not even make it to the table in time, and his pawn did not go below.'

'Where are we?' Aranfal glanced around at the table and

the crowd and the four statues of the Strategist, looming over them all. 'Is this the Underland or the Overland?'

The Strategist laughed. 'The walls are breaking down, Aranfal. Soon, there will be no difference at all.'

There came a great rumble from underneath his feet. *Something is coming.*

'So here we have two of our players,' the Strategist said. 'Aranfal, the torturer, and this girl of Jandell's. That means some are missing, does it not?'

'Yes, mistress, yes!'

It was the woman in green: the wearer of the white mask. *Shirkra.* She was at the Strategist's side, for all the world like a little child, eager to please her mother.

'My one is missing!' she cried, eyes flashing beneath her mask as she locked Aranfal's gaze. 'I watched her on the board. I watched her go into Chaos. Such a beautiful place, such a beautiful girl! Did you see her, Aranfal? Did she live?'

The Watcher's instincts told him that Shirkra, who knew Chaos better than anyone, was aware of what had happened to her pawn.

'She's gone,' he said. His thoughts lingered on the Shadowthings.

'But another one lives,' Shirkra said. She pointed to Aranfal's right. The Watcher turned and saw Canning, being dragged along behind two children. They giggled as they walked. The one-time Tactician for Expansion was encircled in black chains. Aranfal was reminded of the substance that the Shadowthings played with, that dark power of memories. It held Canning tightly, and there was no escape for him.

'But we are missing one, Mother,' said Shirkra. 'We are still missing one!'

'Yes,' said the Strategist. She smiled. 'The pawn of the

Queen. But the Queen is coming. The game is over, and she will fulfil her bargain. She will show us the Machinery, and I will bring forth Ruin.'

Beneath their feet, the table shook again.

*Death is coming.* The words thudded through Aranfal's mind, over and over. *Death is coming. Death is coming.*

He balled his hands into fists. *It's the only thing I have left to give.*

# Chapter Twenty-Two

Brandione was on a table.

It stretched away before him, endless in scope. He knew this thing: a board he had seen, in those hazy moments when he had first entered the Circus and fallen below, to the game. He looked up and saw statues: four loomed overhead, one in each corner of this monstrous sea of stone. *I am back in the Circus, though it has changed. It has changed so much.*

'The game is at an end,' said the three faces to his side.

'What now?' he asked. The Queen seemed very old indeed: three frail women with faces of cracked glass and hair like the tendrils of clouds.

'I must show Mother the Machinery,' she said.

'No.'

Three sets of shoulders shrugged. 'I promised.'

'What have you got from this bargain?'

The Dust Queen smiled. 'I have brought everyone together: Operators and players.' She nodded at him. 'They will all bear witness.'

Brandione did not pretend to understand. He stared out into the distance and could just make out great crowds of people, somewhere far away, moving like shadows on a wall.

'Come,' the Dust Queen said. She reached out with one of her hands, touched him on the shoulder, and took him to another part of the board.

It seemed they were all gathered together, here at the end of the world. The Strategist was a sight to behold: a thing of hungry power. Flickering around her was her servant, Shirkra, that creature in the living mask. Aranfal the Watcher was there, staring at Brandione with a haunted expression. A young boy and girl giggled at the side, laughing at some wretch they held prisoner in a mesh of black chains: Canning, the last Tactician for Expansion.

Lying before Brandione was a figure he knew very well, whose face he had seen on a thousand paintings and statues. It was the Operator, but he was utterly changed. He seemed broken. Another body lay some distance away: a young girl. He could not tell if she was alive or dead.

'All is at an end,' the Strategist said. 'The game is finished. The Machinery is broken.' She pointed at the Dust Queen. 'We have played your game. Now take me to the Machinery, so that I may bring forth Ruin, as was foretold.'

The Dust Queen unleashed a sorrowful moan. 'I promised you this. But do you know what you truly ask, Strategist? Do you know what Ruin will mean for the world, if he is free? Do you know what he will mean for *you*?'

'Glory! Honour! The return of my family's strength!' The Strategist clapped her hands. 'Now: *take me to it*.'

'No,' the Dust Queen said.

Shirkra cursed and seemed ready to attack the Queen, but three hands were raised to silence her.

'I will not take you to the Machinery,' the Dust Queen said. 'I will bring the Machinery to you.'

She raised her arms in the air, and the great table rumbled. 'Ah. So it is happening.'

Wayward had appeared at Brandione's side. The courtier was at his elegant best, clothed in a white robe, with black ribbons tied through his hair. Behind him, in line upon line, stretching off into the far distance, was the army the Dust Queen had given Brandione, those multitudes of sand soldiers, all of them standing to attention in that strange way of theirs. The one-time General was seized by a desperate urge to take command of these troops, to somehow use them at last. But he did not know how, and there was no time to learn. Not now, at the end of everything.

The stone quaked with a new intensity. Wayward took Brandione by the arm and guided him gently backwards. The courtier's eyes were wide, alive with apprehension and excitement. 'The Machinery is coming,' he whispered.

Great cracks appeared across the surface of the table. *Like a mountain crumbling to the ground.* Slabs of stone began to separate, and something new emerged from underneath. *Fire.*

They all retreated; all apart from the Strategist, who spread her arms wide before the inferno, welcoming it. This was no ordinary flame. This was the fire of Selection, that burning beauty of the world, that tempest in which the Operator deposited the names of those who had been favoured by the Machinery. But there were no names here. There was something else in the inferno.

It was a kind of prison cell. *No: not a cell.* It was a *cage*, of the sort that might hold a bird, its twisted bars formed of some strange, dark material. Another segment of this material protruded from the cage itself; it appeared to be a kind of pipe, but it was twisted and broken. Over time, something else emerged before Brandione's eyes: a great wheel, linked to the cage.

In the centre of this structure, in the heart of the flame, something was moving.

The Dust Queen addressed the Strategist.

'I warn you once more,' she said, 'if you bring Ruin upon us, it may not be what you expect.'

The Strategist smiled, and moved forward, towards the Machinery. There came a great scream. From all directions there emerged a howling multitude of beings, rushing towards the flame before falling back, then throwing themselves forward again, screeching in agony and ecstasy.

'The little Operators,' Wayward whispered at his side. 'They have waited for Ruin to return. They sense the vastness of his powers. They want to be here, when he comes. Perhaps they think he will give *them* some power. They are dogs, begging at the feet of their master, hoping he drops some scraps.'

'Why aren't you with them?' Brandione asked.

Wayward only smiled.

As Brandione watched these creatures howling at the side of the burning cage, as he looked upon the Dust Queen, standing before the thing she had made, he felt that old, familiar anger stirring in his gut. *Is this what we worshipped, all these years? This thing of metal and the creatures that scrabble at its base?*

'This army of mine – can I use it now?'

Wayward shrugged. 'You are the Last Doubter, Brandione. The army belongs to you.'

The General looked at his troops, these dead-eyed hordes, and wondered how he could ever muster them into a fighting force, or if they would even be capable of fighting for him.

*What would they be fighting?* He looked at that dark movement in the fire and wondered what lay within. *Ruin,* said a voice in his mind.

The Strategist was at the edge of the flame. She reached out, but the fire did not harm her.

'All of this time, *this* has been the great nightmare.' She looked at the Dust Queen and to Jandell on the ground. 'This is what you made. I feel its strength. But I have thought about it for many ages. I have turned myself into a key. I am ready to open it.'

She walked around the structure, studying it closely, and then came to a halt before a twisted lever of the dark metal.

'The door,' she whispered.

She walked into the flame. She reached out and grasped the lever, turning it to the side, her eyes wide and hungry.

'The time is now,' she whispered. 'Ruin is coming.'

As she struggled with the handle, her face screwed up in bitter confusion.

'It will not open.' She turned to the Dust Queen. 'I cannot open it.'

It did not matter, in the end. The door opened anyway. It opened from the inside.

# Chapter Twenty-Three

There are so many ways to waken.

Sometimes the haze slowly dissipates, consciousness gradually emerging from the confusion. Sometimes it is much more sudden, like a door being flung open. And sometimes a person *feels* awake, yet it is not quite true. It is a dream.

Drayn Thonn was closer to this final state. She remembered attacking the Strategist and being thrown back by a force unlike anything she had ever encountered. She had felt such things since she met Jandell; she had seen such power. She had defeated Squatstout, one of the oldest creatures of memory. She had found *herself* to be a creature of memory, a mother of memory, as all humans were the parents of that strange, febrile power. She had grown to know her hold over it, her abilities. But when she confronted the Strategist, her weakness was exposed. She had simply been dismissed.

'I am still asleep, on the ground,' she said to no one at all.

'Yes,' said another voice. 'But your body does not matter, in this place.'

A light grew from nowhere, and it was before her once again: the Eyeless One. It smiled at her, and for once, that smile seemed *real*.

They were standing in an empty space, just the two of them, floating in a vast sea of nothing.

'Why are you smiling?' Drayn asked. 'Ruin is coming.'

The Eyeless One nodded, but did not cease smiling. Drayn had many questions for this creature.

'How do I stop it?' she asked. 'I don't have the First Memory. No one does. I'd feel it. I know I would.'

'No. No First Memory. But it is not the end.' The Eyeless One smiled. 'We had given up. We were waiting for Ruin. But then we looked at the table, and we saw something. We saw you all, gathered together: mortals. The hope of the world. And we realised, that all is *not* at an end: not while such mortals walk the world. Perhaps the game does not matter. Perhaps even the First Memory does not matter.'

Something had changed in the Eyeless One. When they had last met, the creature seemed full of despair. Now that was gone, replaced with a light-hearted air that was somehow more unnerving.

'You *can* stop it: you, and the others.'

'What others?'

It flicked a finger, and three men appeared. One was a thin, blond-haired creature, glancing around with a look of weasel-like cunning. The second was a large, bald, ruddy man, but he oozed a sense of power. The third man – dark-skinned, muscular – had an appearance of earned strength: in a physical sense, yes, but something more besides. She wondered if she looked like these men, with that same mix of confusion and hope.

'You are the last hopes,' the Eyeless One said. Its words were grand, but its delivery was banal, as if it were giving directions to a lonely traveller. It pointed at each of them in turn, beginning with Drayn. Its voice took on a new, heavy tone. 'This is Drayn Thonn: daughter of a great House. A thing of great courage. Destroyer of Squatstout, and saviour of Jandell.'

It turned to the blond-haired man. 'Aranfal the torturer.' At the last word, the man appeared to wince. 'One of the greatest of the Overland's Watchers. A man of two parts: the man he is, and the man he imagines he once was.'

It turned its attention to the large man; for a moment, it seemed it was actually looking at him. 'Canning. Here is a man who once was weak, but became a leader of two countries: Tactician of the Overland, and the King of the Remnants.'

The man called Canning gave a curt nod. Drayn sensed something in him. *Pride. New pride.*

The Eyeless One swung towards the last remaining man. 'Brandione.' It smiled. 'The Queen sees such things in him.'

It raised its arms before them.

'You are all of you standing at the edge of the precipice,' it said. 'Our strongest child, our most glorious child, our most beautiful and destructive child, is coming for you all.'

The Eyeless One now had eyes, balls of fire that burned in its skull. Drayn found herself staring into them. She saw a shadow there. She saw another place, where the shadow loomed over everything, the physical world and the world of her own mind. She saw herself, with that knife, that terrible, bloody blade: she was turning the knife on the ones she loved. She was cutting Cranwyl's throat. The scene sparkled with a blue light. In the background, the shadow had taken the form of a person, and it was grasping at the light, pulling it into its being. With each moment that passed, the monster appeared to grow stronger.

'We made a creature from all that humanity wanted to *forget*, for they are the strongest of all memories. We threw that beast against the Absence, until our enemy was torn apart. We did not know what we created.'

'It cannot be stopped.'

That was the fat man, the one called Canning. There was something fearful about him, Drayn realised. *He is a king, yet he gives up so easily.*

'Maybe not,' said the one called Aranfal. His voice was strange. It had an icy quality. 'But I'm not going willingly down that road.'

'The door opened from the *inside*,' said Brandione. 'Ruin did not come with the One – it came by itself.'

'The prophecy was wrong,' said Aranfal.

'Perhaps,' said the Eyeless One. 'Perhaps misunderstood. Perhaps a lie, invented for some strange purpose.'

'What purpose?' asked Canning.

The Eyeless One ignored him. It raised a spindly hand and pointed to them all in turn. 'You are all that guards the world: Underland and Overland, Plateau and Habitation and Newlands and everything else that is. We look upon you, now, and we do not see weakness. We see the future.'

It smiled.

'This moment is over. You will not see us again.'

It flicked a finger, and Drayn was filled with hope, a sense that all was still possible. She wondered if the Eyeless One had placed that feeling inside her, or if it came naturally, from looking at these men who were her allies, now, at the end. Perhaps it was not important; perhaps all that mattered was the fact that it was there. She looked to the men, and she saw it in their eyes, too. *It is not over.*

The Eyeless One nodded to them. 'Ruin has come; but Ruin has not yet won.'

The scene faded away.

# Chapter Twenty-Four

'You shouldn't blame yourself.'

Brightling was sitting before her mirror in her quarters in the See House. Candlelight flickered across the room. Behind her, standing where she always had stood, was Katrina Paprissi. The young woman was running a comb through Brightling's white hair, as she had so many times before.

All was familiar, and all was changed.

'You shouldn't blame yourself,' Katrina said again.

Ruin was consuming Brightling. Ruin *had* consumed her. But just now, in this moment, she could not feel him. She felt like herself.

She looked at Katrina. *Beautiful.* A child. No, a young woman – but a child to her, always a child, a lovely creature of black hair and pale skin and *purple eyes*.

'If I blame myself, it's only because all of it is my fault,' Brightling said. She saw another mirror on the table before her, a small one. She lifted it by its golden handle and gazed into the glass. A face of shadow and fire smiled back at her. *I am falling to him. But I have not fallen yet.*

She turned in her chair, and she grasped Katrina by the hand.

'Who is speaking to me? Is it Katrina, or the Strategist?'

Katrina smiled. In that moment, Brightling knew who was before her. This was the girl she had always loved.

'There are monsters inside us, my love,' the former Tactician said. Katrina's eyes widened, and Brightling knew – she knew with such *shame* – that the girl's surprise came not from the mention of monsters, but from the words 'my love'. *She knows about the monsters, but she never knew about the love.*

'You didn't put the monsters there.'

Brightling shook her head. 'I didn't see her, inside you. And I helped her. I formed you in the way she needed. I made you just right for her.'

Katrina smiled. 'I did the same to you.'

Outside, in the night, there came a flash of golden fire.

'Is it too late, now?' Brightling asked. 'Are we lost?'

Katrina walked to the window. Brightling followed, and stared down from the heights of the See House to the world below. The city was gone, and so was the sea. All was fire: golden and purple and *cold, so cold, not like any flame in the world*. Memories flickered across the inferno: moments of terror, and moments of fierce, destructive love.

'This is all that's left of me,' Katrina said. 'All that's left of the real me. I boxed myself away here, in this place.' She glanced around the room, little more than a cell. 'This is *home*. Do you understand?' She took Brightling by the hand. 'I've come home, at the end. And so have you.'

Brightling shook her head. 'It can't be the end.'

There was a noise beyond the door. Light shone through underneath: purple and golden again, glowing together in the beyond.

'They're coming for us,' Katrina said. 'Our new masters.

They know we've come here, together. Both come home.'

Brightling reached out and stroked Katrina's cheek. 'We can fight them,' she whispered. 'We might lose. But it doesn't matter. We need to try.'

Katrina shook her head. 'You don't understand. There is no Brightling any more, and there is no Katrina. We are something more.'

'It's not what I want.'

'It's not what any of us want. But it's *good*.'

'No. It's ... we are horrors.'

'*They* are horrors. But we must let them take us completely. That's the only way.' She looked outside the window again; the flames had now surrounded the tower and were sending thin tendrils in under the door. 'They think everything is moving according to a plan. *Their* plan. But I've seen things, Tactician. Mortals are the masters of this world, not these creatures.' She smiled. 'They can be destroyed. But we must allow them to possess us completely. They must think they have won. *That* is when they will be vulnerable: when they think they are at their strongest.'

Brightling looked to the door, saw it shaking with the force of whatever lay beyond. 'Arrogance births hubris, hubris births defeat.' Katrina smiled at the words. One last Watcher saying, shared between two doomed women.

Together, they walked to the door. Brightling placed her hand upon the handle.

'I have always loved you, my daughter,' she whispered.

Katrina nodded. 'And I you, my mother.'

The girl placed her hand on Brightling's. They pushed the handle down, flung open the door, and vanished into their monsters.

# Chapter Twenty-Five

The Strategist was lost.

She stepped back from the fire, and glanced towards Shirkra, her gaze clouded with confusion. Her lips moved; Aranfal wondered if she was saying anything at all. *Nothing has gone as she expected. She did so much to reach this point, and it's all a lie.*

But no one thought of the Strategist for long. No one looked at her at all as the flames faded away, and the door opened from the inside. Something else was climbing from the Machinery. Someone Aranfal knew only too well.

*Brightling.*

There she was, the former mistress of the See House, the woman who had dominated the Overland for a generation. *The murderer of Aran Fal and the mother of Aranfal.* The one-time Tactician wore robes of blinding red and gold, flowing and twisting like the flames that had recently engulfed her. But this was not truly Brightling, Aranfal knew. His mistress was nothing more than a puppet. This was Ruin. He stood before his cage, smiling amid broken chunks of rock. His eyes were black, with flickers of gold.

'My love,' said the Strategist, falling to her knees.

The other Operators followed suit, the great ones like Shirkra and the minor creatures who had scuttled up from the stands, collapsing to the ground and at the sides of the cage, among the broken rubble of the table.

'Father,' they said in a million jabbering voices. 'Father, father, father.'

Father's gaze twitched between them. He seemed to find the scene amusing, stifling his giggles with Brightling's hand. His expression changed when his gaze fell upon the Dust Queen. That creature was still standing, her heads slightly bowed.

'Father,' said the Strategist, rising to her feet. 'You have … you opened the door yourself.'

Father laughed. 'Yes. I opened it myself.' This was the voice of an old man, a hard-edged voice, a voice like a blunt axe-head. 'Are you surprised?'

The Strategist cringed. *Cringed*. She who had made the earth tremble, not so long before. 'I came for you, Father. I came to release you from the remains of the Machinery, as promised.'

The smile faded from Father's face. 'Prophecies are for fools,' he whispered. 'You have always been a fool, though I love you.'

The Strategist bowed her head.

Father gestured behind him. 'The Machinery did not imprison me. The Machinery *made* me. I am greater now than any of you.' He looked at the Dust Queen. 'Even you.' He raised a hand. 'You should assume a new form, your majesty: one that reflects your status.' He clicked his fingers, and the Dust Queen transformed into three small girls, wide-eyed and innocent and terrified. The other Operators gasped and chattered, as they saw the power Ruin held over the creature they once believed was the greatest of them.

Ruin laughed, and the queen transformed back into her usual self. A dead silence fell across the shattered remnants of the table.

Ruin strode forward, away from his cage. 'Power came to me, my children, one burning at a time, one Selection after another.' He laughed. 'All the while, you danced to my song. All of you – Operators, mortals, and the Old Place itself.'

The Operators stared in wide-eyed awe as Ruin grinned down upon them. He turned his gaze on Mother, and his eyes flickered.

'You *fool*.'

Mother shrank from Father, her hands over her face. She scrabbled back, attempting perhaps to flee. But Father raised a finger, and she was frozen in place.

'How could you allow yourself to be defeated at Jandell's hand?' Ruin shook his head. 'How could you fall prey to such an attack?'

He gazed out at the other Operators. When he spoke again, his voice blew over them like a dry and arid wind.

'I am the greatest creation of the Old Place. I am the weapon that destroyed the Absence. And now I have grown more powerful than the god itself. Soon I will consume it. But first, I will take its children: *my* children. I will take them within me.'

Ruin flicked a finger, and Mother was cast into the air.

'The god will be a weapon; the weapon will be a god. All the world will be Ruin, the world and all its memories.'

Mother remained suspended for a moment, gazing down at Father. Aranfal saw something new in her expression, in the dark eyes of Katrina Paprissi. *She is pleading with him.* But there was no mercy to be had here.

Ruin gestured with his finger, and the flames came again. They coiled around him like burning snakes, and he smiled. Aranfal found himself almost hypnotised by that fire, and the stories it told: he saw moments there, terrible moments from the past, snippets of agony. He saw his own father, dying in the cold, a bloodied …

He forced himself to look at Ruin's eyes. They were burning now, too.

'The flames no longer harm me,' he whispered. He whipped his hand forward, and a coil of fire shot towards the Strategist. She screamed as the flames curled around her, and dragged her towards her lover.

At first, Aranfal seemed to be staring at two separate beings, standing one in front of the other, switching places over and over again. Then the Strategist was surrounded by shadow and flame, a thing with dark and burning claws, pawing at her. Her expression changed, and she began to smile.

'We will be together again,' she whispered. 'We will bring all our children home.'

Ruin was alone. His eyes burned purple.

'Now then,' he said, in the voice of Katrina Paprissi, 'who is next?'

He grinned down at them and spoke again in his own voice.

'Come to me, my children.'

He raised his arms in the air and flame filled the Circus.

Aranfal was in the Bowels of the See House. He knew what this was: a memory, conjured in the flames of Ruin. But there was something different, here.

The memory was not real.

They were in some cell, one of many he frequented in his days as the torturer. This was a small, damp room, with no light of its own, the only illumination coming from a torch in the passageway beyond. Two children sat before him, tied to chairs: two girls, in the silk dresses of the rich, dirty and worn. They were shivering. Perhaps it was the cold. Perhaps.

They were staring at Aranfal, and there was terror in their eyes.

Aranfal looked at his hand. He held a weapon there. *This* was real. It was something he used in the early days. It was an axe, of a kind, though it had a blunted edge. When he looked at it, he heard a howl.

'This is not real,' he said. He looked at the children. 'I never ...'

A shadow filled the room.

**It may not have happened, Aranfal, but who is to say it isn't real? The memory is real.**

'What memory? It didn't happen, so there is no memory.'

**I feel you here, every inch of you, more of you than you know. I sense the pain in this moment. It brings such *energy* to me. We are so alike, Aranfal: both of us torturers. Both of us revelling in the extreme.**

Aranfal felt himself lifting the axe and pointing it towards one of the girls: the more terrified of the pair, if that was possible.

'No,' he said. 'Everything I did had purpose. I am not a sadist.'

Ruin only laughed.

Aranfal had returned to the Circus, and to the flames. They lashed out from Ruin, screeching, grasping tendrils. He saw strange things, as the flames washed over him: memories

208

that belonged to him, memories of cold nights in the North and fetid days in the Bowels. Others that did not: moments of pain and humiliation, of naked exposure and beatings in alleyways. This fire did not burn him, in the physical sense. But the same could not be said for the Operators, who screamed and screeched as it clawed at them. All of them were dragged towards Ruin, and one by one they disappeared.

The weaker ones, those who had once formed the audience, simply vanished within the flame.

Shirkra ran to Father, leering through the fire, and grasped him in a tight embrace. She turned and grinned at Aranfal, smiling from the inferno, before removing her mask and tossing it to the ground.

'Chaos and Ruin belong together,' she said. 'They always have.'

She turned back into Ruin and buried her head in his shoulder, before falling into ash. Ruin's eyes flickered green, and he barked out a laugh in that staccato way of Shirkra's. *The madness is part of a greater whole, now. Shirkra is greater than she ever could have been alone.* The notion filled Aranfal with dread.

The children who held Canning began to creep forward, still grasping the strange chains that held their prisoner. They gazed at Father with expressions that suggested a mix of trepidation and excitement.

'My Boy and Girl,' said the mouth of Father. His voice had changed, as it echoed in the flames; it rang with the cadences of ten thousand speakers. 'Come to me.'

'We don't want to die,' said Girl. Her voice was trembling.

Ruin laughed. 'None of us will ever die. You know that. You will be part of something … *more*.'

He flicked a finger, and Boy and Girl disappeared. He

sucked in a breath, closed his eyes, and roared with triumph. The black chains vanished, and Canning collapsed onto his knees.

Aranfal looked at the remnants of the world: the girl called Drayn, Brandione, Canning, and the torturer himself, standing helpless in the flames. He wondered what had happened to the rest of humanity. Were they all in their homes? Were they ignorant of the new world? *Not for long. They'll find out soon enough.*

All of the Operators were now part of Ruin, and he burned with their power. As Aranfal stared at the flames all around him, he felt that he saw them, standing side by side, gazing out at him, half in pain and half in triumph. All of them were there, living as one creature, apart from Jandell and the Dust Queen.

*Hope is disappearing.*

# Chapter Twenty-Six

Drayn awoke to power. Power that appalled. Power that repelled.

Power that attracted.

*Ruin.* It was now unleashed, before a strange, twisted cage. *Its prison. A prison of fire and metal.* This was not the darkness she had seen before. This creature was part shadow, part human. It had taken the body of a woman: tall, muscular, white-haired. *The woman from Jaco's memory: the one who took the baby.*

Ruin was surrounded by flame, a fire of memory. At first it filled the great stadium, but over time it fell back, gathered around this creature. His clothing seemed part of his burning core, a dress of gold and red that looked ready to eviscerate any who touched it. His eyes were glowering coals. His arms were spread wide, and he seemed *triumphant*.

Something here was strange. It was the *silence*. All the other Autocrats had disappeared. Drayn knew where they had gone, when she looked at Ruin. *He has taken them all within himself.*

No: not all of them. Jandell still lay on the broken table, unmoving. Three women stood nearby, beings cut from the

211

same cloth as Ruin and Jandell himself: strange things, formed of sand or dust, their features shifting in a perpetual dance. *Not three creatures. One creature. A queen ...*

The other mortals were here, too, the ones she had seen with the Eyeless One: *Aranfal, Canning, and Brandione. No one to me a moment ago: now my only friends.*

And she needed friends, in this place. Ruin was different from the others. It wasn't just the power that flowed from him in wave after wave, like sheets of knives. It was the way that power *changed*. The way it evolved. Ruin was all-consuming. Ruin was a fire, and he wanted to burn the world.

Drayn sensed all this with a dead clarity. But more than this, she had a dangerous desire to become *part of it*. It was the feeling of crossing a bridge, and wanting to jump into the waters below.

Ruin gazed upon her. There was a fire in those eyes, two sparks of an inferno dangling in the face of a hard woman. The little flames jumped out of her head and they floated towards Drayn, until the girl was lost inside them.

Mother passed her the butter.

Drayn was back in Thonn House, in the small dining room. Mother was the same as always, a stern figure, hard and unbending, the keeper of some boring secret. She glanced at Drayn with that familiar blend of expectation and disappointment.

Drayn dug out a chunk of butter and dabbed at a piece of black bread. She was vaguely aware of a problem with this scene, some issue that had to be addressed. But the outlines of it were somehow hazy. *It's not clear, it's not clear at all, perhaps nothing will ever be clear again, perhaps clarity was something we had before, before, before it all …*

*Before what?* She could not remember.

An empty chair seized her attention. *Father's chair.* This was after the dark day. He didn't sit in that chair any more. He would never sit there again.

There was a noise downstairs: a great *bang*.

'Someone is at the door,' said Mother. She seemed unconcerned, as if it was not strange that someone should arrive during dinner. *That never happened, in the old days. No one would come during dinner. No one would disturb the House of Thonn while it ate.*

And then he came in through a side door: Cranwyl. He was different. Uneasy. That wasn't like him at all. He usually had the answers to everything.

'What is it?' he asked. He didn't look at Drayn. His gaze was locked on Mother, who slowly sucked at her soupspoon.

'It's the door, Cranwyl,' she whispered.

*This is not a memory.* Drayn found herself on her feet; the chair groaned as she pushed it back across the stone with her behind. *This is not a true memory.*

Mother was looking at her. 'What are you doing?'

'Something's wrong,' she whispered. A pair of eyes appeared in her mind, little drops of fire. 'Can you not feel it?'

The banging noise started up again. This time, though, it wasn't a knock. Someone was attacking the door in the great hall. Someone was trying to force it open.

'They're coming for you,' Mother said. Her eyes were on Cranwyl. A look of real fear crossed his face, but he quickly turned away, and his focus fell on the door from the dining room.

'You've told them I killed Teron,' he said. There was no

emotion in his voice, as if he was describing a change in the weather. *They say it's going to rain tomorrow.* 'They've been wondering what happened, so you told them it was me.'

Mother did not respond, but Drayn knew Cranwyl was right.

Cranwyl ran to the door and disappeared. Drayn tore after him, down the stairs, past the paintings of Thonn after Thonn, their feet thudding on stone and wood. They'd have to run by the main door before finding another way out, another route to escape the badness, whatever it was. But if the door opened before they got there, it would all be too late: the enemy would fall on Cranwyl, and he wouldn't escape their grasp until death came. *And maybe not even then.*

So down they went, under burning torches. They rounded the great door; it was shaking hard, thumped from outside, splinters breaking out and falling on the floor. But it held, and Drayn and Cranwyl were away, through the catacombs of the house, together again, running from the world.

There were so many doors in Thonn House, so many ways in and out, that hardly anyone knew all of them. Not even Drayn and Cranwyl, truth be told, though they knew more than anyone else. They ran through the kitchens and dashed inside the scullery. There, low on the wall, was a little doorway, built into the stone. Drayn always wondered why it was there. Perhaps it was for cats. *Did we have cats? I can't remember.*

Drayn and Cranwyl fell to their knees before the doorway. The servant went first, forcing his body through the opening, with Drayn following quickly behind.

She was only halfway out when she heard the man's voice. 'Stupid. Did you not think we knew about this one?'

There came a great flurry of scrabbling activity and hurried words. Cranwyl urged her to get back inside, but it was too late for that. She looked up, and her gaze fell on a metallic beak. *A Guard.* His mask glowed in the light from the house, and he held Cranwyl tight, squeezed up against his armour.

'This isn't real,' Drayn said. 'This never happened.'

**It doesn't matter.**

The voice spoke from everywhere and nowhere. It grabbed her hard, like a kitten being lifted by the scruff of its neck. She closed her eyes, willing herself to push through this, to fight her way past Ruin. When she opened them again, she saw that the Guard had a knife at Cranwyl's throat. No, not just any knife: *the* knife. The one she had used against her own father.

'Why are you helping this murderer, girl?' asked the Guard. 'Anyone would think you'd something to hide. Your mother told us what happened. This fucker killed your old da.' Drayn imagined the smile under the mask. *Lies, lies, lies, everyone is lying, everyone is always lying.*

Cranwyl nodded frantically. 'He's right, Drayn. Let him take me. I confess. Let him hurt me. I don't mind.'

A storm of emotions: gratitude and love for Cranwyl, hatred for the Guard and Mother, relief that it wasn't her under the knife, and shame at her cowardice.

'We're going to really hurt this little prick for what he … what he did,' the Guard said. *Lies again. He knows he's lying. It's nothing but cruelty.*

'No,' whispered Drayn. 'Don't hurt him.'

And then the scene changed. They were in a cell, somewhere on the island, a dark and hopeless place. Cranwyl was hanging from chains on the ceiling, naked. His body was sweating, trembling, covered in lashes and blood. The Guard was before him, holding a whip. Another false memory, but real enough: too real. *The same ingredients, mixed together into a stew, over and over and …*

'You will always remember this, Drayn.'

Mother was there, at her side, grinning in a way she *never* had before.

'Ruin,' Drayn said. The image of Mother fell away, and the face of that other woman appeared instead, the one with white hair and eyes of fire.

Ruin leaned in close to Drayn. The girl tried to back away, but found she was frozen to the spot.

'I feel such emotions within you, such a cascade, such a torrent.' Ruin grinned. 'Disgust. Hatred. *Fear*. From now until the end, you will hold this image in your mind: the picture of your friend, suffering for a crime that you committed. Dying in your place. Dying for you. It will haunt you, and it does not matter if it is real. I will be there, to drink these memories.'

He reached forward and touched Drayn on the forehead. The girl felt a shock of cold. When Ruin drew back his hand, he held a small, white flame; the creature placed it inside his mouth, sighing with pleasure.

'You are a *power*,' Ruin said. 'Once, there were others like you: they defeated us. Those days are gone. You will not surprise us again. I will take such pleasure from you, from dancing forever through the memories you hold, and the ones we will make together.'

As Drayn gazed at this strange creature, this parasite of pain, she felt a flicker of anger. She knew Ruin's victory was at hand, but she would not go easily into that darkness. She reached into her thoughts and felt the power of memory.

She flicked her wrist. Something was in her hand: a weapon, forged from the power of the past, a thing in the shape of a black sword. She raised it, and she swung it at this beast.

Ruin laughed at her. *Laughed.*

And then she was back on the shattered table, back in the great stadium, helpless before Ruin, who turned his attention elsewhere.

# Chapter Twenty-Seven

The past stretched before Canning, burning in the form of a single being.

In Ruin's eyes he saw only pain: his own, and that of countless unknown others. These things did not present themselves as images or moments, but in the flowing power of memories. He felt it tugging at him, urging him to throw himself at Ruin's feet, to beg him to swallow him up in his fire, as he had done to his children.

He crawled forward, and Ruin saw him. Was the fire in those eyes the same flame that had burned within the cage? Or was it something else – something more? The flames licked their way around the creature, encircling him. Perhaps he *was* the flame.

Ruin turned towards Canning, and he felt himself shrivel before those eyes. *This* was the power of the world, now. This thing could burn the Remnants in a moment. He found Canning amusing. The King of the Remnants could see it. He could see Ruin mocking him. He mocked himself. *How did I ever believe myself great? How could any mortal, when a creature like this exists?*

Ruin blinked, and Canning was somewhere else. A dock.

*The dock*. The place where Annya had fallen, all those years ago. She was on the wall, but this time he was at her side. She looked up at him and, *by the Machinery, why am I here, on this wall?*

Shirkra appeared then, surrounded by shadow. *Two creatures. Not Shirkra alone. Shirkra and Ruin.*

'We are the same, now,' Shirkra said. 'I am Ruin, and Ruin is Chaos.' She walked to him, and pushed a thin finger against his chest. 'Soon, the Old Place will be Ruin: he will drink it all. And then we will all play together. We can dance to Ruin's tune.'

'What is that tune?' Canning asked. He looked at Annya. 'This is not a memory. I was never on the wall.'

'No,' Shirkra said, shrugging slightly. 'But you will remember it. And *that* is what Ruin wants: that pain. That's what he wants from all of you, forever.'

He felt his hand move beyond his control.

'No,' he said.

But his protests did not matter. He could not stop himself, as he pushed Annya into the water.

He was back at the table. Ruin was no longer interested in him.

'You,' Ruin whispered. He raised the hand of Brightling and pointed a finger at the Operator of three bodies. 'Dust Queen. I have *seen* you, *your majesty*.' He said the last two words with a mocking tone. 'I have seen where you came from, long ago, in the days when the Old Place was young. You were formed from the birth of memories. Almost the First Memory ... though not quite.'

The Dust Queen nodded her three heads. 'I sense great power in you now, Ruin. I knew this day would come, when you would walk free among us: the greatest of us all.' A dark look crossed her three sets of eyes. '*Ruin will come with the One.*'

Ruin laughed. '*Wrong*. I did not need the One. I do not need *any*one.'

The Dust Queen smiled. 'But it was true, in a way. She went to the door and was the first Operator you saw when you emerged.'

Ruin shrugged. 'Prophecies, promises, predictions: call them what you will. I have seen so many of them in the great pool of memory. Promises made and broken, over and over again. They are worthless.'

The Dust Queen bowed. 'Ruin,' she said in a quiet voice, 'I am the oldest among us. But *you* are the greatest. You do not understand my intentions.'

Ruin became very still. For once, he seemed surprised.

'I *wanted* you to be free,' the Queen said. 'I created this moment.'

She turned and looked across the shattered table. She gazed at the mortals who remained, locking eyes on Brandione. 'We were losing the war. Before long, the mortals would have destroyed us.' She focused once more on Ruin. 'I knew what to do: how to end the war, and empower you, all at once. I helped Jandell build the Machinery. I *knew* you would grow stronger than the Old Place . But more than that, Ruin – I knew you were not a prisoner. I *aided* you. I saw it would take ten thousand years, for you to reach your true power. Everything I did was aimed at this moment. Everything brought us here, to this place. All your children gathered together, thanks to my words. You have consumed them, and the Old Place is at your feet: all because of *me*.'

Ruin seemed to hesitate.

'I saw that if the Old Place were ever to be a god that

loved Operators above mortals, then it would have to *become* an Operator,' the Dust Queen said. 'We fought a war against the mortals, and the Old Place did not help us – it simply watched. Perhaps, after time, in one of its moments of clarity, it would even have joined the mortals' side. But that danger has now passed. The greatest child of the Old Place will consume it. Ruin will become a god.'

And then this great being, this creature of the most undiluted power, fell to her three sets of knees, and bowed her heads before Ruin.

'I accept your mastery,' she said. 'Take me into you.'

Ruin's eyes widened. 'She bows before me: the Queen of Dust.' He nodded. 'I see, now, that you helped me.' He went to her, and placed a hand on one of the Queen's shoulders. He began to mutter, his eyes burning.

And the Dust Queen fell apart.

She did not collapse into dust all at once, as might have been expected. She disintegrated, chunk by chunk, like plaster from a wall, crashing to the ground and shattering into sand. The piles of dust began to swirl, before forming themselves into a single, narrow pillar.

Ruin opened his mouth, and the dust went down his throat. In his place were three old women, ancient hags clothed in rags with parchment skin and watery eyes. These women turned into three Ruins, arms spread wide. And then there was only one, standing alone before the cage, his eyes gleaming. The power of memory burned through him like fire in a forest.

Canning felt a sense almost of pain, as he gazed upon this thing. Ruin was too much for the world. He was too much for them all, and he had only just begun.

Ruin looked to him with a mix of love and disdain. 'You

are a powerful one,' he said. 'People like you were the *worst*. You almost defeated us.' He shook his head. 'But never again.'

There was a noise from somewhere amid the rubble, and Canning was reminded that not all the Operators had been sucked into the growing power of Ruin. There was one who stood outside his power, one Canning had known longer than any of the others, along with everyone who had lived in the Overland. It was the one they had called Operator, when they thought there was only one. It was Jandell.

He stood, trembling, his cloak curling around him. He seemed younger now, with long, black hair and pale, unlined skin. But there was a terrible weakness there: almost a kind of sickness.

'Father.'

When Ruin looked at Jandell, all the hatred from all the ages of the world seemed to gather in his eyes.

'The boy who betrayed his parents.' He shook his head. 'You almost killed your mother, and you made me a prisoner.'

Jandell pointed at the cage, and there was a look of sorrow in his gaze. 'It would seem not,' he said.

Ruin shook his head. 'You meant to keep me there, and burn me forever.'

Jandell nodded. 'These ten millennia have been a glory of the world, thanks to what we made.'

Ruin laughed. 'What good has it done you? Ten millennia of glory, while I built myself into *this*. While I made myself a *god*. Ten millennia will be a drop in the ocean of my reign.'

Jandell pointed to his cloak. 'The Queen gave me this, long ago, when she agreed to help me. She said it would remind me of all the terrible things I had done.' He sighed. 'I see now what a lie it was. The Queen never helped me. She helped *you*. I have always been a fool.'

He removed the cloak, and the faces screamed without sound. He grasped it in his hands and tore it into shreds, allowing them to fall into the wind. He was naked before them, under a dark, starless sky.

'The Bleak Jandell,' Ruin said. 'Do you know what your failing is? You lost touch with yourself. Your efforts to help the mortals were foolish: they only led to *this moment*.' He pointed at himself. 'When we are one, I will relish your *true* self. I will revel in your bleakness.'

Drayn appeared at Jandell's side and took him by the hand. Jandell turned to the girl and shook his head. She began to back away from him.

'We will die together, Father,' said Jandell. 'Never forget, that I am a weapon as well.'

The Operator – the old Operator, the one they had known forever – swept his arms in the air, and the remnants of his cloak floated before him. They merged together, becoming a great whip, a length of black rope whose surface writhed with sneering and smiling and yelling faces. Jandell grasped the whip. He pulled his arm back and with a sudden movement sent this weapon searing towards Ruin. That creature laughed at Jandell, but he did not laugh for long; he forgot to leap away, and the whip cracked against him.

Ruin yelled with pain and anger. He snatched a hand into the air, and in a heartbeat the cage fell apart. The remnants of his prison rose upwards, dancing in the air, before crashing down on Jandell. The Operator did not attempt to flee. He simply watched as the ruins of his machine fell upon him.

Something began to emerge from the wreckage: a thin line of blackness. Ruin breathed in, and sucked Jandell into his lungs.

'I am Ruin,' he said. 'The last of the Operators.'

# Chapter Twenty-Eight

As Ruin stood triumphant, Brandione thought only of the Dust Queen.

She had engineered all of this. She had helped Ruin, and she had *joined him*. She had betrayed the world. She had betrayed *him*.

He watched Ruin shift from Brightling to the Dust Queen, then to Jandell, then to those little children, then to Shirkra, on and on, over and over, a monstrosity, all the Operators in one. His fire gathered around him, a cold flame that spoke of agonised memories.

Brandione glanced behind. His army was still there, rank after dead rank. The Queen had sucked them dry over ten millennia, turning them into creatures of sand. He felt a pulse of anger. *All this time, I looked to these dead, useless soldiers. I wondered how I would use them. And now – at the end – I see the truth: it was all a trick. She has made a fool of me.*

'It is almost complete.'

Ruin's voice had changed once again. Brandione thought he could see memories forming in the air around his mouth, like gusts of icy breath.

'All that remains is the Old Place itself,' he whispered. 'I must drink the Old Place.'

He fell to his knees and began to whisper, his eyes closed. All around, the world began to change. The broken shards of his cage melted into a river of blackness, then flowed towards Ruin; he drank it in a gulp. The great slabs of the table, the statues of the Strategist: all of it shattered, all of it gathered together, and all of it made its way to *him*, the creature in the flames.

The Circus was gone. Only the Portal to the Machinery remained, though it was nothing more than a hole in the ground. Brandione wondered if he had gone to a memory, and was standing in the ancient past, on the Primary Hill as it would have been before the Operator built the Circus. He soon realised that this was the present, drained of all the power of the Old Place and all the glory of memory. The Circus, the See House, and Memory Hall: the Operator himself built them all. They were gone, now. *No. Not gone. They are part of him.*

Ruin was standing by the Portal, his head twitching as he glanced around with an air of animal fascination. He was seeing the world with new eyes, perhaps. He had been reborn as something new. He ignored them all as he enjoyed the first sense of his new powers, though it would not be long before he gave them his undivided attention.

They were huddled together at the birth of the god: Canning, Aranfal, Drayn, and himself. Lined up behind them was his army of the dead, stretching away in their thousands across the hilltop and down the sides. Ruin paid them no heed. *Perhaps they mean nothing to him.*

'What are you doing here?' he asked his soldiers. There came no reply.

'Who are they?' whispered Canning.

'A gift. An army. Useless.'

'Make them fight,' said Aranfal.

But Brandione shook his head. 'I don't think it's that kind of army.'

And then they all felt it, all at once. There was a presence in their minds: a parasite, burrowing through their memories. Brandione looked to Ruin, and saw that he was burning once more, engulfed in black and red flame, a creature of cold fire. He could see Ruin's eyes, in the flame, and they were laughing at him.

**All of the Old Place is within me.**

The words came from all around and nowhere in particular. Brandione could hear Brightling there as well, her voice mingled with something older by far.

**All of the Old Place is within me, so I am within *you*. I am your memories; your memories are me.**

Brandione placed his hands over his ears, as if that could somehow make it stop.

**From now, until the end, we will all be together: your memories and me. *My memories.***

The former General ground his teeth together. He heard a noise, somewhere, a terrible high-pitched whine, as of steam being released or the cogs of a great machine grinding together.

'Use your army.'

Brandione shook his head. It took a while for him to realise that this was not Aranfal's voice, or Canning's, or Drayn's, or any mortal's. It was not Ruin's, either.

It was the Dust Queen.

Some instinct made him close his eyes, and she was there, smiling at him. He had seen her in many guises, this Queen of Dust: a young girl, an old woman, and everything in between. But now she was the being he had first met all that time ago, in a strange little tower in the Prison of the Doubters: three women in middle age, their faces in constant flux, their thrones and their robes formed of grey swirling dust, wearing crowns of glass. He felt a strange pang of nostalgia for that early part of his journey: a time when he had embarked upon the madness, but was not so far from home.

He sensed, then, that there was more to this story than he understood.

'How do I use them?' he asked. 'Can they fight Ruin?'

The Queen shook her heads. 'No. Only you can do that.'

He felt a spark of anger. 'You betrayed me. Why should I believe you?'

The Dust Queen smiled. 'It is true. I knew that Ruin was not a prisoner. I knew that his powers would grow to dwarf us all, and I gave myself to him. But I did it for a reason. I did it to free you all.'

'Free us? You helped create a new god.'

'He truly is a god. But that will be his downfall. Memory is the god, and the god is memory. If he is destroyed, the power of memory will die.'

Realisation began to dawn on Brandione.

'You will die, too, your majesty.'

'Good. The power of memory has been a curse for mortals. *Destroy it.* Cherish your memories for what they are. But you can no longer live under their thumb. Destroy Ruin, and set yourselves free of us all.'

'How?'

She smiled, and for a moment she seemed to solidify into three real women. 'I told you already. Use your army.'

'I don't know how.'

'You are the Last Doubter. You are the soldier and the scholar.' She smiled at him. 'I stripped out their memories, but I did not leave them empty. I put something inside them, one little bit at a time. Something precious. Something I have possessed for ten millennia: something I kept a secret. The only thing that Ruin fears. Look *inside* your army ...'

The Queen faded away. Brandione opened his eyes, and everything was just as it had been. Ruin was in the same position, burning in his fire. Aranfal, Drayn and Canning watched him with agony writ across their faces, as he played with their memories. With *his own* memories, in truth, for he now was master of them all.

Strange, but Brandione did not feel Ruin within him, in this moment. Had the Queen done something to protect him? *Perhaps I have saved myself.*

He turned towards his troops. He focused his attention on one of the soldiers, a short creature in a yellow cloak, holding a glass spear. *Look inside your army.*

A thought struck him. This was *his* army. These were *his* soldiers. He would order them to do what *he* wanted.

'Army of dust,' he called.

The soldiers stood to attention, slamming their spears into the ground.

'Raise your weapons.'

As one, all the glass spears were raised.

**What are you doing?**

An intense heat flooded him.

**I see you. What are you doing with those dead creatures? Do you think they can help you?**

Brandione struggled to push Ruin from his mind. He felt the god clawing at him with burning fingers, scrabbling through his memories, searching for *something*. He was panicking. The realisation gave Brandione a new sense of strength.

He forced himself to focus on the army. He tried to shout, but found that he could not raise his voice. And so he whispered to them, hoping they could hear him.

'Army of dust, show me what is inside you. I command you.'

At the front of the army, a soldier stepped forward. He saluted, and immediately disintegrated into dust, which floated away around the Circus. But he did not vanish entirely. Something was left behind: a tiny spark of light, flitting through the night air like a firefly.

There was a great murmur through the assembled troops, and they all collapsed into dust, just as the first soldier had done. The spark was joined by hundreds of thousands, millions more, circling each other in the air. Brandione saw that the lights were joining together, forming a greater whole. He knew what he was looking at. The one thing that could destroy Ruin. The weapon he was destined to wield. The Dust Queen had had it in her possession, all this time. She had broken it into little pieces and hidden it within these beings.

It was the First Memory of the Old Place, and it belonged to Brandione.

# Chapter Twenty-Nine

'Something great is happening. Can't you feel it?'

Aranfal swung his head in the direction of the voice. The girl was talking. *Drayn*. She was staring at Brandione, and whatever he had wrought. There was a strange look in her eyes. It was something unnerving, almost primeval: a kind of hunger.

'He's found something, in those ... soldiers,' Aranfal said. *But what it is, I do not know.* He looked at the one-time General of the Overland, standing on the muddy hill with his hands in the air, staring dumbly upwards at whatever he had unleashed: a twisting haze of lights, slowly dancing together.

'A memory,' Aranfal said.

'No,' said Canning. The former Tactician was on the other side of Drayn, gazing up at the dark sky. 'It's not just a memory, Aranfal. Can't you feel its *power*? Doesn't it talk to you?'

'Yes,' said Drayn.

'No,' said Aranfal. Drayn and Canning saw something he did not. *With their magic eyes.* Back when he was a Watcher – a million lifetimes ago – he had been a kind of magician, too. But he had a little instrument to help him: a mask, crafted for him in the Underland, a gift that allowed him to see a person's soul. He knew, now, that it was not their souls he looked at, but their *memories*, the strange essence of their past. *Is it the same thing?* That was a kind of power, was it not? Not everyone could use a mask. You had to feel your way into it: the mask was the tool of the Watcher, not the other way around.

He retrieved the raven from his cloak and held it before him: the infamous mask of Aranfal. Once, it had struck such fear into the Doubters of the world: into *everyone*, truth be told. He lifted it to his face and felt it slide on in that curious way the masks possessed, like a second skin. He turned his gaze upward to the sky, and he concentrated.

The night sky was the same as always, burning with a million stars, a backdrop to the dancing lights. But over time, the picture changed. The lights began to disappear, vanishing inside a growing darkness. This was not the colour of the night. It was not an absence of light. This was a *being*. It had no physical form that he could easily describe. On the contrary, it was defined by its nothingness.

But the longer he stared at this thing, the more he realised his mistake. This was more than nothingness. It was something different: the memory of a creature. Aranfal felt the great movement of time, there, in the depths of this beast of the cosmos. He saw time for what it was: a pitiless expanse, infinite in scope and, until very recently, empty and unchanging. This was the Universe itself. This was the uncaring, unblinking, unchanging stuff of existence.

It seemed to turn its attention to him. He felt something pawing at his mind, delicately twisting his memories, *breaking them apart*. Yet it was only a memory. He wondered what this creature must have been in reality, and he shuddered.

There was a noise. He snatched off his mask, and found that he could still see the darkness. He turned and saw Ruin, his fire gone. His eyes were focused on the sky above.

'I can't feel his hand on my memories,' Canning said. 'Perhaps this thing has weakened him.'

'No,' said Drayn. 'He's just looking somewhere else. He is focused.'

The darkness spread out across the sky, until everything above them was empty and alive, all at the same time.

'The Great Absence,' Canning said, 'or rather, the memory of it. We are looking at the first thing human eyes gazed upon, long ago. The First Memory. That is what they saw: their Creator. *This* is what was in the soldiers.' He laughed. 'The game was a ruse. No one could have found it, because *she* had it this whole time.'

The Watcher spat out a laugh. He felt a sense of administrative awe at the sheer *planning* behind it all.

'What is happening to him?' asked Drayn.

She was pointing at Brandione. The darkness of the memory was contracting, floating downwards and gathering around him, until the man was no longer visible under the haze.

Aranfal turned his focus to Ruin, who regarded the scene with a look of horror, the exact expression Brightling had used when chastising a sloppy Watcher. The longer Aranfal stared, the more clearly he saw the future under Ruin's rule, a world of agonised memories, made exquisite by the power of his imagination. And for the first time, he saw something different in those eyes: *fear*. Whatever was happening to Brandione, Ruin did not like it at all.

*It's not just fear. It's surprise.* He had thought all the

memories of the world were within him, but now he had learned he was missing one. *Perhaps the strongest one. The one that can destroy him.* Suddenly the future was a choice, not an endless, inevitable march of misery.

When the darkness faded, Brandione stood before them. But he was changed. Something seemed to crawl beneath his skin: a worm from the beginning of time. He had a strange air about him, sick and strong all at once.

'He is at one with the memory,' said Canning.

'He is a host,' said Drayn.

Brandione turned to face Ruin.

'You are new,' Ruin said, stepping carefully forward. 'Yet you are so *old*, all at the same time. You are as old as old can be – born of the First Memory.' He shook his head as he edged across the hill. 'I am a fool. I should have known she kept it from the Old Place. What power she has! I never thought to look for it when I burned in the memories of old.' He stifled a laugh. 'Imagine! I never looked for it!'

He sighed. 'You are a beautiful creature. Once, I would have kept you at my side, as a companion. But not now. Now, I will possess you. Not even the First Memory is stronger than me. How could it be, when all other memories are one with my soul?'

He slashed a hand through the air and Brandione fell to his knees, grasping at his throat.

'I thought I was powerful, until this moment. Imagine what I will become when I bring the First Memory into myself.'

He raised a hand, snapped a finger, and plucked a neck shackle out of the air, attached to a chain that came from his own person. The shackle and its chain were constructs of memory, sparkling with the whispers of long ago.

Ruin placed the shackle around Brandione's neck. He flicked a finger in the air and the restraint appeared to tighten; Brandione's eyes bulged in their sockets.

'What will we *call* you?' Ruin asked. He reached out a finger and traced it along Brandione's forehead. 'You are ancient and new, all at once. What about the Old Child? What do you think?'

He raised his arms, and a great axe appeared in his grip, wide and dark, glowing with tendrils of blue flame, like lightning in the sky.

'I made this weapon in a moment,' Ruin whispered, holding the axe aloft. 'I made it only for *you*, Old Child.' He looked at Aranfal. 'I will make weapons for all of you, torturer. Weapons of memory.' He grinned. 'You should understand how wonderful that is, torturer. A special little weapon, for each and every one.'

*Torturer.* The word flooded Aranfal. *Torturer, torturer, torturer.* Life was imbalance: the rule of the strong over the weak, and the Selected over all. Torture was this reality in its most extreme form: one person in shackles, waiting for the blow, a victim of time, which only the torturer controlled. That was to be the fate of the world, under this creature: this Ruin.

A moment forced itself into his memory. There was a woman, on the rack. *But she hadn't done anything wrong. No, it was her son … her son had been …*

He felt the memory crawl across him, like a great slug. It was now beyond the confines of his mind: it was outside of himself. He felt something within it: *power.*

Without knowing what he was doing, he focused on that power. He thought what it would be like to hold it, to play with it, as the Shadowthings had done: not to drain it of its essence, but use it against this Ruin. To turn it into a *weapon*.

Something happened, then. The bounds between imagination and reality began to shift. Aranfal glanced downwards, and saw that he held a staff in his hand, a thing of darkened wood, a thing that burned with the core of the memory.

*You are going to die,* said a voice within. *Make it a good death.*

'Aranfal,' said Canning, somewhere to his side. 'That weapon – how did you …?'

But Aranfal was not listening. *I will do something good, before the end. And then I hope I suffer, somewhere, for all that I have done. But alone. I hope I suffer alone.*

Ruin was smiling at the shackled Brandione. The axe was trembling in his hands.

'It is time,' he whispered.

The axe began to fall, moving slowly, as if it was cutting through some unseen barrier. In that moment, the torturer saw things with greater clarity than he ever had before.

He leapt forward, his staff extended, and he stopped the axe as it fell. The great weapon trembled, and fell to dust.

Ruin turned his gaze upon him. 'That was foolish,' he whispered. 'I will make a special place for you in my new world, Aranfal.'

'Aran *Fal*,' the torturer replied.

He grinned at the God of Memory, and he was gone.

# Chapter Thirty

*A sacrifice in vain.* The words rattled through Canning's mind, as he watched Aranfal die. *A sacrifice in vain.*

The Watcher had stopped nothing. He had merely postponed the inevitable. Canning could feel the power of Ruin. There was no stopping this thing. There was no way to halt its rise.

*A sacrifice in vain.*

Aranfal had simply vanished under Ruin's gaze. The god had turned his eyes on the Watcher, and he was gone. But his memories would never die. They would join with all the others: all of them under Ruin's command, forever, twisted and darkened and turned to bile.

*Ruin.* He now reminded Canning of the Strategist, when he had first seen her on that dark beach. He was warped out of all semblance of normality, a thin, stretched giant. He was bent over Brandione, the Old Child, who remained on his knees, shackled by the neck. He reached out a hand to his new rival, but he did it slowly, hesitantly.

When Canning thought more of what Aranfal had done, his feelings began to shift. The Watcher had shown that the power of memory could still be wielded by mortals.

And he was more powerful in memory than Aranfal had ever been.

He closed his eyes, and he reached out with his mind. Once, he had been able to picture the Underland as a pulsating ball of power. He had been able to snatch power from it, like a cat pulling at a ball of string. Now it was different. The power was there, but it was somehow concentrated, held tight: a balled fist.

Yet as he searched, he saw a weakness. Canning reached out, and he stole a memory from the grip of Ruin.

He was in the Circus once more, though not the giant version with the board. This was the real Circus, or at least the one he remembered, that great lump of misshapen marble with its four statues of Jandell. It was day, and the building was packed full of people. Canning was high above, in his old seat, with all the other Tacticians nearby. There was no sign of Strategist Kane.

A great stage had been built on the lower level, and a woman stood upon it, dressed all in red. Canning knew this moment only too well.

'Sixty-two years,' she said. Her voice was deep, somehow masculine. 'It has been sixty-two years since ...'

This was not a memory; it was a wound. It was branded into his being.

*A play. Brightling's play.*

And there he was: the stage version of himself, under Brightling's boot. She had created this scene, long ago. She had portrayed him on the stage as a simpering mess of a man. Surely it had not moved so quickly, in real life: surely the performance took longer to reach this point? But this was a nightmare. It took him where he least wanted to go, and there were no rules.

Brightling did it to impress the Machinery: to demonstrate his weakness, and highlight her strengths. He realised, now, what a backhanded show of respect this was. She feared him as a rival and wished to destroy him. He didn't see this back then. He *wanted* to believe the worst of himself, in those days. *So much of life is about choices.* It had all become so clear. *I will never choose to hate myself again.*

Yet still this memory held him in its grip. Perhaps a part of him would always be trapped in this moment. Perhaps it would never die.

He looked at the other Tacticians. They were all here, except the only one that mattered. Brightling was not in her usual place, two seats away from him. There was nothing in that chair.

He turned back to the stage, to find that all had changed. Only Canning stood there, now. This was no actor, however. This was the real man, or an image of him. And he was not alone. At his side was Annya, *half-mad Annya, the only thing that mattered* ...

The crowd were cheering. They cheered as the stage Canning lifted his arms. They cheered as he smiled at them. They cheered as he turned his body and kicked out at Annya's legs, knocking her to the ground.

This was *not* a memory. This was something new, a creation made to provoke pain, fashioned by a cruel hand. He tried to avert his gaze, but something held his head in place. Now the stage was cast in shadow. Canning was on top of Annya: he held a cushion, a thing of silver, shaped into a half-moon crown, and he was forcing it over his lover's mouth. *Suffocating her.*

The shadow on the stage gathered together and rose

upwards. It filled Brightling's chair, forming into a perverse outline of a person.

**This will be your life, Canning.** The voice was within him. **This will be life for all of you.**

'But you have not won,' said the former Tactician. He had found courage from somewhere, and it was a marvel to him. 'You will not win.'

**You think you have power. Look where we are. *I* took you here, though you thought you stole it from me. There is no power in you.**

The creature began to flicker between Brightling and shadow, over and over. He knew, then, that he hated one more than the other. It was absurd, but it was always Brightling. She had been *his* ruin long before this creature took her over.

*I will destroy her completely.* Anger swelled inside him like a pustule, bursting open and flooding him with its bile. *She will die: Ruin, Brightling, both of them, forever ...*

He had seized this memory for a weapon. He had not found one. He had only made her mock him more. But perhaps it was enough. Perhaps the *anger* of this memory was all that he needed.

She grinned at him. There was blood on her teeth.

# Chapter Thirty-One

*You are the heir to the House of Thonn, which has stood for ten thousand years.*

*Tick, tick, tock.*

*You will not lose yourself to this place.*

The words came to Drayn in her mother's voice, reaching out from the island. *No. From myself. She's inside me, and she always will be. All of them are in me, all these voices from the past.*

*Tick, tick, tock.*

*I'm a Thonn.*

Canning was gone. Ruin remained, his hand grasping the chain that led to the Old Child. But his mind seemed to be elsewhere. Perhaps he had taken Canning to some place, some memory. The girl looked upwards, to the sky, wondering if they were out there. Only the stars glimmered back at her.

*Tick, tick, tock. It's time to stop the clock.*

A gibberish ditty from childhood. Her thoughts were untethered, as if the anchor that held her to reality was gone, and she was floating away. *Floating to nothing. Floating from myself, and the world ...*

*Tick, tick ...*

She forced herself to concentrate. *I was in a great stadium, vast, the size of a country, with four statues staring down. There was a shattered table and a broken cage. They are gone. Jandell is gone.*

She suppressed an urge to cry out. *Jandell is gone.*

She forced the thought away. *I am on a hill. One god is killing another.*

*Gods.* The word felt strange, but there was nothing else for it.

*The Old Child.* He was nearing death.

*A tick, and a tock.*

She walked to him, studied the shackle that held him in place. It was a gleaming, pointed, dark thing, locked tightly around the neck.

'How do I release him?'

*Tick, tick … Thonn's time ticks down, down to the end …*

She closed her eyes, and Jandell was before her.

'The power of memories must die. I see that now.'

He smiled at her.

'No. That power is the glory of the world,' she said, though she did not believe her own words.

He shook his head. 'Nothing but the shadows of shadows. *You* are the glory.' He closed one of his palms and opened it again: there was a little model there, shaped into a black pyramid. 'The people of the Overland made this by themselves: it is called the Fortress of Expansion. It still stands, even now, when the things I made from memory are long gone.'

Drayn nodded. 'Tell me what to do. Tell me how to free that man.'

Jandell closed his palm. 'He is her prisoner, but she has

not yet destroyed him. Remember that memories come from you, and Canning, and all of humanity. *You* are the gods.'

Her eyes snapped open. Canning had returned. He was at her side, bent over, panting and exhausted.

'I need your help,' she said.

His face was a mask of pain.

'Together,' he heaved. 'We will do everything together.'

The white-haired figure had returned in all his power and was bent over the Old Child once more. Ruin's hands pulled at the black chain and the shackle that coiled around the Old Child, straining at his throat. The scene was changing: the two of them rose into the air. More chains cascaded down, sprung from the darkness and fire of Ruin, crashing around the mortals below. Each chain was a memory of another life. *Dark memories. Hidden moments. The treasures of Ruin.*

'We have to follow,' said the girl. 'But I don't know how.'

'Yes,' said Canning. He was a strange man, even now. He *gleamed* with fear; it shone on his skin like sweat. But even so, something pushed him forward, onwards into danger. Anger. Ambition. *Hate.*

He moved towards the chains, and he ran his fingers along them.

'She's crushing him,' Drayn said.

'She hasn't killed him yet. He's strong. He's holding her back.'

Drayn looked upwards. 'Let's go to him,' she whispered. 'Let's help.'

She grasped the chains, and nodded as Canning did the same.

'Take us to your mistress,' she whispered. 'Take us to Ruin and Brandione.'

And up the chains they went, up through the treasures of Ruin.

Death was near for the Old Child.

They were floating in the night sky, atop the heaped piles of chains. Ruin stood before them, encircled by his fire and his chains; he was bent over, and his white hair covered his face. He was pointing towards Brandione.

The Old Child was on his knees. His face was contorted in pain, his eyes screwed tight, his mouth curled into a snarl. He now wore a pale-blue gown, which rippled like water in the moonlight. He was the endless sea, and Ruin was the fire of the world.

The chains were alive. They gathered around the Old Child, cutting into him. He was not fighting back, as the shackle and the chains and *memories* suffocated him. *Strangled by pain*. Ruin would consume him, and the memory he held.

'Take my hand,' Drayn said, turning to look at Canning, whose gaze was fixed on Brandione. He did not seem to hear. 'Take my hand,' she repeated.

'Beautiful,' Canning whispered. 'Can't you feel the power inside him? That memory is a glory.'

He seemed to shake himself, and looked at Drayn.

'We need to help him,' he said.

The girl nodded. She took Canning by the hand. She did not know where she was going, but she somehow knew the way.

They were on a wall.

They had come to a fortress, a vast thing of towers and stone. The wall was a great defensive structure, taller by far than the buildings behind. Brandione stood alone, staring out through a small opening. His hands were pressed up against the stone, as if he was attempting to physically hold something back, something fierce and unrelenting. Drayn and Canning ran to his side, to gaze through eyeholes of their own.

The land below them was a bowl of fire: roiling, endless flame. Occasionally Drayn could *see* things there, in that conflagration: a pair of eyes, unblinking, burning with a fire of their own. There were chains, too, in the fire: they gathered together and shot forward, crashing against the wall and making the fortress shake.

'I need to protect it,' Brandione said. He did not look at them, but jabbed a thumb over his shoulder. 'I need to guard the wall, or he will take it.'

Canning touched Drayn on the shoulder. She looked where he was pointing; behind them, below the wall and in a kind of courtyard, was a great cannon, lying useless on the ground.

'That's the wrong approach, Brandione,' said Canning. 'You need to *attack* him with it, not protect it.'

Brandione did not respond.

'He can't hear you,' Drayn said. 'Ruin is destroying him.' Drayn looked once more through an eyehole at that fire below. 'Something's wrong here.'

Canning was staring at the former General.

'This is Brandione,' he said.

'Yes. I don't know what you—'

He swung his head towards her.

'I mean, this is *Brandione*. It is *not* the Old Child.' He turned back to Brandione. 'He needs to give himself over to the memory. He must allow himself to be consumed. Do you understand, Charls? Ruin will kill you if you don't.'

But the man simply stared out, out beyond the wall. There came another barrage of chains: the wall shook again, and great chunks of stone began to fall to the ground.

'He's losing,' Drayn said. 'He needs time.'

Canning looked at her. He reached out a hand.

'Then we will give him time.'

They turned as one towards the wall. They climbed upon the edge, and they jumped down into the fire and the chains.

# Chapter Thirty-Two

The flames burned and the chains tightened around Brandione. *Closer, closer, closer.*

He was nowhere at all, but he saw everything. He flickered through memory, along the roads and lanes of the Overland, that land of his birth. There he was, in a dusty village of the South; now in the College; now in the Fortress; now in the damned, benighted West. Little shards of the past, prickling his skin.

*Was there ever an Overland at all? Perhaps it was a fantasy: perhaps the Underland is reality.* He did not know if these thoughts were his own, or those of the *new* creature. *The Old Child.*

He was a host for this being. Together, they would destroy Ruin. But he did not *feel* it. Sometimes he thought he heard something. A different voice spoke within him, a whisper from the shadows of the ancient world. *Fight it. Fight him.* The memory was within him, but it was not yet a part of him. He felt an urge to protect it from Ruin, though he knew this was foolish. *I can't stop him taking it, until I become one with it.*

But he did not know how. Before long, *he* would be there;

he would burn away Brandione's ignorance and strangle it with his chains.

*We can do great things,* the memory told him. *Allow me to become one with you.*

The Queen was there again.

'You are the Last Doubter. Do you know what that means? I have seen you in the storm of memory. It speaks to me in a thousand voices, and sometimes it deceives. But I know *this* to be true. The Last Doubter will *destroy* Ruin. You must accept the First Memory into your heart. You must throw your old self away.'

The Dust Queen faded away. Brandione did not know it then, but this was the last time he would ever see that creature, that power of the world who had called him the Last Doubter, who had found him in a prison in the desert and placed the world in his hands.

And so Brandione wandered through memory and time. The First Memory was at his side, sometimes appearing as a thin line of smoke, sometimes assuming the form of a person, a vision of darkness, of *Absence*. He willed himself to embrace this thing: to truly become a host. He knew this would end his mortal life, but he was not afraid of that. He had always known that an early death awaited him, from the day he walked out of the College and into the armies of the Overland. This would be glory on an unrivalled scale.

But he could not do it, and he did not know why. He was lost, now, lost in the world, lost within himself. He felt helpless: a piece of wood on a surging stream, carried by forces he could never control.

As this thought took hold of him, an old anger began to grow, the same rage he had felt all his life. *I am Charls Brandione.*

He was not like others of the world. He had clawed his way to the pinnacle of the Overland, not through the whims of some machine, but thanks to his own efforts, his own talents. He would no longer call for aid to the Dust Queen, or any other being of the Old Place. He would win by being Charls Brandione.

He felt a fire burn at him: the fire of Ruin. But he paid it no mind.

'Who is Charls Brandione?'

There were two others at either side of him, sitting at a table. But there were not three of them in this room; there was only one.

The room was divided into two sections. To his left, it had the appearance of a library, a cluttered space of books and dust. The Brandione at this side of the table was young, and wore the dark cloak of a scholar.

To the right was the Map Room of the Overland, a dark, marble space with the borders of the country engraved upon the ground. The Brandione of this place was closer to today's man, a weary figure in a battered leather breastplate, his eyes locked on his younger self.

*The soldier and the scholar.*

The two men turned and stared at him. All was silent here; even the flames of Ruin seemed to die away, their harsh light fading from the memory world of Charls Brandione.

'She waited for both of you,' he said to the men. 'Ten millennia ago, she saw us, and she waited for us. We are the Last Doubter.'

The two men spoke as one.

'We must use both sides.'

Brandione nodded. 'I am a soldier. I am a scholar. And I am more besides. I am ... I am ...'

He felt something appear in his grasp. It was a book: *The Days Before the Fall*. He found it long ago, in the Museum of Older Times, when all this madness had begun. He flicked through its pages, gazing once more at the painted images of the Operators, Jandell and Squatstout and Shirkra and all the rest of them. But then he came to two others, ones he had not recognised before: a grown man and woman, hand in hand. They had changed: the woman was now in the form of Katrina Paprissi, staring out at him with purple eyes. The man, though, took no form at all; he was only a thing of fire and shadow, formed roughly into the contours of a person. This man seemed to change under Brandione's gaze, shifting from one creature to another, flickering from the shadow to Brightling to other, stranger beings. Brandione saw power when he looked at this thing, power beyond anything in this world. He saw a creature that held all memories in its grasp, and could not be tricked or overwhelmed.

'He owns the world,' said the two other Brandiones. 'He owns all the world, except *one thing*: the First Memory.'

A new page had been opened, though he did not remember turning it. A great heart was painted there, black and festering, pumping streams of putrid blood that ran off the paper and into his lap.

'It has a heart,' he whispered. 'All things with a heart can die.'

The book fell away into dust, and was reborn as something else: a dagger, old and worn. *His* dagger, a little weapon he had carried for half his life. He knew, though, that the dagger was not for Ruin. Steel would not harm that thing. Only memory could do that. Only the First Memory.

'You must truly become a host,' said the scholar. 'You must become a weapon.'

'I am ready,' said Brandione.

'You are not ready,' said the soldier. 'You will only be ready when you are *gone*.'

Brandione looked at the dagger.

'A part of you resists,' said the scholar.

'Kill it,' said the soldier.

Brandione nodded.

'The blade is not for Ruin,' he whispered.

He looked at the two younger versions of himself, and all of them shared a smile, as Charls Brandione plunged a dagger into his neck.

The Old Child sat on a platform of chains.

Ruin stood before him, wreathed by flame. The Old Child was held firm by the shackle and the chains, countless chains, all of them wrapped around him, squeezing the life from him. The chains fell away, far down to the ground below. They were a part of Ruin, and they were formed of all the Old Place. The Old Child could not escape these bonds, while Ruin put all his heart into them. But the Old Child felt no fear. He knew that all would be well. Soon Ruin would turn away. He would drop his guard, and loosen his grip. The Old Child knew it.

A movement seized his attention. Two mortals were standing at the side of Ruin. He did not know where they had come from, but he remembered seeing them, somewhere else. *They came to help my host. They are helping me.*

Ruin had not noticed them; all his focus was on the Old Child. He did not see them, as they each raised their right hands towards him, palms open. Power formed there: a little blue flame in the man's hand, and a swirling storm in miniature in the girl's. As one, they pulled those hands back and pushed them against Ruin.

At first, the gaze of Ruin remained resolutely focused on the Old Child. But after a moment he seemed to acknowledge these creatures at his side. They were not harming him, the Old Child saw. They were simply *annoying* him. The Old Child felt such love for these mortals in that moment. He saw what they had achieved, at such risk to themselves.

And that was enough. Ruin turned his gaze from the Old Child for a moment, and slackened his grip. The Old Child stood, and cast aside his chains.

Ruin swung back towards him, his eyes burning black and red. But it was too late. The Old Child was unleashed.

# Chapter Thirty-Three

The man called Brandione was gone.

Drayn was on her knees, exhausted, her power spent. She looked to the other side of Ruin and saw Canning there, in the same condition as her. Ruin had only *glanced* at them in anger, and it had almost destroyed them.

But it did not matter any more: the Old Child was here.

The Old Child began to walk forward, his gaze set intently on Ruin. Darkness gathered around him like a smoke; he held it in his hands. It *came* from his hands. His neck shackle was gone. He raised a hand in the air, and the rest of the chains collapsed as well, until the platform was gone and they stood on nothing but air. He clicked his fingers together and they all began to float downwards, back onto the hill.

Ruin faced the Old Child and smiled, though it was uncertain. The stars seemed more numerous than before, and the hill was bathed in their light.

Canning was at Drayn's side.

'We did it,' he whispered.

Drayn nodded. 'We did something. But it's not over.' A new thought came to her. 'The Old Child is separate from Ruin. That woman – that Queen – took it away from the

Old Place. There are two gods now: two gods of memory.' She could feel both of them in her memories, melded with all the magic of the past. 'These creatures *are* the power of memory. If they die, so does our power.'

She felt a surge of relief. She did not *want* any power. Not any more. She wanted only to return to normal, to her island, to her Cranwyl. But when she looked at Canning, she saw a fear in his eyes that she had never seen before.

Ruin took a step towards the Old Child. His flames were gone, but there was a fire in his eyes.

'I destroyed the Great Absence. How could a *memory* of the Absence ever hurt me?'

The Old Child shook his head. The darkness swirled around him, this memory of something older than any of them. It was a nothingness, but it was not empty. It was a hunger that wanted to throw them all in its jaws.

'I am not the Absence,' said the Old Child. It was the voice of Brandione, though there was something else there besides. 'I am the First Memory. I will destroy us both.'

The Old Child smiled, and the man that was Brandione fell into smoke. The smoke gathered together, into the shape of a person, and ran forward, towards Ruin.

# Chapter Thirty-Four

Canning watched with a blend of horror and hope as Ruin raised a hand and cast the Old Child to the ground, like a supplicant before him. Horror, because he *knew* what was going to happen: Ruin would defeat the Old Child. The First Memory would be consumed by the god, and the world would belong to *him*, the endless past and the tortured future, all of it forevermore. But there was hope, too: a strange, splintered kind of hope. *If Ruin lives, the power of memories lives. My power lives.*

'How could one memory alone threaten me? You will not destroy us; you will live on, within me.' Ruin laughed. 'You are a beautiful thing. I will enjoy bringing you inside me.'

He gestured with a finger, and the Old Child was dragged forward. Ruin became a flame, golden and black, and the darkness of the Old Child vanished into his fury.

Canning wept, then. He wept with joy and sadness, as the story of the mortal world came to an end, but the power of memory lived on.

# Chapter Thirty-Five

The Old Child was lost in flame and shadow.

A name surfaced in the swirling mist of his mind. *Charls Brandione. The Last Doubter. A soldier and a scholar.* The words seemed to hold some significance. *Words of the host. Words of my body.*

He was so young, and so old, all at once. He felt the weight of time within his being, but looked at the world through fresh eyes. He was the youngest of the Operators, and the oldest.

He had come now to Ruin. So much memory was here, in this creature. It had swallowed the Old Place. It held the power of the world in its grip, *like a spider in its web*. Oh, and what a web that must be, stretching through the Old Place and into every mortal mind. Memory was tied to it, and it was tied to memory.

A storm of power surrounded him, formed of flame and darkness. The Old Child smiled. He did not know how to feel fear. He looked upwards, and saw a great patch of darkness. That was the centre of the beast: the heart of this god. It floated downwards, until it hung over the Old Child.

**There has never been a creature like me. All memory is within me, and I am within all memory.**

'No,' said the Old Child. 'Not all memory. Not *me*.'

The Old Child had a vague recollection of its mortal self: a man, a soldier, a scholar. That man seemed to be there, at the Old Child's side. He was of the Old Place, and beyond it. He gave a slight nod. Both parts of the Old Child knew the lie of the road ahead, and were agreed on the direction.

*A soldier is always willing to die.*

'You have allowed me inside your being,' said the Old Child. 'You have allowed me inside. And now you will fall.'

There was a great shudder, in the flaming darkness. **I sense your power. But you cannot harm me.**

'There is something you do not know, Ruin; something that has always been hidden from the children of the Old Place.'

There came an uneasy laugh.

**Your tricks will not help you now.**

'I will tell you, Ruin. You see, only one thing is more powerful than memory,' the Old Child said. 'The Absence told mortals this secret, in the beginning of everything. It has been hidden from you, but I know the truth.'

There was a tremor in the maelstrom: a tremble of *fear*.

The Old Child looked within itself to the very core of the First Memory: the beautiful wasteland of the Absence, the first thing that mortal eyes ever saw. This was the centre of its existence, the blood that flowed through its veins. It was the stuff of creation, and the febrile matter of destruction.

'The only thing more powerful than a memory,' the Old Child said, 'is the *death* of a memory.'

The Old Child took this power in its hands, and set itself aflame.

# Chapter Thirty-Six

The flames died, and Ruin stood alone. Canning looked from this creature to Drayn, and knew what she was thinking. *It is over. The god has won.*

But when he looked once more at Ruin, he saw there was a certain look in his eye. A *fearful* look. The god glanced around the hill; his eyes burned, but not with their usual flame. This was the darkness of the Old Child. It was the blackness of creation, a cosmic emptiness. It was the memory of a creature that was older than all the ages of the universe. All of Ruin's being now crawled with this thing: this memory of Absence.

Ruin looked upwards to the starry sky, and he screamed. He screamed as the darkness burned through the skin of Brightling. He screamed as his body was rent apart. He screamed as he fell into a broken corpse of fire and shadow, rolling out over the hill and away on the winds of the mortal world.

There came a sound in the air: a great grinding, like the movement of some terrible machine. It reached a screeching pitch, and then fell silent, never to be heard again.

\*

Memories whispered past Canning. He opened his eyes, and he saw *them*: the real Brightling, and the real Katrina Paprissi, hand in hand on the hilltop, smiling at him. There was a look in their eyes he had never seen in either of them. *They are content.*

But then they were gone. All of it was gone.

All that was left was the Old Child, on his knees. He looked up at Canning, and he smiled. The memory of Absence danced across his skin, uncontrolled, searing into him.

'I'm dying,' he said. 'The First Memory, become the last.' He lay on the ground.

'No,' said Canning. He ran to the side of this man, the man he had once known as Charls Brandione. 'No. I can see you … you are here, despite everything you unleashed. Ruin is gone, but you're still here. You have such strength!'

There was a hazy look in the Old Child's eyes. 'The god is dead,' he said.

'You're a god, too,' Canning whispered.

'I am dying.' The Old Child nodded at Canning. 'The King of the Remnants and the First Memory: together at the end.'

Canning felt a surge of desperation. *The death of the power of memory. The death of my own power.* His mind turned to the future, a future where he was just a man. He thought of the things he had done since he'd been a prisoner in the Bowels. All of it would soon be gone.

He would never know, in later years, where the thought came from. Perhaps it was born from some dark recess of himself. Perhaps it was not *his* thought at all. But something happened to him, as he stood on that hill, watching the thing that was once Charls Brandione, the last power in the world, slowly dying.

He knew that he had to stop it.

He searched within himself, in the deepest recesses of his soul, scrabbling for some trace of that power he had once felt. It was useless. It was gone.

But then he saw it.

'What are you doing?' Drayn asked.

Canning hurried across the hill and picked it up: the white mask of Shirkra.

'There's still some power in this,' he whispered. He turned to Drayn. 'It's the only bit left in the world. This, and *him*.' He pointed his finger at the dying Old Child.

'Let it go, Canning,' Drayn said. 'The world doesn't need it any more.'

But Canning shook his head. 'It's *our* power, Drayn. Those creatures stole it from us. But it's *ours*. The Absence gave it to *us*.'

He gazed at the mask. With everything he had left, he willed it to respond to him.

'There's nothing you can do,' said Drayn. 'I don't feel anything any more. It's all gone.'

Canning shook his head. 'I am the King of the Remnants,' he whispered. 'I will make this thing of memory obey me.'

The mask broke into a smile, grinning at Canning. He smiled back. *It hears me.*

He turned, and he threw the mask at the Old Child. It changed and grew as it sailed through the air, until it ceased to be a mask at all and became a storm cloud. For a moment, Canning thought he saw words there, repeating over and over: *Death. Life. Death* ...

The Old Child glanced up with heavy eyes.

'No,' he said. 'Let me die.'

But the mask did not listen, and neither did Canning. The

cloud fell upon the Old Child and the world filled with light and darkness: the white of the mask, and the black emptiness of the First Memory, twisting together, flickering across the hill.

When it was over, all that remained was a small ball, white with patches of black, like a pearl the size of a fist. Canning lifted it.

'The power of memory is still in here,' he whispered. 'The last power of memory. I've got it. It's *mine*.'

Drayn shook her head. 'Destroy it, as the Old Child wanted.'

'Why? All these years they've used the power of memory to control us. Why can't *we* use it for ourselves?' He laughed. 'We have all the magic left in the world, here – in a prison.'

'It's just a husk,' said Drayn, though she seemed unsure of her own words. 'You won't be able to do anything with it, except put it on a shelf. There's nothing there. When I search my memories I feel *nothing*. They died, and so did their power. So did *our* power. That's nothing but a stone.'

*No. She is wrong.* Canning could feel something there. Something they could use to start again. And this time, *he* would control it.

'We will find out. I will study it.' He glanced at her. 'For the good of the Overland. For the good of mortals.' He locked eyes with Drayn. There was such a power in her, or there had once been. *There could be again.*

'You need to leave,' he whispered.

The girl hesitated for a moment, before nodding. She turned away from him, and began to walk away. But she stopped, further along the hill. She stooped to pick something up, before looking back at Canning.

He could not see what she held in her hand. But it didn't matter.

The new world was coming.

# Chapter Thirty-Seven

Cranwyl climbed and climbed, huffing and puffing until he came to the very top of the island: the very top of the *world*.

The old tower loomed before him, fat and shadowy against the light of the sun. It was squat and stout. That was appropriate, for once this had been Squatstout's Keep. The Autocrat had sat here, dispensing his justice, ruling over them all, doing whatever it was that majestic beings like him actually *did*. It wasn't any concern of old Cranwyl's. Oh no. He never asked what *they* did.

That was just the way it was. He'd always worked for the families on the island. *The* families. The great ones. The ones that ran the place. They always needed people like him, and he did what they needed. That's how it worked.

The Thonns had been the best of them. Especially Drayn. He liked to think he'd *really* helped her, over the years. He'd helped her see things the way they were supposed to be seen. Helped her deal with bad thoughts – dark thoughts – things you wanted rid of. He was proud of it. *Friends*, some people called them. He didn't like the word. She was his master. Friends were for ale and cards. Oh, she wasn't a *friend*.

That was the way it'd always been, before she'd left the

island. And that was the way it was now, after she'd come back.

A Guard nodded at him before the big door, then shifted out of his way. It still felt odd, seeing these fellas without their big beak masks. *But they're not the same people at all, are they? Silly Cranwyl.* They were just normal folk now.

Cranwyl nodded at the man and moved into the keep. Dusty, strange, horrible place it was. He would've preferred they'd managed things from one of the nice houses, a bit further down the island – Thonn House, now that would've been ideal. But no, he supposed some traditions had to be kept. After the end of Squatstout, everything had gone bad. Until Drayn had come back, that was. *The House of Thonn, back on top.* He sucked in a satisfied breath.

He came to the door of the throne room and gave it a gentle knock.

'Come in,' she said from beyond.

Cranwyl grasped the old doorknob (it was shaped in the likeness of Squatstout; they still hadn't got rid of it – they probably never would, he reckoned) and pushed inside.

Drayn smiled. She looked the same to him, in many ways, though maybe he just *wanted* her to look the same. She wasn't a girl now. *Twenty-five years old.* In truth, she hadn't been a girl for a long time, and age had nothing to do with it. All the childishness had been knocked out of her by whatever happened in the world beyond the island. She was sitting at the great table, staring down at a few papers that were scattered around. *Messy.* Cranwyl hated a mess.

But he didn't say anything. He was too busy looking at the stranger who sat at the table with Drayn. He was a funny-looking thing, dressed up like he was going to a costume party, with ribbons in his hair and a fancy blue coat. There was nothing unusual about his presence. Drayn was always bringing strangers to this room. Still, there was a lot that felt unusual about *him*.

Cranwyl looked to Drayn, and he felt reassured. They'd put her in charge when she came back to the island. *A Thonn,* they'd said. *We need a Thonn. And she's seen the world outside.* There was more to it than that, though. She was a smart one, and everyone knew it. She'd got them on the right path. She'd set up trade with other places. You could even leave the island, now, if you liked, though few ever did, unless they had to.

'Cranwyl!' Drayn shouted. She still had that happiness in her voice, the joy he remembered from when she was young, chasing after him round the big house. All right, maybe it was different, now: a bit older, a bit wearier. But it was there.

He gave her a little bow, and he took a seat at the table, at Drayn's side and opposite the strange man. He glanced around the throne room. Squatstout's old chair was long gone, now, that thing in the shape of the letter 'A'. Cranwyl thought it was a pity. Drayn would have suited a throne, not that she'd ever sit in one.

He nodded at the pair of them, and the strange man grinned back. There was something off about him. He seemed ... *thoughtfully devious*, if that was an expression.

Cranwyl stuck out a hand. 'I'm Cranwyl,' he said. 'The servant of Madam Thonn.'

'Servant!' Drayn laughed. 'So much more than that. My chief adviser.'

He blushed. 'If you say so.'

The man took his hand, and smiled. 'Wayward,' he said.

'Come again?'

'Wayward is my name.'

Cranwyl shrugged. 'Suit yourself.' He shifted his focus to Drayn. 'Anything you need doing today?' He cast a glance at Wayward. Drayn would know what he meant. *Is this man bothering you?*

Drayn gave a slight shake of her head. 'Something strange happened recently, Cranwyl. It happened, and then Wayward arrived. I don't think the two are unconnected.'

Cranwyl glanced between them. 'What happened?'

Drayn reached under the table and lifted something up, placing it before them. It was some kind of object, covered by a cloth.

'I found this ... back then,' she said. He knew what she meant, though she rarely talked about it. 'I took it with me.'

She pulled the cloth away. Sitting on the table was a mask, shaped into the likeness of a smiling man. It was a strange thing, fashioned from some material that was darker than anything Cranwyl had seen before. No: it wasn't *dark*. It was somehow *empty*.

'This mask,' said Wayward, 'is all that remains of an old power. The oldest power: the being that created the world, before trying to devour it. It was destroyed long ago, and this is a shard of its corpse. It's called the Absence.'

Cranwyl frowned. There was no good here, in this thing. This was something that would eat him all up, if it could.

He looked up at Drayn. 'It has a bit of power in it, doesn't it? A bit of power like Squatstout used to have.' He gestured at Wayward. 'This fella has it too.' *Cranwyl ain't always so dumb.*

'I took it with me, from the Overland,' Drayn said. 'And now something is happening to it. It's always been a bit funny, like it's watching me. But now ... it's as if it's *alive*.

There's such power in it, and it's growing stronger all the time.'

'Death never dies,' whispered Wayward.

Cranwyl looked once more at the mask. As he stared at it, he felt something in his mind, something unwelcome, picking at the core of him.

The mask of Absence smiled at Cranwyl, and it winked.